Rise of the Remnant

Book 1 of the Issur Trilogy

Dedication

For my students and other daydreamers

For a colored map of Issur and more information concerning
the trilogy, please visit brianagriffen.com

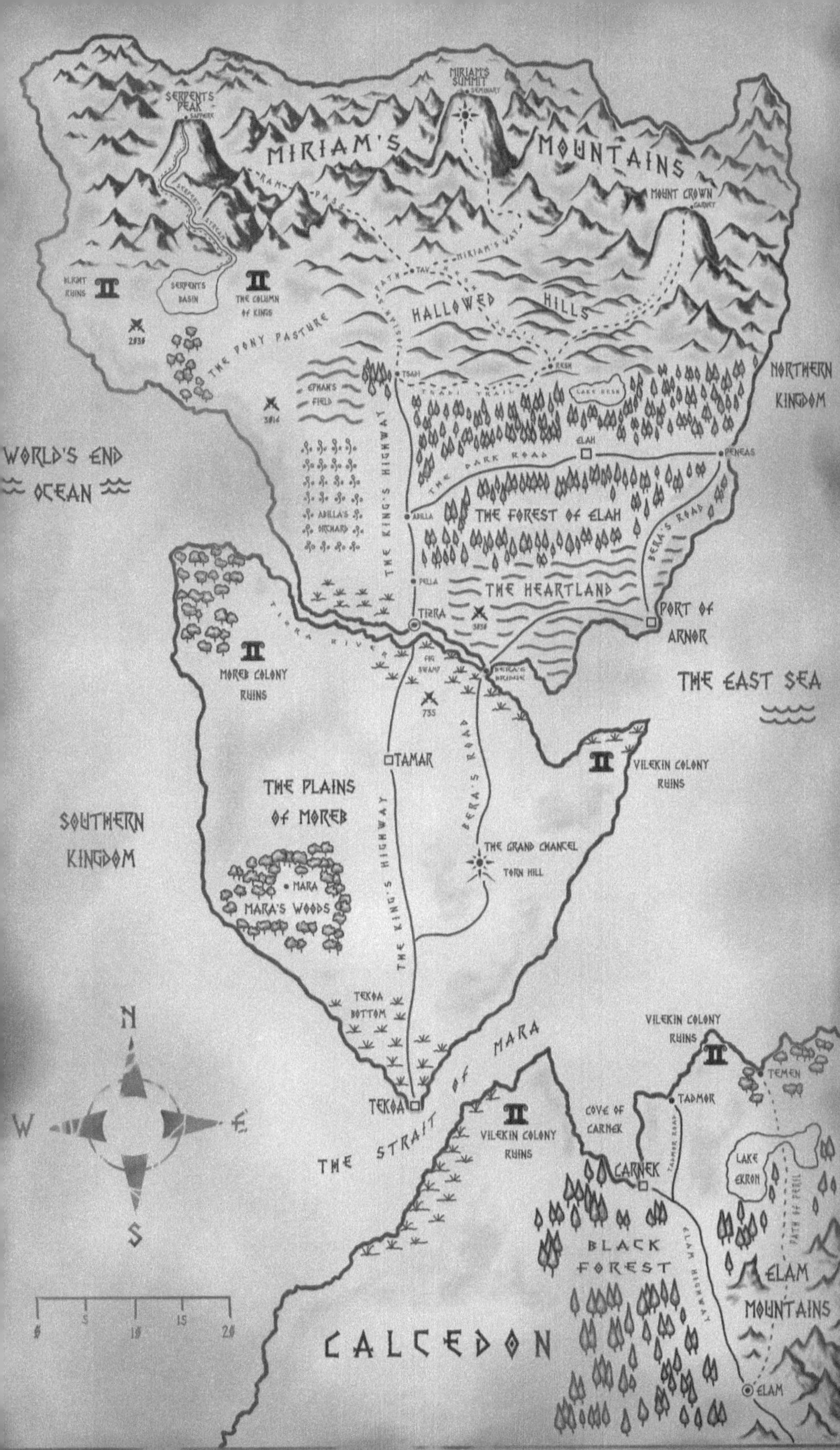

MIRIAM'S MOUNTAINS
SERPENT'S PEAK
SAPPHIRE
MIRIAM'S SUMMIT
SEMINARY
MOUNT CROWN
GARNET
RAM PASS
SERPENT'S STREAM
MIRIAM'S WAY
PATH
TAV
KESH
HALLOWED HILLS
BLIGHT RUINS
SERPENT'S BASIN
THE COLUMN OF KINGS
2835
THE PONY PASTURE
EPHAH'S FIELD
TSAH
TRADE TRAIL
LAKE KESH
NORTHERN KINGDOM
WORLD'S END OCEAN
3814
ABILLA'S ORCHARD
THE KING'S HIGHWAY
THE PARK ROAD
ELAH
PENEAS
ABILLA
THE FOREST OF ELAH
BERA'S ROAD
PELLA
THE HEARTLAND
MOREB COLONY RUINS
TIRRA RIVER
TIRRA
3856
PORT OF ARNOR
FIG SWAMP
BERA'S BRIDGE
THE EAST SEA
735
BERA'S ROAD
TAMAR
VILEKIN COLONY RUINS
THE PLAINS OF MOREB
SOUTHERN KINGDOM
THE KING'S HIGHWAY
THE GRAND CHANCEL
TORN HILL
MARA
MARA'S WOODS
TEKOA BOTTOM
OF MARA
VILEKIN COLONY RUINS
TEMEN
N
TEKOA
TADMOR
TADMOR ROAD
W
E
THE STRAIT
VILEKIN COLONY RUINS
COVE OF CARNEK
S
CARNEK
LAKE EKRON
PATH OF PERIL
ELAM HIGHWAY
5
10
15
20
BLACK FOREST
ELAM MOUNTAINS
CALCEDON
ELAM

Table of Contents

A Night to Remember

Spring 3016 of the 4th Age

Stars dotted about the black expanse dazzle the curious brown eyes of a restless boy. He rustles about the thick matted grass underneath his grey wool blanket. Reaching under his back, he strains his arm to remove a jagged stone. He rolls over and finds himself interfaced with his wide-eyed father, bothered by his antsy son.

"Benjamin, you must rest. Dawn will break soon."

"Why must we sleep in the grass? Why can't we go inside to our beds?"

"You have to get used to this. Shepherds sleep in the grass more nights than they sleep in their beds." The smell from the sheep stall atop the hill lingers in the night air to remind Benjamin of the family business.

Oren Tav rolls onto his grey wool blanket and repositions the waves of his thick dark hair. Benjamin mirrors his father's features and movements. They place both hands behind their heads and fix their gazes on the infinite stars.

A loner by nature, little Benjamin was at odds with the children of Tav. The only friend near his age was his younger sister, Jael, who didn't have much say in the matter. Raising an isolated son meant that Oren had to assume the role of best friend. Still, Benjamin always felt alone, even in the presence of family.

"Father, where did the world come from?"

"If I tell you, will you go to sleep?"

Benjamin's innocent smile offers his father a shred of hope.

"In the beginning, Neshama created the ether world and the nephesh. In the latter, Neshama created the world and the humans."

"Where's the ether world?"

"Beyond the stars, I suppose. It's where Neshama reigns."

"What's a nephesh?"

"They're heavenly beings. They taught humans about language, farming - useful kinds of things. Most importantly, they taught us about our creator and how she wants us to care for her creation and for one another."

"Why aren't there any more nephesh in Issur?"

"According to legend, they returned to Neshama after the humans forgot their creator. A time when the world was very evil. Humans were cruel to animals, and cruel to one another."

"How do you know all of this?"

"Thankfully, a young shepherd girl named Miriam from the days of old made a decision to remember Neshama."

"Does everyone remember Neshama?"

The weight of the question crushes Oren's chest and restricts his breath. The chirps of crickets replace the rhythm of questions and answers.

"Father?"

"No, Son… There are those who have forgotten."

Benjamin senses the desperation in his father's voice so he puts his curiosity to rest and closes his eyes.

Oren jostles Benjamin's shoulder, and his son jolts up.

"Don't be startled, the sheep in the stall are spooked."

Once Benjamin regains his senses, he realizes that it's still night and he hears the chorus of bahs.

"It's probably Nabal's ghastly cat again. Stay here, I'll be right back."

Within seconds, Oren vanishes into the night, and Benjamin tracks his father with his ears. He listens to Oren's feet lightly tread upon the grass. He hears a word of calm go out to the flock, followed by some curses at the ghastly cat. Then, the little shepherd hears a sound that he will never forget.

A shallow growl bellows behind him, before a heavy breath exhales the thunder.

Benjamin gradually twists his neck and finds two yellow eyes glowing in the night. He carefully gets to his feet clutching his grey blanket. He doesn't flinch a muscle as his stalker comes into vision. Saliva drips from the fangs of the brown wolf as the beast's nose draws him closer to his isolated prey.

Most children aren't conditioned to understand death, but shepherd boys aren't like other children in Issur. They grow up enthralled with the tales of their fathers, stories crafted with grim and guts - shepherd heroes triumphing over the pack. Most children lack the wisdom to understand fate, but shepherd boys can sense it stalking them like their starving rivals. Is it a premonition from his father's stories nudging him or is it the chill of fate biting him?

Benjamin knows not.

Out of instinct he tosses his blanket, and it swallows the wolf's head as Benjamin darts into a maze of boulders. The wolf thrashes his head about before using his front paw to remove the distraction.

The hunter tracks his meal into the maze of boulders.

Benjamin makes his way through the boulders taking tiny steps - his vision sharp, too terrified for tears.

The brown wolf considers unleashing a dreadful howl to dislodge his prey but reconsiders drawing the attention of a potential competitor.

Benjamin knows the way through the boulder maze; he's played in it too many times to count, but always in the sunlight - never in the dark. Under the light of the moon, the boulders seem taller and the maze seems to reverse the pattern.

Benjamin is lost, even worse - cornered. His missteps land him with boulders on both sides and to his back. At the end of the path - the glowing yellow eyes of his predator.

The impatient beast charges his easy target.

The little shepherd's knees lock first, then his hips. His shoulders tense, leaving his arms to dangle at his side. His neck muscles loosen slightly, enough to allow his small face to look to the stars. In the dire moment he screams, "Neshama!"

The soles of Oren Tav's boots graze the top of Benjamin's head when his father leaps down from the boulders above with his longsword aimed at the wolf. He clinches the black leather hilt and shifts all of his weight onto his blade as he impales the night-stalker. The wolf's death yelp is quick, soon replaced with the swirling sound of the night breeze.

Benjamin releases his repressed breath as terror exits his eyes. Soft tears slowly slide down his cheeks.

Oren removes his sword from the wolf's back, gives a nod of confidence to his son, and admires his kill.

"Never a dull moment in Tav, eh Benjamin."

Suddenly, the sheen of a steel blade glistens through the night as it swiftly swipes at Oren's neck. He ducks the blow and steel shards spark off the boulder behind him.

Oren gets into a defensive stance, separating Benjamin from the assassin.

The swift breeze rustles the assassin's black longcoat and sends ripples through his black hood. The assassin swings furiously and maintains his initiative from the surprise attack. Oren's steel longsword absorbs the attacks, allowing him time to size up his opponent.

Benjamin reverts back to his paralyzed state.

Once the assassin's momentum slows, Oren puts his nemesis to the test. His powerful strikes blow the assassin backwards, driving him down the path away from his offspring. The killer slashes wildly and grazes Oren's right shoulder, causing a crimson flower to bloom on his white shirt.

Oren retaliates with rage and rips his sword across the left side of the assassin's face; blood spatter dots the boulders as the maimed foe lets out a squall. Oren rips the black hood from his bloody head, and Benjamin winces at the man's disfigured face before the coward flees into the hills.

Oren's pride urges him to pursue his attacker, but his compassion brings him to the realization that he can't leave his rattled son alone a second time.

Dawn breaks and the black of night fades, but the recent brushes with death loom over the shepherds as Oren holds Benjamin on his lap and the two stare at the wolf carcass at their feet.

"I'm sorry about tonight. Your first night under the stars wasn't supposed to be like this."

Oren's apology dangles in the silence.

Then, Benjamin asks another crushing question, the type of question that only he could ask. "The man who tried to kill you, he doesn't remember, does he?"

Like the assassin's blade, the question catches Oren off guard. Once he considers the question, he fears answering it. For the night his boy endured - he feels impelled to answer.

"No, Son. He doesn't remember."

Oren stands Benjamin on his feet and kneels in front of him to connect with his troubled eyes. "I brought you out here tonight to spend some extra time with you because I have to go away today."

"To shepherd?"

"Yes, but not sheep. I've been called to be a shepherd of men, to protect my people from a wolf."

"But why do you have to be the one to face the wolf?"

"So you won't have to."

Benjamin looks down at the felled wolf, trying to make sense of his father's plans.

Oren gently lifts Benjamin's chin. "Tyranny is a wolf that lurks in the darkness of a man's soul. It devours his humility and gratitude. Therefore, power and greed afflict his heart with a hunger that can never be filled. Tyranny will never claim enough authority, never enough taxes. Like the wolf stalks the flock, tyranny preys on liberty. It's always been up to us, the shepherds, to snatch the innocent from the jaws of tyranny."

Oren wipes away Benjamin's tears before staring tenderly into his son's soul. "There are so many truths about the Goddess I want you to remember, but I know you can't. Humans are too forgetful. But promise me that you'll never forget Neshama because she'll never forget you. And Son, promise me that you'll never stop asking questions."

Benjamin's sleepy brown eyes well up once more as he nods his head to affirm his promises.

Oren embraces Benjamin, and his son returns to his lap, curling up and laying his head on his father's thigh. Oren whispers, "Goddess keep you, Son."

Benjamin drifts into a deep sleep.

Chapter 2

The Children of Oren Tav

Fifteen Years Later

Benjamin Tav wakens from a restless sleep on a rickety wooden pew and stares into a cobweb-filled cathedral ceiling. Sparrows stir in the rafters above, and the stained glass sun in the front of the chancel glows dimly from the rays rising with the dawn.

Now that the chancel sits empty, it's the perfect place for twenty-year-old Benjamin to escape the social pressures of Hallowed Hills. Five years before receiving the full rights of adulthood, five years before being single is considered dishonorable to one's family lineage.

The chancel was always a place of comfort for Benjamin. The very place where he lay his head was comforting even more so - that was his father's place on the pew, and as a child, during the lengthy sermonizing of the precept, his little head would often end up on his father's lap.

"You're definitely the son of Oren Tav," the old wives

would always tell Benjamin when he and his father exited the chancel - wavy dark hair, humble brown eyes, kind smile. As Benjamin grew to become a young man, the resemblance grew even more - same good height, same solid build. Same on the outside, not so much the inside.

Oren Tav and his wife, Rachel, are revered patriots in Hallowed Hills. Their younger son works the hills ignored by the elder shepherds, the way Benjamin likes it.

Benjamin stands and straightens his shepherd's garb- loose white cotton shirt flowing into his waistline, black woolen pants tucked into leather boots of wolf skin. He straps an iron sword to his side and slings a quiver of yellow- feathered arrows over his back. He tightens his black-leather bracers around his wrists before grabbing his longbow and moving towards the front of the chancel.

Benjamin runs his hands across the grey stone cover sealed atop the ether font. Etched in the stone seal, symbols of the moon in all its various stages encircle the cover.

The symbols of the moon exercise the passions of every Issurian. For many, they invoke feelings of liberation and pleasure. For others, like the shepherds, they invoke feelings of oppression and pain. For Melek worship is the reason that the chancel collects cobwebs and the pews remain empty.

The weight of the moment collapses Benjamin to one knee; he bows his head and prays softly.

"Neshama. Are you there? Are you listening?"

A sudden crash beneath the floor breaks Benjamin's concentration. He gets to his feet and quickly removes an arrow from his quiver as a stone panel near the ether font shifts.

"You wouldn't shoot a precept of Neshama," speaks the gruff voice beneath the floor.

"A precept?" questions Benjamin, slowly lowering his bow.

The stone slab gets pushed aside when an older man

emerges; his crystal blue eyes glow from within his dark sunken eyes underneath his wrinkled dome.

"How'd you know I wouldn't shoot you?"

"You're the only shepherd in this town, who visits the chancel. More than that, you're the only shepherd who sleeps in the chancel."

Anxiety bites Benjamin's confidence, and he recoils.

"Why do you cower in the corner?"

Benjamin looks over the precept draped in a filthy grey cloak with a yellow sun embroidered into the chest. "How long have you been living under the chancel?"

"A decade at least."

"A decade! How come I never heard you under there!?"

"I've never tripped over my pots when you were in here."

"So you eavesdropped on my prayers for the last decade?"

"I never looked at it that way," speaks the older precept in a gentle tone. "I know most shepherds prefer to pray in nature, always have. But not you, you like to pray in the shadows of an abandoned chancel. Regardless, your prayers give me a bit of hope and for that I'm grateful."

"But you must know everything about me," says Benjamin, his timid nature making his stomach sour. "How much do you know?"

"I know a lot. I know you love your parents and you miss them dearly. Your brother is the sorest spot in your soul. You love both your sisters, but you're closer to your younger sister, not just in age but in friendship. I know your hopes, regrets, doubts…"

"Doubts?"

"Oh yes, you're riddled with doubt. The Goddess cannot be pleased with your lack of faith."

Benjamin's legs feel weary, so he retreats back to the pews. He plops down and hangs his head. The precept allows the shepherd a moment to recover.

"What's your name?" asks Benjamin.

The precept is hesitant to answer. The sounds of flapping sparrows fill the quiet chancel as they flutter about the rafters.

"Shamgar Ram," exhales the precept.

Benjamin's body stiffens with reverence as an awe-inspiring bolt of faith strikes his soul.

"The High Precept!"

"Former High Precept. I was assassinated; at least that's what's believed."

"How did you survive the assassination?"

"Know your enemy, young shepherd. Know your enemy well… When King Zimri and the High Magi Zidon declared war on the prophets, it was only a matter of time before he went after the Synod of Paladin Precepts. The assassins trapped me in a barn loft. They sliced me up pretty good. I was armed with my mace and shield, so they had to work for what they cut. I fell from the loft about four stories high and was swallowed in a sea of seed corn. The assassins presumed I was dead."

"You know about the Scarlet Winter, then?"

"Of course I do! And don't you think a day has passed that I've forgotten my fallen brethren!"

Benjamin backs off.

Shamgar calms himself.

"Yes, I know of the fate of the precepts. Yes, I know the Grand Chancel has been converted into the Temple of Melek. And I'm aware that five precepts survived - those cowardly five," admits Shamgar, remorse softening his rough voice.

"Cowardly?"

"Yes, cowardly. They hide, protected in The Southern Kingdom, more interested in raising another Grand Chancel than raising a crusade against Melek worship."

Benjamin catches Shamgar in his hypocrisy, "How is that any different than hiding under an ether chancel for a decade?"

Shamgar's wrinkled face sours at the question.

"You were elected High Precept to defend Issur from this corruption."

Benjamin stands tall, his blood rushing.

"You failed as High Precept and now you hide! My parents are dead because leaders like you failed Issur!"

"Who are you to question me, to blame me!?"

"Then tell me why, out of all the chancels in Issur, why did you pick this one? Tell me why you listened to my prayers for the last decade?"

Shamgar's stubborn nature urges him to lash out at Benjamin. Instead, the seasoned precept closes his eyes for a moment of meditation.

"You're the son of Oren Tav, the only hero of The Fourth Age. Yes, I failed. The Synod failed."

Benjamin's left speechless by precept's confession.

"I came here seeking the sons of Oren Tav hoping to find a hero. I found disappointment instead. The older son hasn't a bit of faith in Neshama. The younger son is a troubled soul riddled with doubt."

The stained glass sun in the front of the chancel glows brighter, reminding the shepherd of his duty. "I've got work to do."

Benjamin moves slowly towards the exit.

"Sorry I'm not my father, sorry to disappoint you."

Shamgar moves quickly to the door, blocking the exit. He reaches into a pocket in his robe and produces a small stone statuette of the prophetess.

"Miriam go with you."

Benjamin suspiciously accepts the gift.

"And Benjamin, it's not just this old relic under the chancel who hears your prayers. Neshama is listening."

Inside a suffocating sheep stall, Benjamin gasps for air and wipes sweat from his brow.

The Summer of 3031 punishes Issur with a sweltering heat. It's a link in the chain of three brutally hot summers, and this makes the toil in Hallowed Hills harsher than it already is for the shepherds. To make matters worse, it's halfway through the summer season and Issur hasn't felt a drop of rain since the end of spring.

There's a buzz in the air as a shepherd rotation will soon take place in Tav. This happens on a weekly to monthly basis depending on how far the flocks graze. For other shepherds, though, it's a bittersweet occasion. They're grateful to see their companions return, but troubled that they have to leave their families for what seems like an endless amount of time. Benjamin counts himself among the troubled for it's his turn to graze a flock.

Benjamin labors hard, preparing the stalls for his brother's return. It's filthy work, shoveling manure-soaked hay. It's monotonous work, hauling buckets of water from the shallow wells to the deep troughs.

The day seems to have a good pace, and he spends much of it lost in his thoughts more than his work. Thoughts of embarrassment from bearing his soul to whom he thought was only the Goddess. Thoughts of hope from the Miriam relic that hugs his front pocket. The story of Miriam offers him hope and inspires him to keep praying. The weightiest thought pressing down on Benjamin's mind is the return of his brother from the hills.

Evan Tav had a straightforward approach to shepherd life. He was either feared or revered by the elders in Hallowed Hills. Like Oren Tav, he rarely lost a lamb because he refused to tolerate apathy from the shepherds around him, but unlike his father's personality, he was cold and unapproachable. His allegiance was to family and flock. His top priority was to protect the integrity of his last name for nothing mattered more to Evan than Tav.

The sky prepares for the moon's arrival as disappointment and worry creep into the families waiting to see their shepherd heroes return home. Then, in the horizon, the faint barks of a sheep dog echo throughout the hills.

"They're home!" shouts a freckled-faced boy atop a large boulder. Mothers and children fly from their hovels and run to greet their long lost fathers with embraces, kisses, laughter.

This was the way shepherds always returned, the way they wanted it. Once the sound of joy subsided, there was an uncomfortable pause, a pause that silenced every hovel in Tav. If the silence went uninterrupted then the merriment could continue; if the silence was swallowed up by sadness, the families knew that the return was not joyous for all.

On this particular return, the awkward silence is met with the screams of a wailing widow. The faces of the fortunate families hide their delight and pay their respects with a slow, somber walk to their hovels.

Shepherd deaths are commonplace in Hallowed Hills; shepherd funerals are not. Any remains of the dead are simply buried in the countryside as tribute to a good death. No eulogy needs to be spoken. To die protecting the flock - there's no higher honor in Hallowed Hills.

Benjamin and his two sisters sit quietly around a fire pit in the middle of their obscure hovel. Nerves get tense as they await the return of Evan.

Jael rhythmically pets Smoke, her fat, fluffy grey cat.

Benjamin gets lost in his thoughts as he runs his fingers across the Miriam relic. The statuette is no taller than his index finger, yet the intricate model details her solemn face.

The grains of her hair flow into a long ponytail that rests on her long dress, which ends at her bare feet.

Judith diligently sews a seam on her wedding dress as a delicious aroma lifts from her boiling broth in the small cauldron simmering over the fire pit; the hearty steam from the broth alleviates the tension in the air.

The hovel's original purpose was to quarter servants, but the space always had a sense of comfort about it. Judith worked hard to keep it that way from the time their uncle, Nabal Tav, allowed them to reside in the small hovel. Evan sectioned off a small bedroom for Judith and Jael to allow for a modicum of privacy. The two brothers were rarely in the hovel at the same time, and if need be, they would simply throw furs or blankets on the floor in the main room.

"Can we eat?" begs Jael.

"We should wait for Evan," says Judith.

"Please… We've worked hard all day, and it's well beyond supper time."

Judith turns to her little brother to break the stalemate.

"Let's eat, Evan will understand," answers Benjamin with his stomach.

Judith serves Benjamin and Jael a stew of mutton, carrot, and potato with a slice of cornbread for dipping. They waste no time slurping the stew to their mouths.

Judith prepares to serve herself a bowl when the door flings open.

Evan Tav is home.

Evan's presence in the doorway intimidates his siblings inside. He wears the traditional shepherd's garb - white shirt, leather bracers, black-woolen pants, wolf skin boots. His father's steel longsword straps to his back. He's slightly taller and much thicker than his little brother. Short dark hair grows from his thick neck to his chiseled forehead, and the dark eyes in his stone face seal in any emotion.

Jael is the first to wrap her arms around her brother; he hugs her tight, lifting her feet from the floor. Her fingernails rake his brown stubble like they once did her father's trimmed beard.

Judith patiently waits for her moment to embrace her brother. Her guarded hug protects her dress from Evan's sweat.

Before Benjamin can offer a greeting, Evan questions his table manners, "Had to dive in. Couldn't wait for your brother?"

The stew settles in Benjamin's throat as he tries to digest the insult.

Judith returns to serving the stew, and the shamed shepherd waits until everyone is seated on the floor before he resumes eating.

"We heard sounds of weeping, so we stayed inside," says Judith.

"Eman Pe. He vanished in the night. Found his bones three days later, ripped clean of his flesh."

"Nasty," says Jael with a grimace.

"Show some respect," demands Evan.

Benjamin's soul retreats in fear at Eman Pe's fate; his heart accelerates and breath deepens. Ever since his near-death experience as a boy, his deepest fear is being torn to pieces by wolves. No thought sickens him to his core like the thought of wolves.

"Well, Benjamin. What's the news on Uncle Nabal?" asks Evan.

"No news, I guess."

"Didn't I ask you to keep tabs on him and the guild hall? I knew you couldn't handle something as easy as that."

Benjamin hangs his head and silently sips his stew while Evan turns to Judith.

Evan always felt that he could trust Judith being that they were so close in age. He was approaching thirty and she was only two years behind.

Judith Tav was reliable and respected among the women in the village. She had the face of royalty, and her silken-straight dark-blonde hair was never out of place. Her clothes were stain free and perfectly pressed - a near impossible feat for the women in shepherd families. Some of the jealous women accused Judith of not doing her chores to avoid the filth, that she pawned them off on Jael.

The jealousy may have stemmed from Judith's good fortune. Oren Tav arranged a marriage for her with the Tsadi family not long after her eighth birthday. The Tsadi family was the most influential in Hallowed Hills, and her betrothed, Daniel Tsadi, wasn't the oldest son in the Tsadi line, but the women always thought him the most charming.

Judith would never consider forcing her duties on her little sister like the jealous women accused. Regardless, if the task involved dirt, sweat, or manure - Jael Tav would be more than delighted to do it. She was a free spirit, a shepherd at heart, and reckless at times. As a child she would run free with her curly, dark-blonde hair flowing behind her, her wild eyes ignoring the stares of suspicious onlookers. Maybe it was because Judith never had the time or because she didn't want to, but Benjamin was the one always chasing after her.

Because Jael was only a couple years younger than Benjamin, the two siblings formed an inseparable bond in their childhood. Jael remained a free spirit at heart - wrinkled dresses, wild curly hair, boyish interests, still drawing the ire of suspicious onlookers, set in contrast to her dutiful sister Judith.

"Well, Judith. Tell me about Uncle Nabal," requests Evan.

"It's getting worse, much worse."

Evan sighs deeply as he prepares himself for the bad news.

"Of course we all know of his drunkenness. He drinks all night and lays passed out in the guild hall all day. We know that Ruth Gimel has been after Nabal since her husband died, but her visits increase; she sneaks in unnoticed under the cover of dark and well… You know."

"Just say the word, Judith. We're all adults," interrupts Jael.

Evan clears his throat, "Two of us are."

Jael's demeanor sinks to match Benjamin's.

"As I was saying, I think it's only a matter of time before they marry and she moves in. Her two sons, Merlen and Melvin, seem to be buttering up Nabal as well."

"This is bad, real bad, if they end up in the will. The Tav Guild Hall has bore our family name for thousands of years. The Gimels, talk about a lazy lot. Merlen runs the worst bakery in town and Melvin does nothing but sloth outside the bakery," laments Evan.

Jael snickers at the insult.

"This isn't funny, Jael! The guild hall could fall into the hands of those two pigs. It makes me sick to think that a couple of lazy bakers would live in our guild hall… What do they know about shepherding? What does Nabal remember about shepherding?"

A dark aura clouds Judith's radiance. Benjamin and Jael watch the eerie transformation with dire faces; they reposition themselves with backs straight.

In the midst of his rant, Evan takes note of her bleak face, "Are you ill?"

"No, but what I'm about to share will make you so. King Zimri has proclaimed that Tizra will host a grand moon festival in honor of Melek at the end of the summer season."

"How is that news?" asks Benjamin.

"Some of the king's men visited the guild hall yesterday," informs Judith.

"That fool!" curses Evan. "He signed a contract didn't he?"

"Ruth Gimel has been boasting about it!"

"How many?" questions Evan.

Judith swallows deep and her aura grows darker.

Evan stands to receive the contract request.

"Five hundred," answers Judith, leaning away from Evan's impending wrath.

"Five hundred head! That's nearly the whole flock! He can't deliver that!"

"Doesn't Tsadi usually handle Zimri's orders?" asks Benjamin. "So why Tav?"

"Zimri learned of a weakness and wants to expose it," notes Evan.

"What will happen if Nabal fails?" asks Judith.

"*When* he fails, Zimri will take the guild hall and put a regiment in Tav. Eventually, our guild will go the way of the other guilds. Under his control and into ruin."

The hovel fills with an awkward silence as Evan, Benjamin, and Judith ponder thoughts of Zimri's tyranny.

Jael's attention escaped the grave conversation a while back; her focus shifts to a mouse scrounging food atop a barrel. She softly steps into her room and emerges with a readied longbow. She quietly draws string, and lets loose the arrow.

The vermin gets sliced in two.

Jael's cat flies under her bed as Benjamin and Judith jump to their feet.

"Nice shot," says Benjamin.

"Jael, you could have hit one of us!" scolds Judith.

"I need the practice if I'm going to bullseye my way to another blue ribbon at the bazaar."

Unphased by the fired arrow, Evan's thoughts shift quickly back to Nabal. "That's it, the summer bazaar."

"What of it?" asks Benjamin.

"No worries, Brother, but that's the day we take the guild hall back."

"Benjamin, will you practice with me in the morning before your rotation starts?" requests Jael.

"Sure."

"No. He won't be practicing; he won't be here in the morning," interjects Evan.

"Why not?" asks Jael.

"He's going into Hallowed Hills, to the flock at the base of Miriam's Mountains."

"By myself!"

"Yes. You're a Tav, you'll be fine… Now listen, only the people in this hovel can know of this plan."

Judith and Jael look upon Benjamin with pity.

"What plan?" asks Benjamin.

"You tell Bo Baladan to bring the mountain flock to Tav."

"Fine, I'll lead them back here."

"No! You're the messenger boy, that's it. Besides you can't handle a flock that size. And don't act tough with these shepherds. Bo and his brothers are a rugged lot; tell them I sent you and they'll do what I say."

Benjamin tries to mask his disappointment, but Evan senses it, so he puts his arm around him.

"Trust me on this, Brother. You deal with those shepherds; I'll deal with Uncle Nabal. Eat up and get some rest, you'll have to leave soon, under the cover of dark. I'll find another shepherd to take your rotation."

Chapter 3

Old Friends

Night breaks and darkness fades as Benjamin stands on a rocky outcrop overlooking the landscape of Hallowed Hills and the town of Tav. The sun gently rises over the rolling slopes. Wide and narrow ravines meander around the windblown grass and stoic boulders.

Benjamin sorts a thousand memories in his mind as he gazes upon the guild hall that his ancestors built on the highest point in Tav - happy memories of watching his father bring in the flock and listening to his mother hum the anthems of ancient shepherds, the choir of sheep bleating their own hymns to the Goddess. Sad memories as well, especially the day his parents never returned home to the guild hall.

Benjamin kneels down to pluck a stem of lavender. He breathes in the scent of the flower and exhales the painful memory.

Surrounded by stables, the guild hall rests on the east hill overlooking the town. The shops outline the town square where pings from the blacksmith's hammer echo off the boulders. The hovels form the next circle, creating crooked alleys and walkways. West of town, the corroding ether chancel bookends the dwellings. The wealthy among of Tav reside in manors on the outskirts of town; their servant-hovels dot the terrain around the manors.

Tav is a town on the crossroads. Miners from Sapphire, atop Serpents Peak, travel south down Ram Pass to barter for food. Before The Scarlet Revenge, prophets traveled north and south along Miriam's Way to do the bidding of the master prophets housed in Summit Seminary.

Josiah's Path and Resh Trail roll south to the other guild halls in Hallowed Hills.

Benjamin surveys the various paths and trails that he hopes to travel one day, but not this day, for he must travel through the lonely hills and forge a way that his brother sees fit.

Benjamin struggles to put his memories and Tav behind him. He stands and turns north to face Miriam's Mountains. He marvels at Miriam's Summit, the queen of the mountain range. Miriam's Mountains dominate the horizon; they span the entire north of the isle all the way across Hallowed Hills. Their purplish tone blends in with the rising sun that peeks through the perpetual light mist decorating the snow-capped mountains.

Benjamin takes a deep breath and tastes traces of the crisp mountain air flowing over his lips. The oxygen invigorates his lungs as he begins his brother's errand.

The midday sun swelters high above Benjamin, but he cleverly avoids the heat by staying in the shadows deep within the ravines.

Benjamin does his best to keep Evan out of his thoughts. To focus his busy mind, he draws energy from Jael's excitement for the archery contest.

His consciousness quickly snaps back to the ravine when he hears the howl of a wolf. Benjamin stops dead in his tracks, readies his bow, and scans the terrain. He catches the slightest glimpse of a wolf's back in the tall grass atop a hill, but he quickly loses track of the wolf as it ventures deeper into the thick grass.

The brown wolves of Hallowed Hills lost their pack mentality a millennia ago when the shepherds of old beat it out of them. They now stalk isolated animals and shepherds. Their constant hunger pangs keep them on the move, and when they eye a lone target - they never blink. If more than one howl is heard, it's not because they've rallied together as allies. These hunters have eyed the same prey and will compete for their prize, to sink their fangs into the skin of an animal or the flesh of a shepherd.

After a long day of traversing ravines and hills at a spirited pace, Benjamin draws near to the base of the Miriam's Mountains. As he stands atop a steep hill, he gauges the setting sun against the distance to the Baladans and the mountain flock. His calculations halt when the howls of wolves rise up to welcome the first glimpse of the moon.

Benjamin listens closely to distinguish the howls.

"Three," laments the shepherd under his breath. He scans the hills and sees a fortress of boulders embedded into the side of an adjacent hill; he makes a rash decision to end his day in the cluster of boulders.

Benjamin skids down to the base of the steep hill. The excursion down the hill takes longer than anticipated, and he finds himself at the mercy of the moonlight. He plants his foot into the adjacent hillside to make his final push to the boulders, but his boot slips on a loose rock and he plants his face into the dirt. The sting of the fall steals the last of his energy. He rolls over on his back and looks up at the moon. Within a few breaths, the dangerous thought of falling asleep enters his head.

Unexpectedly, a faint cry of desperation rings out in the night air, "Run, you imbecile, run!"

Benjamin stands and sees a shadow of a younger man scurrying down the hillside above. The flares of his torch flicker behind him. The flight of embers reveal a wolf's head nipping at the man's back.

Benjamin strings an arrow. He calms his breath, takes aim, and looses the bolt. The yellow-feathered arrow sails up the hill, gaining velocity as it glides through the dark night. The arrow sinks into the hind leg of the wolf, flipping the beast into the air. The wolf bounces down the hill smacking against stone.

The panicked man leaps into the cluster of boulders.

Benjamin smiles with relief, but the relief fades in an instant when another wolf charges down the hill toward him. He doesn't have time to ready his bow, so he draws his sword instead, planting his foot into a boulder and stretching out with his iron sword.

The wolf leaps at the shepherd.

The eager beast jumps onto the sword with such force that Benjamin gets knocked backward. The wolf is dead, but Benjamin aches on the ground from the collision.

A determined howl terrorizes the shepherd when he realizes the third wolf bears down on him. Benjamin labors to get out from under the carcass when he hears a mystical chant floating down from the hilltop. The wolf's ears perk up at the sound of the chant, and the stalker slides to a stop in front of the shepherd's face.

Benjamin locks eyes with the wolf.

The wolf howls loudly before transforming into a tame pup.

Benjamin cautiously approaches the timid creature.

The wolf tucks his front paws under his belly and bows low to the shepherd. Benjamin's initial inkling is to kill the wolf, but as he draws nearer, he can't bring himself to put it down. The wolf looks deep into Benjamin's eyes; the beast tilts his head as to acknowledge the shepherd's mercy. The pup calmly retreats and vanishes into the night.

"Shepherd?" calls out an older man from atop the hill. "Can you help an old prophet find his student? Neshama only knows how many more wolves lurk in the night."

Benjamin identifies the voice and his countenance lifts.

"Othniel, is that you?"

The pulsing adrenaline in his body mellows as he recalls the fond childhood memories of Othniel 'Wayfarer' visits with his father. Even though Oren Tav had passed fifteen years ago, Othniel made sure to visit Benjamin when occasion would permit.

"I do believe I hear the voice of the apple of Oren Tav's eye."

"Your student is on the hillside, in the boulders."

The circle of boulders conceals the shepherd and two prophets. Benjamin warms some cornbread and deer jerky over the fading torch. He divides his meal between the three of them, the prophets accepting the food with gracious faces.

A dark brown robe with a thick hood envelops Othniel- a leather-bound book and a few scrolls of scripture dangle from his side. A knotted-ponytail gathers together his full head of grey hair. Cornbread crumbs collect in his thick beard; he shakes them free by jostling the knot at the tip of his beard.

His oak staff leans against his shoulder. The peculiar staff is shaved to a point on the bottom end, and masterfully engraved vines grow up the staff to form a uniquely-notched orb on top. Othniel's aged face reveals a profound wisdom and his eyes twinkle with a mysterious charm.

Ezekiel, Othniel's understudy, still trembles from the near death attack, his shaky hands feeding his little mouth a bite of jerky. A smaller man, his thick brown robes consume his slender frame. The humble-eyed prophet senses the shepherd's stare of intrigue; he looks up with a grateful smile on his kind face.

"I apologize for my rudeness," says Othniel. "This is my one and only student, Ezekiel."

Benjamin extends his hand, and Ezekiel gently shakes it.

"I found Ezekiel roaming in Mara's Woods when he was just a boy, his parents killed by bandits. He's trained as a prophet his whole twenty years of this life and hasn't gained a speck of knowledge," voices Othniel with a hint of exaggeration.

"Not true, Master. I've memorized The Book of Neshama and The Book of Miriam."

"Fair enough. You thrive at the story arts but as for the ether arts, you're pitiful. This wolf debacle is the last in a long line of mistakes."

"What ether arts?"

"Such matters are best left to the prophets. Shepherds need not know of such secrets."

"I've heard that line before, ever since I was five."

The three men finish their supper and recline against the boulders.

"What news of our tyrant, Zimri? Still trampling the head of the poor into the dust of the earth, I presume," asks Othniel.

"He's holding another grand moon festival at summer's end in honor of Melek. Uncle Nabal signed a contract to deliver five hundred head for the party."

"Was the dimwit drunk to agree to such a contract?"

"Of course," says Benjamin.

The thought of a drink makes the old prophet feel a bit antsy. "You wouldn't happen to have any honey mead in that canteen, would you?"

"Sorry, only water," answers Benjamin with a bit of sarcasm.

"I could go for some of that honey mead you shepherds brew so well."

Ezekiel rolls his eyes, annoyed by his teacher's inquiry of alcohol.

"They're brewing plenty for the bazaar. You should hang around for Evan's plan to oust Nabal. I'm retrieving the mountain flock while he arranges his scheme."

"Evan still bossing you around, I see. Like you were his puppy… I'm certain Evan has a plan with his best interest in mind."

Ezekiel hangs onto every word of Othniel and notices Benjamin's dislike of being compared to a puppy.

"Never a dull moment in Tav, your father would always say to me."

"I've got bigger news still," offers Benjamin with a glint in his eyes.

"Out with it. I'm not getting any younger."

"I don't know. Such matters are best left for the shepherds. Prophets need not know of such secrets"

Othniel's eyes twinkle at Benjamin's sarcasm, "Well played, young shepherd."

Benjamin leans over to tell his news, and the prophets straighten with anticipation.

"Shamgar Ram lives."

Othniel exhales a sigh so deep that it brightens the embers of the fading torch.

Ezekiel attempts to read his master's blank face, "Who's Shamgar Ram?"

Benjamin waits for Othniel to answer.

"He once served as High Precept to the Synod of Paladin Precepts."

Ezekiel frowns as if the answer puts a bad taste in his mouth.

"Where did you see him?" asks Othniel.

"Hiding under the chancel, he's been there a decade."

"I want to burn with hate knowing that he lives, but I can't in good conscience."

"I've never heard you speak a kind word about the precepts, but hate, Master?"

"The Synod didn't stand with the prophets when we stood with the shepherds to confront Zimri."

"Why not?" asks Ezekiel.

"We'll have to ask Shamgar Ram that question when we get to Tav."

"Wait. Shamgar failed the shepherds, failed my parents, failed the prophets too. Why would you see him?"

"Our allies grow thin, and we must rely on grace if we have any chance to revive the Covenant."

Benjamin's exhaustion overrides his will to debate.

"Best we get some sleep. In the morning you will continue on to the mountain flock. We'll travel to Tav to find Shamgar Ram, doing our very best to avoid your brother."

The herd in the stalls rumbles against the wooden enclosures rousing Evan's keen connection to his flock. He pulls up his black trousers, steps into his boots, and dashes from his hovel. The moonlight shines across his strong shoulders and cut chest. Seasoned at sensing danger in the night, he uses his ears first - ewes nagging, night bugs bickering, guild master groaning.

Nabal.

Too skilled in his senses, his nostrils activate; the smell of liver and onions emanates from Nabal's armpits to overpower the earthy smells of Tav.

Evan walks toward the smell that's torturing his flock. His uncle gets off his mistress, and reaches over for his wooden mug of ale. Nabal chugs loudly before roaring a belch.

"Enjoying the view, Nephew?"

Ruth Gimel pops up from the matted grass to hastily straighten her dress. "Well… I never. Evan Tav, you are most perverted!" shouts the embarrassed widow, before plodding her thick thighs back to her bakery.

Moonbeams glisten off Nabal's hunched shoulders and greasy sheen across his chest.

"Good morning, Uncle." Evan quickly notices Nabal's rapidly contracting chest, "You gonna be alright?"

Nabal doubles over and rubs his heart.

"That woman sure can wear me out."

"So can all that red meat and beer."

The insult stiffens the guild master's frame to a familiar disposition that attempts to shame Evan.

"You sure Ruth has your best at heart?"

"Ruth's a good woman, waited patiently for her infested husband to rot away so she could be with me."

"You sure that contract with Zimri was best?"

"You're an ungrateful mutt, Evan Tav. After all I did for you and your siblings."

"Sorry. I should be grateful that you kicked us out of our home and shoved us into that little hovel. That you made me take double rotations so you could stay drunk, so drunk that you groped Judith like she was a wench. For laughs, you kicked Benjamin down the guild hall steps and put spiders in Jael's hair. We had so much to be grateful for."

"That's not how I remember it," says Nabal, tilting his

cup upside down to catch the last drop of mead with the tip of his tongue.

"It's time for me to get mine. That's what Zimri believes about Melek, so why shouldn't I believe the same way too? Ruth will be my bride. Merlen and Melven will be the sons that you and Benjamin never wanted to be. Delivering that flock by myself will make me a legend in these hills."

"No shepherd could drive five hundred head from Tav to Tizra. That's madness, Uncle."

"Madness is living in the shadow of a younger brother. Maybe I should've gone out to battle Zimri that morning, maybe I return to Tav a hero. I couldn't buy into all that liberty versus tyranny talk. At least I didn't return in a box. But Oren has become more powerful in death.

You know of what I speak, your brother too, it's not easy to live under a shadow. Benjamin flees its reach, but not you, you war with your father's shadow. And you've done well for a young man. Some shepherds say you're a greater man than me, that you should be guild master.

Now hear this, Evan Tav… You'll never lead the guild; no issue of Oren Tav's loins will take my hall. This time, my pride will be satisfied."

Nabal adjusts his trousers and takes aim at Evan's boots. "To be clear on this, here's your inheritance." The filthy herdsman relieves himself on Evan's boots.

Benjamin exchanges stares with five grisly shepherds guarding the mountain flock. The Baladan brothers block the serene view of the glade behind them. He tries to look around them to get a view of the flock, but they tighten their stance to hinder his view.

Feelings of intimidation bear down on him and he recalls Evan's instruction to invoke his name. If he invokes Evan's name, he will command the obedience of the Baladan brothers. The instruction puts a strain on Benjamin's humility, so he refuses to speak the name Evan Tav.

"What business brings you all the way out here, boy?" asks the black-bearded Bo Baladan.

Benjamin refuses to speak Evan's name as delusions of leading the flock flicker in his thoughts.

Another brother breaks rank and grabs Benjamin by the back of his head, "Speak, boy!"

"Evan Tav sent me, he's my brother," acknowledges Benjamin, regretfully invoking Evan's name.

"Why didn't you just say that?" wonders Bo with a spark in his black irises, for the oldest Baladan brother shares a hateful respect with Evan Tav.

The ancient Baladan Clan refused to take part in building Tav, claiming that shepherds should live under the stars and among their flocks. As the centuries passed, they became more and more isolated from civilization, similar to the nomadic Tinkers who roamed Hallowed Hills – Though, the Baladans held themselves to a higher standard than the lawless Tinkers.

Oren Tav was the first and only shepherd to befriend the Baladans, for he admired their unrivaled herdsman skills and quickly found them to be an asset to his guild and to his bottom line. Though Oren held one regret about his partnership - The summer that Evan turned thirteen and ran wild with Bo blazing a trail of trouble across Hallowed Hills.

When confronted by the other guild masters, Oren simply wrote it off as sowing oats and forked over a handful of coin for the damages. Only Evan and Bo know what happened at the end of that summer to cause Evan to come back home. Ever since that day, they never trusted each other, but they always maintained their hateful respect.

"What does my old friend want?" asks Bo.

"He wants you to bring the flock to Tav. Nabal signed a

contract with King Zimri for five hundred head and he needs the three hundred out here. Evan wants to oust Nabal and reclaim the guild hall."

The brothers exchange opportunistic looks with one another.

Evan's command of secrecy shames Benjamin's conscience and a familiar anxiety swirls in his stomach. The nerves spawn from his hunger to be his brother's equal, a longing for a place at the table, a place that Evan was hesitant to prepare for his unproven little brother.

The scream of an eagle blasts Benjamin's eardrums, redirecting his hands from his churching stomach to his ringing lobes. The scruffy shepherds shake their heads at the green herder as they cease to obstruct his view.

Shadows from the mountains above cover the glade, and crystal clear springs run down the mountain into a shallow stream allowing the sheep graze on lush grass. The serenity of the shadows, the sound of the trickling brook, and the smell of the spinning breeze sweeps his shepherd senses into absolute tranquility.

WHACK! Bo Baladan smacks Benjamin across the back of his head ending the brief moment of serenity.

"Look at the size of that flock. Your drunken uncle can't deliver that, and certainly not five hundred… So your brother will deliver the flock, huh? If Evan's in charge, he'll deliver. He always delivers."

Bo's affirmation of Evan makes Benjamin feel small in the mountain of his brother's shadow.

Chapter 4 — The Bizarre Bazaar

ocking onto the black bullseye of the target, Jael squints with sharp focus. Benjamin studies his little sister's form with similar focus. The crowd behind them holds their breath in anticipation of her shot. Jael frees the arrow.

A slender man, donning a pointed black-feathered cap, examines the target with his beady eyes.

"Dead Center!" announces the judge and the crowd releases a collective gasp of amazement. Benjamin doubles over in relief.

The spectators vigorously applaud when the judge awards Jael with a blue ribbon. "She's definitely the daughter of Rachel Tav," the old wives cackle.

Jael beams with pride, but Benjamin's smile is much wider than his sister's. The proud brother puts his arm around his sister and they walk in stride to the finale.

Festive black and yellow banners decorate the shops in the town square. The crowd thickens as the remaining townspeople gather for the finale. The judge emerges from the crowd to stand on a boulder in the middle of the town square.

"It's time for the Feats of Fortitude!" trumpets the judge.

The merry crowd cheers the announcement, but their cheers quickly turn to chatter about the two competitors - the challenger, Halvar Hammer, a blacksmith, and the reigning champion, Evan Tav.

Nabal sits at the head of a very long table of prominent people in Tav for the guild master always held the seat of honor at the bazaars. Nabal's scraggly beard frays in all directions, and his flabby physique fills out his sweat-stained shirt. Those sitting next to him keep their distance to avoid the onion odor lifting off his greasy skin. He nervously taps the table with his dirty fingernails while eyeing the corked barrels of honey mead.

Put, the sooty-faced Tav blacksmith, sits to Nabal's left observing Nabal's jitters, "Lousy tradition, eh. No brew until the Feats are through."

Nabal shrugs his shoulders to blow off Put. He never cared much for the braggart, maybe because they were so similar, at least in hygiene or lack thereof.

"You're the guild master, why not break with tradition?"

Nabal thinks on the suggestion with a swallow of his dry throat.

"Eh, the Feats will be quick this year. Evan is no match for my apprentice, Halvar."

Not fond of his nephew but loyal to his guild, Nabal matches the boast, "Evan will win, shepherds always win. Evan's been champ three years runnin' – never once sniffed defeat."

"He's had nothing to drink all day?" asks Evan of Judith on secluded path leading to the town square.

"Nothing. I hope you appreciate how hard it was to keep him from his vice. One boring story after the other… I'll never get the stench of his skin out of my hair."

"I knew you could do it. The first part of the plan worked, let's hope the second does."

Evan wraps his arm around Judith, and they walk in stride to the finale.

They take a few steps before Bo Baladan blocks their path.

"The mountain flock grazes but a couple lengths from the outskirts of Tav," informs Bo.

"I know. Benjamin told me. You should've waited for me in the fields. You better go back; the elders are still ticked about the butcher."

"Still? That was two seasons ago. And I thought you people liked to eat roe deer?"

"We do, Bo. Dead ones. Not ones that buck off the table and kill butchers."

"Guess he had it comin'."

The crass shepherd troubles Judith, so she keeps her head down. Evan grins at his rival's response, "I'll be out for the flock in the morning."

"Who said anything about putting the flock under your control? Nabal might be interested to know that we brought the mountain flock back to Tav. I'd hate to ruin your plan," says Bo with a crooked shine in his eye.

Evan grinds his teeth, frustrated by Benjamin's big mouth.

"There'll be something extra in it for you and your brothers if you leave town right now and return to the flock."

Bo gives a sly nod and follows orders.

"What was that about?" asks Judith.

"That was about Benjamin's folly, yet again."

Before Evan makes his way through the large crowd

assembled in the town square, Judith wraps his right arm in a sling of white cloth.

Evan leaves Judith's side and the crowd cheers loudly at the first sign of the shepherd champion. Gasps of concern for Evan's arm quickly replace the cheers.

Benjamin and Jael look at one another in disbelief.

The white cloth supporting Evan's arm befuddles Nabal, "Evan, my boy. How did this happen?"

"Bad luck. I spared the sheep from the ravine, but my arm was yanked from the socket. I can't compete in the Feats."

Disappointment washes over the faces of the shepherds in the crowd while Put stands and boastfully gawks his head about his wide shoulders.

"That means Halvar wins!" arrogantly proclaims Put.

All of the shepherd families in the crowd grumble with indignation.

Evan raises his left arm to protest Put's declaration of victory and quiet the crowd, "Wait! No need to declare a winner in such a cowardly manner, not while Nabal Tav sits in the seat of honor."

"Nabal? Ha! Are you serious? This is a young man's game," mocks Put.

"I disagree. The Feats are about pride," says Evan.

Nabal furrows his brow and tries to make sense of how he got roped into the dilemma. Baffling more so, is his nephew's newfound respect.

Put and Halvar draw blank faces.

Evan appeals to the shepherds who form the majority of the crowd, "Come on, a round of encouragement… Nabal. Nabal. Nabal."

The crowd takes up the Nabal chant, which echoes loudly off the shops. Evan moves to his uncle's side and lifts his arm to the sky. The roar of the shepherds crescendos into one final thunderous *Nabal*; the cheers lift from the crowd bloating Nabal's ego.

Othniel taps the floor of the ether chancel with his staff. "Shamgar Ram, show yourself."

The balding precept emerges from a dark corner. Othniel turns and engages Shamgar in a long stare down. The disdain in their eyes for one another thickens with bitterness.

"Sorry, I am but a poor prophet. Precept, I have no coin for your coffer…" chides Othniel, gliding toward Shamgar.

"Benjamin Tav told me that you live. What do you want from him?"

"I want him to have faith in Neshama and cease his doubt. Maybe then, he can pick up the mantle of his father," answers Shamgar.

"Doubt, always the enemy of the precepts. Stowing yourself beneath this chancel for a decade hasn't changed you."

"You don't see how doubt ruins him?"

"Doubt is natural, even the Prophetess Miriam had doubts. If we didn't have doubts, what good would Neshama be to humans?"

"Tell me, then, doubting prophet. What troubles you most about Benjamin?"

"The same thing that troubles me about the precepts, that troubles me about the people of Issur. A lack of an imagination. He has no sense of wonder about how awesome Neshama can be. He reduces her to a concept, like he reduces himself to a concept. He can't imagine being anything more than Evan Tav's little brother."

"He lacks holy fervor as well," snaps Shamgar.

"For what cause, collecting coins for your ether chancels? Your holy fervor availed nothing when you abandoned the prophets and shepherds."

"We were in a difficult position. I don't recall much grace from you when the precepts were slaughtered in The Scarlet Winter."

"I don't know why I bothered coming here. I've little grace left, and what I do have, I won't waste on an old zealot like you."

Ezekiel rushes through the door toward the front of the chancel. He puts his hands on his knees and breathes heavily.

"Master, I've come to tell you the news you've longed for… Nabal Tav ordered the barrels of honey mead uncorked."

Shamgar looks over Othniel with suspicion. "Prophet, you tell me who hasn't changed?"

Ezekiel's proclamation breaks Othniel's concentration, "How can this be? Are the Feats through already?"

"You must see this," implores the shocked prophet.

Honey mead gushes from a wooden barrel like a waterfall drenching Nabal's cracked lips and fuzzy beard.

"Best hydrate, Uncle. Maybe knock the edge off. The rock throw was close; you can take him in the barrel stack," encourages Evan.

Nabal removes his face from the barrel as mead streams down his neck and across his greasy chest.

The elder shepherds stand with crossed arms in disgust that Nabal Tav cast aside their ancient tradition.

Ruth Gimel, Nabal's wide-hipped sweetheart, waddles over with an angry scowl.

"Evan! This nonsense must stop! My man's not in good health, for Tav's sake look at him!"

"His honor's on the line, not that an adulteress would know anything of honor," rebukes Evan.

Nabal, emboldened by the mead, rears up like a bear. "Woman! Get behind me! Don't rob me of my honor!" commands Nabal storming off to the barrel stack.

Evan swiftly follows.

Ruth stomps her foot and shuffles behind them.

✦ ✦ ✦

Benjamin and Jael cheer loudly for Nabal as he feverishly stacks another barrel on the pile.

A drunken buffoon drapes his arm around Ezekiel, his beer-breath stinging the eyes of the cramped prophet. Othniel flanks his understudy with an arm draped around the other shoulder. The two prophets mingle in the rear of the crowd avoiding Evan's line of sight. Othniel downs a wooden mug of mead and belches into Ezekiel's ear.

Evan and Judith stand next to the suspicious mistress and stoically watch the scheme unfold. Ruth rings her wrinkled hands watching Nabal labor for air.

Sweat drains from Halvar's freckled bald head down to his thick red beard. His abs ache as he stacks one more barrel. Halvar looks upon Nabal in disbelief, "That mead gives you unnatural strength, old man. Is this some kind of trick?"

"Shut your mouth and keep stacking," coaches Put.

Halvar and Nabal wobble back for their final barrel of grain. They reach down in unison and lift the heavy barrels above their heads and make way back to the pile.

Halvar picks up the pace and takes the lead. Put encourages his apprentice with boastful acclamations.

An explosive CRACK! startles the crowd when Halvar's left knee buckles.

The challenger drops to the ground and his weighty barrel shatters across the back of his skull. Grain sprays in all direction.

Nabal tosses the final drum onto his pile, and the crowd chants his name once more.

The judge rushes to Halvar with such haste that his feathered-hat flies away. He rolls Halvar over, taps his face, and waves his hand above his mouth.

Put slides in and grabs hold of Halvar's body, "Halvar, wake up!" shouts the mentor forcefully jostling his apprentice, who shows no signs of life.

Nabal draws near to gloat over Put and his dead apprentice. "Fools, honey mead is the lifeblood of shepherds."

Nabal grinds his palm into his chest as a sharp pain stings his heart. An unhealthy grimace surfaces on his face.

Evan's unsteady hand serves his uncle a foaming mug of brew. Nabal chugs the mead, lets out a deathly belch, and falls headlong next to the corpse of Halvar.

The crowd goes hush.

Benjamin, Jael, and Judith sprint to their uncle's side. Ruth Gimel pushes onlookers out of the way and waddles to her beau. Merlen and Melvin Gimel drag their feet to the scene, nudged along by obligation.

"Evan! Look what you've done to my precious Nabal!"

"Did he ink your name in his will, Ruth?" whispers Evan so that only Ruth, her sons, and his siblings can hear.

Her mouth drops to the ground.

"You snake!" curses Ruth.

"Who's the snake, Ruth?"

Merlen and Melven attend to their brokenhearted mother as she weeps over the corpse of Nabal.

"Why don't you and your boys dig elsewhere for gold? The guild hall is mine."

The air in Benjamin's and Jael's lungs freeze, iced over by Evan's sinister scheme. Judith dries her tears with a handkerchief and releases a warm sigh of relief.

Othniel pulls Ezekiel from the embrace of the drunken buffoon. He looks upon his understudy with the most sober of stares. "Take notice, my young apprentice. We must be wary of Evan Tav."

Chapter 5 | The Prophet Hunter

Ezekiel sits on a rock surrounded by a handful of children, two mothers, and a small flock of sheep. He shares The Book of Miriam from memory, captivating his audience with his eloquent storytelling.

Benjamin stares at the Miriam idol in the palm of his hand. He peels his eyes from the statuette and sees hope in the faces of the children - a pulse of promise thumps in his soul. He places the idol back into his pocket and nervously scans the horizon for Evan. Instead, he locates two rapidly approaching objects out in the distance. Within moments of squinting, he spots two lightly armored horsemen in black galloping across the hills.

"Grab your children! Run! Hide!" shouts Benjamin.

The mothers follow orders, but two boys remain unclaimed. Benjamin catches sight of their mother at the highest point of the hill, screaming down to her two sons. He looks upon his flock then looks at the two boys. He tucks a child under each arm and makes a run for the frantic mother.

Ezekiel labors to keep up with Benjamin.

The flock scatters as the two horsemen plow through the sheep in pursuit of Benjamin and Ezekiel.

Benjamin safely delivers the two sons to their mother, who gathers her boys into her arms and hides between two large boulders.

The horsemen pursue the fleeing shepherd and prophet.

Benjamin feels the breath of the steeds ruffle his hair as the hunters draw swords and take aim. Before the blades fall, Benjamin grabs Ezekiel. They leap off a ridge and tumble down a hill.

A dozen children gather together on a ragged carpet in the guild hall, listening intently as Othniel reads from The Book of Miriam. The captivated children lean forward to receive the climax of the story.

Large oak doors etched with the tales of shepherds welcome visitors into the guild hall. Green tapestries line the stone walls along the near side and three wooden doors line the far side. The hall is replete with a long oak table, barrels, and sacks. A cast iron cauldron bookends the hall and boils in the large fireplace. Loud pops and cracks from the fireplace startle the enthralled children, but the thickening aroma of Judith's mutton stew restores their nerves.

The gravestone in a memorial garden near the hall and the mess in the master bedroom are the only evidence of Nabal Tav existence. Judith and Jael worked all week to get the hall back to how their mother left it. Judith's wedding was approaching, and there was much to prepare. The master bedroom would have to wait.

As Othniel concludes his story, he's delighted that the tale enraptures the children. He slides to the edge of his seat and leans over the children.

"Yet in the quiet of the dawn, a whisper wanders in the morning breeze, and a wish of remembrance ascends to Neshama. It is in the darkest hours of our history that remnants rise like the sun to shine the daylight of liberty. Therefore, in these dark times, we pray to Neshama with the hope that she will remember us, with the hope that the nephesh will return to Issur."

Othniel offers the children a kind smile, "You've been the most pleasant audience."

Judith moves about the carpet and rewards the children with candy, "Thank you, and thank your mothers for letting you help with the wedding decorations."

After a week of cleaning with Judith, Jael tires of hearing about the wedding. She makes a face mocking Judith's happiness, but Judith pretends to ignore her sister. Jael returns to petting Smoke, her bushy grey cat. He sits on her lap watching her flip through Othniel's book, a leather-bound book chock-full of sacred writ and drawings.

Evan enters the hall earlier than expected and everyone takes notice. His stone face intimidates the children.

Judith exhales a worrisome gasp.

Evan catches sight of Othniel and becomes as hot as the boiling cauldron.

"I knew you had something to do with this. Bo told me that he saw Benjamin and some stranger in a brown robe running south."

Suddenly, Benjamin and Ezekiel bolt into the hall wrecking into Evan.

"They're coming… Here," wheezes Benjamin.

Evan looks out the guild hall doors and sees four men approaching on horseback followed by four soldiers on foot.

Two of the infantrymen hold the leashes of shaggy black dogs. The hunting party wears the colors of purple and black. An ominous black wolf head on the standard bearer's purple banner warns Evan of King Zimri's presence.

"They fly king's banner," says Evan as Judith quickly opens the chamber door to the master bedroom; she motions to Benjamin, Othniel, and Ezekiel to enter.

The stench from the room holds them at bay.

As the galloping thunder and barking bites get louder, they realize there's no choice. They slide into the chamber and crawl under the bed.

King Zimri Tizra and Captain Rezon Scar dismount from their black steeds. With a flick of his wrist, Scar orders his soldiers to patrol the domain surrounding the guild hall. Zimri arrogantly tromps up the stairs and enters the hall.

Zimri's flabby physique forms a layer over his once muscular build. Long, black, scraggly hair falls over his sunken eyes and unshaven cheekbones. Planted firmly on Zimri's right hand, the Signet Ring of Issur glows shades of gold.

Rezon takes his place at his lord's side, wiping his thin, black, scraggly hair from his grotesque face. He lacks a left eye, and mangled scar tissue reddens the left side of his face. The terrified children shelter behind Judith. The little ones huddle in the far corner, shuddering at the sight of the two ruffians.

"Hail, King Zimri. What business brings you to my hall?" asks Evan.

"Your hall? What has become of Nabal Tav?"

"His heart failed him, about a week ago at the bazaar."

"That's unfortunate news," says Zimri, his black armor clinking ominously as he struts about the guild hall. After pondering the unfortunate news about Nabal, he walks to the cauldron, reaches for the stirring spoon, and breathes in broth from the stew.

"Are you aware of Nabal's contract?"

"I'll honor it. I always commit to my plans," affirms Evan.

"Twas true of your father," admits Zimri with a twitch in his eye.

"Have you come here to discuss the contract, Sire?"

"No. We've been tracking a couple of prophets. Two of my men were about to capture one until a shepherd decided to be a hero. The dogs picked up their scent and led us to *your* guild hall," says Zimri, investigating the hall for any signs of the prophets.

"Let me remind you that Neshama worship is outlawed and punishable by death."

Zimri eyes Jael for a lengthy moment before noticing a crack in the chamber door. Keeping a lustful eye on Jael, he walks slowly toward the master bedroom.

The soles of Benjamin's boots stick out from under the bed. In an attempt to investigate the dirty boots, Zimri steps into room, but the odor of rotten liver halts his investigation. He squints through the heaps of dirty clothes and pile of mead bottles cluttering the room. The stench of vomit lifts from the floorboards to repel the king.

"Nabal Tav's quarters, I presume," gags Zimri, retreating from the odor.

Jael's wit alerts her that she's reading an outlawed book. She swiftly plops Smoke on top of the potential evidence that could link the prophets to the guild hall.

Zimri notices the sudden movement; he moves toward Jael and plays with the tip of her curled-ponytail, his fingers spiraling further into her thick hair. She despises his caress but can't move for fear of revealing the book.

Evan suppresses his fury as he watches the tyrant touch his little sister. Zimri flicks the tips of Jael's hair as he removes his fingers - the chills fold her toes.

Zimri lords over Evan once more, but the stoic shepherd refuses to be intimidated.

"Evan Tav… I know the shepherd hero is your little brother. I know he adores Othniel 'Wayfarer,' the same way your father adored him," says Zimri turning a dark shade of red at the thought of Oren Tav. Memories cause his veins to burn with hate.

A soldier enters the hall; his back stiffens as he awaits permission to report. Zimri disconnects from his unpleasant reminiscence. Rezon Scar tilts his head to acknowledge the soldier.

"Sire. We checked the premise and there's no sign of the prophets, but we did find a garden out back."

Zimri presses his armor into Evan's chest and huffs like a bull, "Is this so? Just because you're in these hills doesn't mean that you can disobey the law. Everyone, including the shepherds, must purchase produce from my farms."

Rezon steals a couple of empty sacks from the hall and tosses them to the soldier, "Take what we can use, then destroy the garden."

Evan musters every ounce of patience to control the fury that boils within as Zimri turns to Rezon, "Captain, get the tax log."

Rezon steps outside the open doors and pulls a large leather-bound book from a saddlebag. He returns to the hall and rudely clears a portion of the table before slamming the tax log.

"People have problems coming up with taxes these days, let's hope your family is not delinquent," says Zimri, slowly thumbing through the log. "Here you are, the Guild Hall of Tav… How prestigious."

Zimri gets back in Evan's face, "Paid in full… Lucky… You better stay in my good graces, and that flock better arrive in time for the moon festival. I'd hate to return and take your little sister as payment."

Zimri's eyes lust after Jael for another lengthy moment.

"Like the produce from your garden, I share all my spoils with my men."

Rezon grins with approval.

Evan stoically stares down the tyrant while Zimri breathes down the guild master's neck.

"I have a message for Benjamin. If I catch him with the prophets, then he will burn with the prophets."

Zimri exits the hall slowly with Rezon following behind.

They mount their horses, and at the blast of a horn ride off with their hunting pack following after.

Judith consoles each child with a hug and more candy as she sends them on their way.

Frantically gasping for fresh air, Benjamin, Othniel, and Ezekiel flee the bedroom and return to the hall.

Evan rushes Othniel and slams him against the wall, "You're not welcome here! Stay away from my family! Get out!"

Judith secretly slips Othniel some cornbread in a folded cloth, trying hard to hold back her tears. Jael hands Ezekiel Othniel's holy book without making eye contact with her brother.

Once the prophets exit, Evan directs his fury at his siblings, "Benjamin! I told you to stop being friendly to the prophets and to stop believing those worthless stories… Judith! Why would you allow that old fool in our hall?"

Knowing her brother's temper, Judith withholds any words that may flame his fury. She simply stirs the stew as her answer.

Benjamin isn't as suave and his eyes stay engaged with Evan's red eyes.

"Where's your flock?"

The temptation to lie tickles Benjamin's soul, but he's a terrible liar, so he comes clean with the truth.

"Scattered."

"I told you about this before. Never abandon your flock!"

Judith steps in to rescue her little brother, "Let's eat."

Jael puts bowls and spoons on the table to speed up the process of getting her siblings to the table. Everyone seats themselves and they enjoy a quiet meal of Judith's mutton, carrot, and potato stew served with a slice of warm cornbread.

After the sons of Oren Tav finish their meal, they make way to their hovel across from the guild hall. They clear the last step when Evan takes hold of Benjamin's shoulders.

"What's wrong with you? Wasting time with that old fool, losing your flock. How could you disrespect me like that? After Father's death, I was forced to provide for you and our sisters. Nabal removed us from the hall, cast us out like orphans. Even worse, he soiled our family name. We have to prove to every shepherd in Hallowed Hills that we can lead this guild hall the way our father did. Apparently, you've forgotten his instruction. Shepherds never abandon their flock."

Evan cools his temper when the rush of the night breeze fills the silence.

"What excuse are you going to make this time?"

Benjamin hangs his head.

Evan grabs his chin and pushes his head up. "It's about time you grow up."

"I guess I should go reclaim my flock, then."

"I'll get someone else to clean up your mess. Bo can send one of his brothers."

Evan storms off leaving Benjamin to regret yet another mistake under the shadow of the guild hall.

Evan, Benjamin, Judith, and Jael finish a quiet breakfast as the prophet incident from the night before lingers in the air. Benjamin and Jael eye one another, still feeling the resentment that festers within Evan. Judith seems to have forgotten the incident, her mind floating on clouds of romance as her wedding date nears.

Judith's wedding excitement often annoyed her siblings but rightfully so. She was forced to play the role of mother at a young age and she was well beyond the marriage age due to the expensive wedding sum set by her father.

"Daniel is the tallest of his brothers, best looking too," announces Judith, unable to contain her inner thoughts.

"Ardon Tsadi is a good man. Daniel comes from a long line of capable shepherds. I'm sure that's why father arranged this marriage," says Evan.

"And that's why father set the wedding sum so high."

"It's an honest sum, Judith. I'm sure Daniel is good for the other half. I look forward to having him be part of our guild hall. He doesn't abandon his flocks."

Benjamin pretends to ignore the comment, but it stings his heart.

"The next archery contest is at the fall estival," says Jael prodding Benjamin's ribs. "You should enter, give me a challenge."

"I'm better with a sword."

"Let's see about that."

To Benjamin's surprise, Jael gets up and draws a ceremonial sword from the mantel over the fireplace.

"Let's settle this now."

Judith rolls her eyes as all the attention shifts to her unruly sister.

"Jael! Sit down and act normal!" commands Evan.

"So sorry for interrupting Princess Judith."

Judith fancies the sarcastic comment. She revisits her childhood dreams filled with flowing gowns and sparkling tiaras.

An emphatic rapping rattles the door and interrupts the siblings.

"Come in!" shouts Evan, nervous from the heavy knock.

Bo Baladan's face appears bearing grim greetings.

"What happened?" sighs Evan.

"My brother did the best he could to gather Benjamin's flock, but a sheep did stray. We found its bones at the watering hole. We spotted two wolves on the outskirts of town, wise enough to be out of bow range… They're getting bolder."

"Desperate. They're searching for water too."

A look of concern pours over Benjamin's face, and Jael takes notice, "You're sad. A shepherd that's afraid of wolves."

"I should've been in the field last night, should've dragged my brother along to clean up his own mess," admits Evan, his face returning to stone.

Evan's resolute demeanor demands everyone's attention.

"I'll take the flock to Tizra for the moon festival. Bo and his brothers will come with me. We'll return in a couple weeks. Benjamin, reclaim your flock and watch over them at the watering hole. Make sure you cover the hole, those wolves will drink it dry. And promise me that you won't abandon your flock."

"I promise," affirms Benjamin with halfhearted conviction.

"Can I help him?" asks Jael.

"You need to help Judith get ready for her wedding; maybe you'll learn something about being a lady."

Evan's comment cuts Jael's confidence.

Evan, with his longsword tightly fastened to his back and a staff at his feet, slings a burlap sack over one shoulder and a leather canteen over the other. He hesitates for a moment, taking in the grandeur of the guild hall and reflecting on the shepherds of old. The rising sun highlights the craftsmanship of the guild hall. The boulders of Hallowed Hills undergird the masculine structure, triangular oak planks frame the truss, and layers of green wood shingles span the roof.

Judith and Jael marvel at the sight of five hundred sheep.

The Baladan Brothers marvel at the sight of Judith and Jael.

A nasty look from Evan dulls the gleam in their wild eyes, "Boys! Keep your eyes on the flock."

Benjamin attempts to hide behind Judith when Evan calls him out, "You understand your task?"

"Yes."

"Not too hard for you?"

"No."

"All you have to do is cover a hole."

"I got it," affirms Benjamin with wide eyes.

The Baladan Brothers bite their lips to withhold their laughter as Evan runs down Benjamin.

"One more thing. Stay away from Othniel, he's poisoning your mind," commands Evan with an edge to his warning.

"Othniel was a friend of our father."

"I don't care if he was. He's not a friend of mine."

"Maybe one of the brothers could tend my flock and I could go with you to Tizra?"

"You wouldn't survive two steps. Pickpockets, prostitutes, drunkards. It gets worse every year. Tizra would swallow you whole."

Judith and Jael intervene on Benjamin's behalf by saying goodbye to Evan with warm farewell embraces. Benjamin retreats to lengthen his distance from his brother.

"Don't part in bitterness, Evan," pleads Judith into his ear.

Evan closes the distance with his brother and puts his arm around him. "Next time…" The affectionate act puts Judith at ease, but it seems an insincere and forced gesture to Benjamin.

Evan's powerful voice commands the flock and the sheep spring into motion as if a roar from a mountain lion threatens them. The motivated flock meanders south down Josiah's Path toward Tizra.

Chapter 6
The City of Kings

van and the Baladans halt the flock on a mound that stretches half a length across the King's Highway north of Pella. They look toward Tizra with a sense of awe - the very sight of the city of kings steals a heartbeat from the shepherds.

Lengths upon lengths of crops roll west of Tizra across The Heartland. The rising sun sparkles off the mighty Tizra River flowing across the south of the city dividing the isle into two islands.

A magnificent palace dominates the cityscape with its round bastilles towers forming an inner sanctum within the capital. Architects spared no expense in creating a palace worthy of the Goddess and protective of King Josiah Tizra.

Townhomes and apartments of matching grey stone speckled in black surround the palace. The dwellings allow Tizrites easy access to the market districts - one in the north plaza and the other in the south plaza.

Two grand landmarks flank the palace - The Pit, a hastily built wooden stadium to the west, and the Temple of Melek, an alluring pantheon of worship to the east. Once the Grand Chancel, it now serves as a den of immorality for the Melek worshipping nobility of Tizra.

Four thick walls joined together by four large towers on each corner guard the city of kings. The south gate, with its formidable drawbridge, seals off Tizra from southern Issur. Merchants move freely about northern Issur under the watchful eye of the tower guard in the north gate.

Evan allows the brothers to gaze upon Tizra for another moment before issuing a stern warning, "She's beautiful, no doubt. On the outside. On the inside - not so much. Shepherds of your lot, I'm certain you can handle most of the filth in Tizra. But if one of you crosses the crown, we'll be heading home a man down. Careful where you piss."

"We're outsiders, not hermits," says Bo.

"On second thought, I might enjoy seeing you tossed in the dungeon. Don't worry. I'll visit you… To laugh in your face."

Evan looks Bo in the eyes and flares a screaming whistle that summons the flock back to action.

King Zimri looks out a palace window into the streets of Tizra. Hungry women and children beg on hands and knees in hopes that their king will throw down food.

"These are hard times for my people," laments Zimri turning to his table filled with heaps of food - hotcakes stacked high, lush fruits, cured meats.

The decadence of his table matches his hall. Colorful tapestries tell of his triumphs over the guilds that revolted against him, streamers of purple and black line the barren spaces in the hall, assorted treasures and weapons offer a shine to the space.

Queen Rizpah sits at the foot of the table. The grace that once charmed her eyes fades into dark circles of depression. A frail woman, her heavy blue gown strains to grasp her thin frame. Her small brown dog snacks on table scraps at her feet.

"Zimri, my love. Please tell me this is your last hunt for a while. I worry when you're away. Aren't you afraid when you leave Tizra?"

"Never. There are those in Issur who despise my reign, but they won't rise up against me. Fear keeps them in line."

Zimri notices that tears cloud Rizpah's blue eyes. He walks to his queen, kneels at her side, and gently swipes the tears away. "If I didn't go on my hunts, how could I gather opal orchids?"

"Don't tease me."

Zimri pulls an opal orchid stem from behind his back. The queen's dark circles lighten and her cheeks glow as she accepts the rare flower. She locks onto her love's eyes as she savors the smell of romance. The fragrance transports her back to her youth - lying on the bare chest of Zimri, listening to the rushing waters of the Tizra River, the tranquil prince gliding the opal petals of an orchid stem down her smooth shoulders to her elbows.

"It's perfect!"

"I knew you'd love it, so I brought the whole plant!" Zimri stands and whisks a white cloth off the orchid plant in the center of the table.

Rizpah leaps up and kisses him. The romantic moment lightens his features and invigorates his health, providing the queen a glimpse of the king before the age of Melek.

Prince Aden Tizra the Fifth enters the hall. Immediately, tension replaces the romantic notions floating about the orchid plant. Zimri returns to his view of hungry children begging in the streets below while Aden sits next to Rizpah.

The prince was an only child and mothered accordingly. His approachable demeanor was cultivated by a responsive queen, who knew her subjects by name and provided for their needs by her own hand. From a young age he was taught to defend those who could not defend themselves.

Aden looks nothing like his father. He's handsome with piercing blue eyes and a muscular build; his thick, dark-blond hair was passed down to him from the spitting image of his namesake, and grandfather, King Aden Tizra the Fourth 'The Deerstalker.' Not only does he resemble his grandfather, he excels in hunting and the military arts like his beloved mentor. Of all the virtues that emanate from Aden, none are more prominent than his pure heart.

"Maybe you could spare a morsel of your meal with those starving children," suggests Aden to his hoggish father.

"Maybe you could keep your mouth shut for one meal. Besides, I have it on good authority that you loot my kitchen on behalf of the poor."

Rizpah takes little time to poke the hole in her son's heart for the question springs forth from the hole in hers.

"When are you going to settle down with that nice girl from the Bel family? It'd be nice to cradle a grandson in my arms. What's wrong? Your father has agreed to terms with her father."

"I haven't agreed, and by the way she's not a nice girl."

"We sew for hours in the afternoon. She doesn't say much and likes things quiet, but she's so thoughtful, always brings a pitcher of tomato juice. Poor thing suffers from those awful headaches and backaches."

"Because she's hung over, Mother. She's into Melek worship and gets hammered at the temple. And I can list a dozen reasons why her back hurts."

"Enough!" shouts Zimri smashing his fist on the table. "You're still stuck on Abigail Locke. What you need is a woman who bends her knees to the moon god. A woman who will make a man of you, help mold you into the image of Melek."

"Like the Queen Mother, Isavel," says Aden with a bite to his words.

The insult hurts Rizpah more than it does Zimri, and Aden regrets his disrespectful words.

The High Magi Zidon 'The Absolute' enters the hall.

"Here's a man who can mold you into the image of Melek," says Zimri embracing his councilor and head of the Order of the Magi.

Zidon glides to his seat under his long grey robe with a thick grey hood. The shades of his grey knotted-beard match his cloak. Despite a crooked nose, he bears a similar but darker resemblance to Othniel.

Zidon's presence forces Rizpah to nervously tap her nails on the cedar table.

"My wise councilor, maybe you can tutor my misguided son in the ways of Melek."

Aden looks upon his father with disdain. He glances over to his comrade, Caleb Glade. His best friend and scout plays the role of palace guard. Aden had Caleb infiltrate Zimri's bodyguard in hopes of discovering Zimri's deepest secrets because his father refuses to share his mind with his son.

Caleb's shoulder-length brown hair pulls into a ponytail behind his long face etched with a brown goatee. Due to his extensive efforts as a scout, he has no fat on his body. Caleb has covered every square of terrain in Issur and canvassed the streets of every town.

"You were coming along so nicely, Aden. Your sixteenth year was so full of potential for Melek," reminds Zidon.

"That was a long time ago," acknowledges the prince,

forcing the hellish memories back to the depths before they can torment his soul.

Zimri sits and breakfast begins.

Aden prepares a frugal plate, Rizpah picks at some fruit, and Zimri stacks his plate.

"Emmerick still doesn't recognize my rule. With each year The Southern Kingdom slips further from my grip," complains Zimri.

"Your brother and The Southern Kingdom will fall; they lack the resources to succeed. Their fall has been foreseen… How was your hunt?"

"I had him, Zidon. Him and his understudy. Had them cornered in Tav, but they escaped yet again."

"I hate those dreadful hunts. Why can't you hunt elk like your father used to?" questions Rizpah.

"A quiet queen is a cordial queen," says Zidon, causing Rizpah to sink back into her chair.

Aden resents the comment with a crossed look.

"Deer pose no threat to your kingship. Prophets do. You must continue to hunt them."

"What of the moon festival? Will Evan Tav deliver on time?" asks Zimri.

"Based on Rezon Scar's most recent report, it appears so," informs Zidon.

"Nabal Tav's untimely death was most unfortunate. I was so close to overtaking the Tav guild hall. If I could somehow link the shepherds to the prophets, I could arouse such a frenzy in Tizra that I could seize their guild as I did the others…

Curse the shepherds and the foresters, how they reject my reign. My army is twenty-five thousand strong; I could crush them all at once."

"The guilds are divided, and you must conquer them as such. Then you can rout the southern separatists from Issur. All will be yours in time, my King."

Zimri shovels hotcakes into his mouth and chews like a horse. The butter sinks into the warm bread atop his tongue and slides down his throat to ease the tension twisting in his gut.

Zimri's main obsession is killing prophets; his second obsession is food. A handful of misfortunate chefs have found themselves at the wrong end of Zimri's fork, like the previous head chef who made a blackberry tart a little too tart. Zimri stuck a fork in the chef's eye and threw him in the dungeon for thirty seasons.

The replacement head chef, Ruben, frantically dices carrots. His knife rapidly taps the cutting board like a woodpecker drills a log, his baggy white clothes and fluffy white hat flittering about his short and skinny frame. Ruben chops with a puckered face, annoyed that the kitchen runs inefficiently under his direction.

His cooks focus more on the wrath of Zimri's appetite than their duty at hand. Ruben's crew stumbles about the claustrophobic kitchen, huffing on the oven fumes lifting out the sole window. Despite the cramped space, the stations follow a proper order - the prep area stands next to the cauldrons and the stovetops, the bread racks stack next to the brick oven.

Chef Ruben mumbles orders to his men nervously prepping the evening meal. Failing to inspire the crew, he directs his ire toward the only female in the kitchen.

"You know Ardon Tsadi and his boys usually deliver the big flocks for the grand festivals? Can that boyfriend of yours from Tav handle such a large flock?"

"He learned from the best," humbly answers Evan's betrothed.

A sweaty, gorgeous mess - Ashira Keros pulls her long, silky, raven-colored hair into a bun. She wears a white outfit similar to the other chefs, but with the sleeves rolled up her olive-colored arms. Her cheekbones cut perfectly below her playful brown eyes. The baggy clothes cover her curves and she blends in well with the male cooks. Unlike the male cooks, Ashira has an intense aura, focused on her duty instead of fear.

"I heard Zimri has it out for the Tav guild hall," taunts Ruben.

Focused on her work, Ashira ignores him.

"Girl! I'm talkin' to you!"

"When are you gonna shut up and cook?" blurts Ashira, annoyed by her boss and his inefficient staff.

She removes Chef Ruben's hat and places it on her head.

"I'm your superior. How dare you touch me?"

Ashira rips a knife from the butcher's hand.

"Do something about it."

The bold move silences Ruben and his frantic staff.

"I don't know about you, but I want to keep my eyes. And while I take meals to the dungeon, I'd rather not end up a permanent resident like my last boss. Not to mention, I've never missed one of my brother's fights and today won't be the first."

Chef Ruben backs down and allows Ashira to take control of the kitchen. She points out orders with her knife, "You two, on prep. You, stir. You, scour that oven. You, knead that dough. And you… Get washing," orders Ashira, pointing her knife at Ruben - directing him to the dish pit.

In short time, Ashira's operation runs efficiently.

A sickly rat attempts to escape the dank training room in The Pit. It hobbles across a ledge, dodging a thrust of a dagger and a whack of a mace. A tiny lantern dangles from the ceiling, expanding the shadows of the instruments of doom.

The unscathed vermin plops into a sewer grate, causing Seth Keros to slam his weapons against the metal grate before returning to his bench.

Seth stares at the dirt floor while Og, the pit boss, eyes the behemoth with disgust.

Sweat beads atop Seth's buzzed black hair and olive-colored forehead. The sweat flows over his brown eyes, and slides down the dark stubble on his cheeks. A brewing rage stirs beneath his gentle eyes.

Og, with his horrid breath, badgers the pitfighter, "You ever gonna fight with honor?" accuses the pit boss, spitting a meteor of black tobacco that splatters on the wall.

Seth stands and towers over his superior, "Your breath smells worse than the sewer."

Seth shrivels his nose as he walks over the sewer grate, more appalled by the rats that scavenge in the sewer than the smell.

"Honor has forsaken this city. Two more fights and my debt's paid."

"And after your debt's paid?" asks Og.

"The family business."

"What's that?"

"Pottery."

Og laughs uncontrollably at Seth's trade. The pitfighter furls his nose and places his hand over Og's mouth; the aggressive gesture silences the jovial laughter.

"Who am I facing? The usual… thieves, bandits, disgraced vets?"

Og removes Seth's paw from his tobacco-stained teeth to reveal his snakish grin, "A Vilekin Corsair, no clue where Zimri fished her out."

"Her? And what's a Vilekin?"

"An ancient menace of Issur. You best watch out for this one, she's a bit on the wild side."

Seafarers from the east, the Vilekin Corsairs first arrived on the shores of Issur in 531. Their superior navy, knowledge of metallurgy, and mastery of toxins made them a formidable foe, but their lust for gold drove them to ruin. The Vilekin maritime empire expanded too quickly and enslaved too many; the slave revolts could not be contained and there were not enough warriors to defend their colonies. In time, they were driven from their homeland and now exist in roving bands of mercenaries.

Seth enters the arena of The Pit wearing traditional pitfighter garb - sleeves of iron armor protect his shoulders and arms, iron greaves protect his legs. His chest and abs appear as if they're chiseled from stone. Peacemaker, a large, steel warhammer with intricate etchings of doves in the head of the hammer, rests across his shoulders.

Vendors scale the rickety bleachers to offer spectators steaming mugs of almonds. The shoddy planks creak with each step. The wooden bleachers form a horseshoe around The Pit and Zimri's cement box seat seals off the arena on the south side of the stadium. Four execution-posts firmly stake their claim in the center of the dirt floor arena.

The crowd chants their champion's name at the first sight of Seth. Zimri sits in his box seat and pretends to ignore the praise. Ashira arrives in her food-stained chef's coat. She's out of breath and unable to shout her brother's name.

Seth marvels for a moment when his unusual opponent enters the arena. The presence of the unique enemy hushes the crowd, pulling a rare smile from Zimri.

Purple linen wraps scantily clothe the lean form of the Vilekin corsair. Black runes canvass her forearms and biceps. She wears a shark tooth necklace around her neck, the jagged diamonds sparkling from a coat of a mysterious metal alloy. She wields a curved dagger in her right hand and a poisonous choral-blue sea snake in her left hand. She squeezes the snake's mouth and anoints her dagger with toxins.

Seth charges the corsair like a wild bull.

She spits an acidic substance causing her to grimace in pain as the chemicals exit her mouth. Seth halts to block the acid with his left sleeve of armor. The toxic substance slowly devours the iron armor and burns the surface his flesh. He throws his corroded sleeve of iron to the ground.

The corsair takes the initiative and attacks Seth with wild dagger swings. The behemoth shows some quickness as he swerves through the wooden posts, dodging the poisonous attacks.

The corsair removes her shark tooth necklace and connects it to the butt of her dagger. She takes the sea snake and secures it around her neck. With her left hand balancing the onslaught of whip lashes, the whip cuts Seth and blood runs from his chest. She cracks the whip across the pitfighter's left leg greaves, the triangles ripping through his defenses like a saw.

The corsair moves to capitalize on his unarmored left side. Seth makes a bold and painful move to disarm the woman of her whip when he catches the lash with his right forearm. He sneers in the tug of war with his enemy, but this works to Seth's strength as he reels her in like a fish. The corsair hits a mechanism on her dagger that releases the whip-necklace.

In one fluid motion, the corsair releases the snake from her neck and flings it at Seth. His right leg greaves are thick enough to block the bite, but the snake's fangs stick in the iron.

The seafarer leaps and takes aim at his throat.

Seth rolls out of the way while grabbing a fistful of dirt and throwing it into her eyes.

Seth swings Peacemaker though the dirt cloud and connects with the corsair's head. A resounding THUD! echoes across the bleachers as Peacemaker wrecks the corsair.

Seth does not swing a second time.

The stunned crowd releases a sickening gasp.

The silence dies quickly when a section of bloodthirsty fans muster a rousing ovation for the carnage.

Zimri wears his usual placid mask to hide his embarrassment at yet another failed attempt to end the life of Seth Keros.

Ashira exhales her anxiety and mouths a thank you to the Goddess.

The cheers strengthen as Seth's name echoes across the arena, but the pitfighter refuses to pander to the crowd and humbly exits.

As Seth exits the arena, four executioners enter with four shackled peasants.

Seth turns to Og, "What's this about?"

"Three Neshama worshippers and a scribe. Zimri fished them out of the sewers the other night."

The crowd awaits Zimri's proclamation while the executioners hook the shackles of the prisoners on the posts and pour oil over the logs underneath their feet.

"Glory be to Melek, god of the dark, god of the moon! Neshama will not be worshipped! Burn them!" shouts Zimri flashing a sadistic smile as the mob cheers their mad king.

Seth stares at the ground, and Ashira releases a prayer for the martyrs into the starry night.

Chapter 7 | Not-So-Simple Instructions

enjamin waters his flock on the outskirts of Tav. A wolf sends a howl of anticipation into the night sky after she spots her prey. A competitor throws down a challenge with a vicious bawl. The wails at the moon unnerve Benjamin as he plots his next move - to cover the hole with a small boulder or to move the flock to safety. The security of the bow in his grip makes him hesitant to move the boulder - a two-handed task - so he strings an arrow and directs the flock to safety on a crest of a hill about a quarter-length away from the water source.

Benjamin musters the courage to hunt the wolves. With his yellow-feathered arrow pointing his direction, he parts the tall grass with long, soft strides.

Jael springs from the tall grass onto Benjamin's back, and the siblings crash to the ground.

She laughs at his fearful face, and once a moment of relief settles Benjamin, he cracks a smile at her prank.

The joke ends when a wolf lunges at Jael's head. An apt Benjamin shoves her to the grass. Jael rolls to her feet, draws her bow, and nails the wolf between the eyes.

The second wolf leaps from the tall grass at Benjamin. He fires an arrow into its hind leg to drop the beast. He finishes the wolf with an arrow to the heart.

Benjamin inspects his kill while Jael admires her bolt firmly planted in the wolf's skull, "One shot, thought you should know."

Adrenaline gives way to tired legs forcing Benjamin and Jael to lie down among the sheep and take in the warm summer air. They position their hands behind their heads and gaze into the endless stars.

A foreign scent overpowers the earthy smells of the hills, and Benjamin's eyes begin to water.

"Are you crying about the wolves?" asks Jael.

"No… What perfume is that?"

"Jasmine. Judith spilled it on me by accident… I think."

"It burns my eyes."

"Who's the girl that revealed this allergy?"

"Nobody, forget it."

"You're wrecking this wholesome image I have of you. Tell me, you know I'll find out sooner or later."

"Ashira wears Jasmine," admits Benjamin in a bashful voice.

"Evan better not find about your infatuation with her."

"It's not like that."

"If you say so… Evan wants to marry me off to one of Daniel's brother, Jacob Tsadi. I keep making excuses to avoid meeting him, but I won't have a choice at the wedding."

"Daniel seems like a good guy. I'm sure his brother is nice."

"It's not about that. I know Evan wishes that I were more like Judith, but I want to make my own choices." Jael's words pierce Benjamin, and she realizes that something troubles him.

"What's wrong, Benjamin?"

He's hesitant to answer, but his fondness for Jael softens his defenses, "Do you believe in Neshama, in the Covenant?"

"More so as a child. I really don't think about it like you always have. You were always spiritual, Judith too. I barely remember those late fireside chats with papa, sitting next to you, fighting to keep my eyes open as papa went on and on answering your questions."

"I miss those nights... Othniel says father should have been a prophet but he had too much shepherd in him. After his death, I assumed that Evan would be that voice in my life, but I never realized how much he resented that father was a spiritual man. At least I had Othniel to talk with from time to time. I often wonder if Evan has it right, that all the Neshama talk from Othniel is nothing but foolishness."

"So you're telling me that you're giving up on your faith?"

"I want to believe, and I feel guilty for doubting. There seems to be freedom in the stories that Othniel tells, a freedom I crave."

"Freedom!? You have a much better chance of finding faith than freedom."

"Why, because of King Zimri?"

"No. Because of the way things are in Hallowed Hills. To be free to choose who I love - to be a woman shepherd, not bound to live my sister's life... Keep your faith, forget about freedom."

"What if we find freedom through faith?"

"Like Evan will ever allow that!" voices Jael in a tone that unnerves the flock.

"I hate that I don't stand up to him; I want to feel free," laments Benjamin.

"Me too."

The somber siblings quiet their minds and watch the moon fade and the stars dim. Benjamin suppresses his warm sentiments for Jael, fearful of one of her brash badgerings.

"I better get back home," says Jael with regret, wishing that the night would last a little longer so she wouldn't have to return to scrubbing Nabal's stench out of the guild hall and crafting more wedding decorations - both tasks equally troublesome.

"It won't always be like this," says Benjamin.

Jael smiles at Benjamin's optimism as she heads for Tav. Benjamin's eyes get heavy scanning for potential wolves in Jael's path. Once she reaches the outskirts of town, he sinks back into his soft grassy spot, and drifts into a deep sleep.

Benjamin wakes up to a lamb chewing on his hair. He squints at the blaring sun above and immediately regrets his decision to sleep.

Benjamin returns the flock to the watering hole only to find the cistern empty; he curses the well then curses himself under his breath. A faint sound of cow bells rings out from a nearby ravine. He runs to a large boulder and scales it for a better view.

Tinkers!

These shifty clansmen with their herds of sheep, goats, and cattle roam Hallowed Hills as nomads; they scavenge for supplies and graze their flocks wherever they please. There are more laws against Tinkers in Issur than any other group.

Benjamin crawls down from a boulder when a sick feeling punches him in the gut. He will now face Evan's wrath. He gently pats a thirsty sheep on the head. She looks up at him and lets out a "bah" as if she understands that Benjamin is in deep trouble.

Evan pats a sheep on the head before he hands over the flock to Rezon Scar; the captain pays the shepherd and gives him a scrolled receipt. Rezon nods to his company of soldiers, and they prod the flock into the palace stable. As harsh as Evan appears on the outside, like every shepherd, it saddens him on the inside to part ways with his flock.

Evan pays the Baladan Brothers their wages; he waits for them to disperse, but Bo flashes his sly smile to remind Evan of Benjamin's blunder.

"You win this time, but you'll always be the one bested by Tinkers," says Evan forking over more coin. Bo clenches his fist at the boast, but one of his brothers yanks his arm and they make for the nearest tavern.

Evan scans the chaotic north plaza marketplace, filled with more beggars and hustlers than customers. The consumers complain about the high prices and sparse produce. The excitement of the exchange stirs Evan's homesickness, and speeds his desire to return to Hallowed Hills.

Ashira runs to meet Evan and instantly cures his longing for home. She throws her arms around his shoulders, and they share a long kiss. The energy of their kiss enraptures the couple. Time stops and their troubles vanish.

Oren Tav knew from a young age that his son had an edge to him. He was sharp, keener to the ways of flock than other shepherd boys. Oren marveled at his child prodigy; not only was Evan gifted with skill, but he worked harder than every man in Hallowed Hills.

Laud Keros knew from a young age that his daughter had an edge to her. She was sassy and spirited, not exactly the proper qualities to run a pottery business. He knew his daughter would one day grow to appreciate rural life; he witnessed her transformation as a child when they traveled beyond the walls of Tizra - the sense of adventure that stirred within her. Oren and Laud trusted that the arranged marriage would bring out the best in Evan and Ashira.

The couple's lips separate, their minds exit the brief moment of paradise, and the shepherd senses the uneasiness of his surroundings once more.

"The city is on the brink of chaos, worse than I've ever seen. How can you live here?"

"It's home. Always has been," says Ashira with a sense of pride.

"Your home could be with me, in the hills, away from this noise. Your parents promised you to me, remember."

"I'm an indentured servant, remember."

"Ashira, you know I'm willing to pay your debt," pleads Evan.

"No. For the hundredth time, I won't allow you."

"I'm five years beyond the age for marriage. Do you realize the yoke of dishonor that I bear among my people?"

"Poor Evan Tav, can't handle a little dishonor while his fiancé finishes six more seasons in the kitchen. After what Seth and I suffered, you might show a little empathy."

Evan points his eyes to his boots. The way Ashira talks to him humbles his pride, shrinks his ego, and a boyish grin reveals he adores her for it.

"Is that a smile… on Evan Tav's face? We must mark this down in the Issurian records."

Ashira gives him a soft kiss on the cheek in appreciation for his apology.

Chef Ruben nervously searches the market place for Ashira when he marches into the middle of their conversation, "Ashira! Where have you been? I command you to return to the kitchen!"

Evan glares at Ruben and the nervous chef loses the attitude and gently pulls Ashira to the side, "The kitchen's a mess without you, please return quickly."

Ashira returns to Evan and nestles into him, "Sorry for the short visit, I better go." Ashira gives Evan a quick goodbye kiss and hurries back to the kitchen with Ruben.

Evan's look of frustration follows her.

King Zimri salivates at the sight and smell of his meal. He sinks his teeth into his bloody steak. "Perfection… no one cooks a rare steak like Ashira Keros. It's a shame she has that beast for a brother."

Queen Rizpah rolls a grape around the rim of her plate with her index finger as her mind drifts to the pleasant past. The High Magi Zidon grinds dry tobacco leaves into his pipe with his thumb. Caleb Glade strikes a sulphur match for the councilor; Zidon puffs the pipe as he separates the peas from his carrots.

"To be young again," complains Zidon. "My stomach only tolerates vegetables these days."

Prince Aden rolls his blue eyes at the pointless table talk. "Calcedon laid siege to the port of Tekoa. Maybe you should make peace with Uncle Emmerick and lend some troops."

"Your traitor's talk ruins my meal… Do you hear this nonsense, Zidon? I suffer for the sake of my country, and my son spews traitor's talk at my table."

"Suffer?" questions Aden. "You're a drunkard, gambler, backstabber."

"All that which Melek desires," declares Zimri, ripping his steak with his teeth as if he were a mountain lion.

"I defend our people from robbers and murderers."

"No one speaks of your quality."

"You choose not to listen."

Zidon cracks a smile underneath his crooked nose,

relishing the argument more than his pipe. Rizpah continues to pick at her grapes in a catatonic state.

Aden eyes the Signet Ring of Issur shining on Zimri's hand.

"Madness drove you to claim that ring long before it was to be yours. Melek makes you mad."

Zimri smashes his fist down on the table. "You will speak no more of my god!"

Zidon furrows his black eyebrows with concern for Aden's accusation.

"In fact, you will never speak in my presence again. Your words mean nothing to me," warns Zimri behind his grey eyes.

Aden takes a swig of merlot and swirls it down his throat.

"Reconcile with Emmerick, unite Issur, remember the Covenant!"

"I told you to keep your mouth shut!"

Zimri stands in protest of his son's radical ideas. He lunges at Aden and yanks him from his chair, "You are dismissed from my table! Forever!"

Zidon nods with approval of the dismissal.

Rizpah's love for her son livens her being, and she stands in defiance of the dismissal, "Zimri! No! Don't do this!"

The sullen king turns his back on his wife and son.

Aden tightly embraces his frail mother in hopes of easing her misery.

"I love you, Mother. But my convictions can no longer tolerate the sins of my father."

He exits the hall, making a slight nod to Caleb.

Rizpah's heart breaks as Zimri banishes their only child from the hall. She lifts her gown from the floor and darts away from her dinner in the opposite direction toward the embroidery. Her yappy table-dog follows.

She swiftly moves down the palace hallway, the open-air

walkway offering a crisp view of the night sky.

Zimri quickly catches up to her.

"Rizpah! Wait! Melek foretold that Aden would betray me."

Anger halts Rizpah's flight.

"I curse the day you began to worship that god. Melek worship has done nothing but ruin Issur."

"What are you saying?"

"It was the voice of Melek, or should I say the voice of Zidon, who told you to seize the guilds."

"To assert my dominance."

"You murdered the scribes and burned the Hall of Knowledge. Now there are but a handful of people in Tizra who can read and write or teach others to do likewise."

"The scribes were Neshama worshippers faithful to Emmerick; they spread lies about me."

"Then, you looted the Merchants Guild. You put businesses out of commission, killed capable merchants, and now the country is on the verge of bankruptcy."

"The merchants were illegally funding a plot to dethrone me."

"You angered the farmers because you charged them a tax to irrigate their crops and when they couldn't afford the tax, your soldiers cut off their water supply. Yet another revolt against King Zimri."

"That I easily crushed. I dedicated a monument to honor my courage."

"It took a lot of courage to kill starving men, women, and children armed with pitchforks. Issur suffers from a food shortage, not that you would know anything about that," states Rizpah before continuing her march toward the embroidery.

Zimri and the yappy table-dog labor to keep up.

Rizpah stops to gather herself at a well that comes up out of the palace depths. A well filled with faded reveries.

"This is the well where we fell in love."

Rizpah softly caresses the stones as she once did Zimri in their youth.

"I worry about you… You go on those long hunts. You rarely sleep. You've become so cruel that you'd disown your only son… I know in my heart that there's a secret between you and Isavel too; it's more than an affair with the Queen Mother. I know your soul better than anyone."

Rizpah's rebuke convicts her unfaithful husband.

"What do you want from me?"

"All I'm asking is that you return to the good man I married, and be a father to Aden. Forget about Zidon and Isavel. Take a break from Melek worship."

Zimri's ego steams at Rizpah's request to take a break from Melek worship. It heats to a swelter then ignites into a flame, his pride bursting into a conflagration of resentment. "I do remember that this is the place where we fell in love." Zimri reaches for his wife's hands. He gently caresses her fingers and the couple locks eyes. To Rizpah's dismay, the blazing malice consumes Zimri's tranquil gaze. "And this will be the place where we fell out of love."

The hateful proclamation bewilders Rizpah.

"Farewell."

Zimri pushes Rizpah into the well.

Her screams go from loud, to faint, to nothing as she vanishes into the deep cistern.

Rizpah's dog angrily yaps at the tyrant. Zimri picks up the little brown dog, looks it over with disdain, and nonchalantly tosses it into the well. The barks go from loud, to faint, to nothing.

✦ ✦ ✦

Zimri enters the throne room in an emotionless state. Zidon and his four magi - Zoheth, Zur, Zalmon, and Zatu - kneel before their king. The magi wear matching grey hoodless robes. Zoheth and Zur, the more experienced of the four magi, train closely with Zidon. Seldom do they leave the sanctuary located within the throne room. Zalmon and Zatu, the portly ones, supervise the worship services and moon festivals at the Temple of Melek.

An abundance of treasures and tapestries fill the throne room, and the gaudy marble throne reflects Zimri's excessive kingship. The dim room casts the dark shadow of a grey stone statue of Melek nearly twenty feet tall. Melek wears a flowing robe with etchings of the stages of the moon engraved into his robe. A thick hood hides his face. His large hands rest on the pommel of his sword pointing to the floor.

Zimri approaches the statue and kneels in a circle outlined by candles. Zidon and the magi surround him on the edge of the circle.

Korah emerges from behind the Melek statue, his tall dark figure blends with the shadow cast from the tall idol. Korah appears similar to Melek, draped in a hooded black robe trimmed in crimson - his height reaching to eight feet.

"Most wise Korah... You were right about my son's betrayal, and my wife's intentions to turn me against Melek."

"Melek is pleased with your sacrifice. The steps you take bring you closer to liberation... Though, I come here tonight to offer caution. Melek sends warning about a shepherd from Tav; he may be a threat to your kingdom."

"Yes, I know of this shepherd. He's the son of Oren Tav. I will run my sword though his back the exact same way I killed his father."

A guileful delight washes over Zimri's face as he proclaims his promise to Melek.

Chapter **8**

The Call of Neshama

enjamin walks among the flock counting sheep with thoughts of the empty watering hole weighing on his conscience. Pausing his count, he prays into the pitch night, "Neshama. It's been months since the last drop of rain, please water your flock, help me out on this one."

A rustle in the grass interrupts his prayer; he readies his bow and moves towards the noise. The fear of wolves drive his initial thought, but the flock remains as calm as the night breeze. Jael enters his second thought, and he turns around anticipating her antics. A lone firefly blinks in his eye, so he lowers his defenses and calls out to the dark, "Jael, is that you?"

Benjamin trembles when he notices a glowing light burning brightly behind his back. He raises his bow and turns in a flash. The radiant light forces his face to the ground. He drops his weapon, puts one hand over his face, and stretches out the other as a show of surrender.

"You have nothing to fear, human… Rise."

Benjamin prepares to lift his face as a twist of faith stirs within his soul. Could it be possible? Would the deepest imagination of his childhood come to life when he looked up?

His brown eyes lift, and there before him stands a nephesh.

Benjamin scoops dirt from the ground and lets it sift through his fingers to affirm that he's not dreaming. He stands to behold the nephesh.

"Greetings, my name is Azor."

Benjamin struggles to find words to offer the celestial creature as he marvels at the size of the nephesh.

A white robe with gold trim flows down from a white hood that covers Azor's silvery hair atop his deep purple irises - intricate circular patterns engrave the fabric of the robes. Azor measures nearly eight feet tall, yet somehow the serenity of the divine being puts Benjamin at ease.

"Are you a nephesh?" asks Benjamin like a timid child.

"Yes. Your fairy tales are true after all." Benjamin's reverence for the divine being forbids his face to smile. "I believe your kind calls that a joke…"

Azor's humor lessens the shepherd's stress.

"I found that Benjamin's a common name for a shepherd. I gave an elderly gentleman a good scare before I realized that I had the wrong person." Azor grins underneath his hood with hopes to put the shepherd at ease. "You must forgive my tact, or lack thereof, it's been thousands of years since I spoke with a human."

"How did you get here?" blurts Benjamin.

"Neshama created an ether vortex so that I could come to your world from the ether world. The reason that I appear so bright is that I came directly from her presence."

"An ether vortex?"

"It's like a tunnel that connects the physical world to the ether world."

"Why have you come to Issur?"

"I've been given a mission by Neshama. I've come to find Korah."

Benjamin runs the men of Tav through his memory.

"I don't know of any man by that name."

"It's not of your concern, as it's my call to fulfill."

"What do you want with me, then?" asks Benjamin out of his burning curiosity, yet fearful to know the answer.

Azor kneels to be at eye level with Benjamin. "Neshama has called you to overthrow King Zimri and end the worship of Melek."

The call knocks the air out of Benjamin. He retreats from Azor and tries to catch his breath. In the midst of the heavy moment, Evan comes to his mind. What would he think of such a call? Benjamin's breathing steadies as Azor stands to receive the shepherd's answer.

"I can't. I won't leave my flock and besides, my brother will never allow me to leave these hills."

"You have free will, but I caution you, those who don't follow their call may find regret instead... I must honor Neshama's call to find Korah."

Disappointment washes over Benjamin as Azor vanishes into the night.

Othniel and Ezekiel appear soon after. 'Wayfarer' pauses, sensing an unusual presence. He runs his fingers through the air and begins to rub them together as if he can feel some kind of residue on his fingertips.

Ether.

Othniel approaches the antsy shepherd, "An elderly man on the outskirts of Tav by the name of Benjamin claims to have seen a nephesh."

"So, why would I know anything about it?" snaps Benjamin.

Othniel senses that Benjamin has experienced something phenomenal - the trace of ether on his fingertips and the shepherd's defensive nature provide the evidence needed to confirm his suspicions. Othniel looks to Ezekiel, who nods his head in agreement.

"You saw the nephesh," presses Othniel.

"I'm out here tending my sheep, that's it. I'm a shepherd, that's all I know."

"That's Evan talking. You've been called, I can sense it."

"Evan told me not to talk to you. I think you should be on your way."

"I must know, Benjamin. You were called, to what end?"

Benjamin tries hard to hold it in, but the call spills out,

"To overthrow Zimri and put an end to Melek worship."

The call transports Othniel's soul to the past, and for a brief moment he feels a faint brush with eternity.

"That's the same call your parents answered all those years ago. That's the call that led them to revolt against Zimri. I fought with them in the Battle of Ephah's Field. The shepherds fought valiantly, but the battle ended in a draw. The shepherds kept their guild, but Zimri kept his throne. You, your brother, and your sisters became war orphans."

"The story is true… How did my parents die?"

"Your mother bravely held the line swarmed by enemies on all sides, and your father made a valiant attempt to rescue her when Zimri, that coward, stabbed your father in the back. The moment his sword pierced Oren, Rachel was swallowed by the mayhem. Their eyes connected for their final breath; they fell in unison, and arrived in the ether world as one spirit."

The painful history lesson collapses Benjamin's emotions and reduces him to tears.

"Why didn't you save them?"

"I failed them. I'm so sorry," says Othniel placing his hand on Benjamin's shoulder.

"I remember hearing this story once before when I was a boy, but Evan refused to speak of it ever again."

"Did the nephesh mention anything else?"

"He said that he was on a mission to find someone named Korah."

Othniel 'Wayfarer' never met a stranger in Issur, so it feels odd to him to stand quietly and stroke his beard, hoping to put a face on the foreign name.

"We should start by looking for this man as well. You must leave your flock and come with us."

"I can't leave my flock; they're helpless without me."

"Fine. We'll help you return them to the stalls."

"If we did return them, there's no way Evan approves this."

"You'll never find freedom under your brother's thumb, trapped in these hills."

Benjamin agrees in his heart, but his fear of Evan will not allow him to follow the prophets.

"Sorry, I can't."

"Your answer disappoints me, but if you change your mind you can find us at the Columns of Kings. Ezekiel and I will prayerfully seek Neshama's council before we start this search."

Benjamin feels more regret watching Ezekiel's torch vanish in the darkness than he did Azor's celestial light fading into the night.

"Wait here," says Othniel to Ezekiel before entering the darkened ether chancel. Ezekiel hands him the torch.

The embers light a silhouette on bended knee. Shamgar Ram rises and approaches Othniel - an uncertain energy currents between prophet and precept.

"I must walk the way of forgiveness as is required by my synod vows. Forgive me for not coming to aid your order. If I only knew how awful Zimri and his Melek worship would ruin Issur, I would've done more," admits Shamgar.

"There's a chance for redemption, a call has gone out."

"You know this to be true."

"Benjamin Tav received the call of Neshama."

Shamgar rolls his eyes and the ounce of hope that musters in his soul exits the chancel, "Neshama forsakes Miriam's Covenant."

"Oren Tav nearly succeeded in dethroning Zimri. Is it out of the realm of your possibility that his offspring can do likewise?"

"He hasn't the faith of his father, and Zimri is far more zealous than when Oren faced him. He can't win."

"That's why we need your help."

"I offered you forgiveness; I'm not obligated to offer my mace."

Othniel releases a sigh of disgust. His face reddens to match the embers flickering off the torch.

"Then you can shift with the shadows until death comes and this chancel becomes your tomb. As for me, death will come atop a flaming pyre in The Pit. My burning flesh will proclaim the Covenant to the thousands who have forsaken it. When the journey of my soul ends at the feet of Neshama, my judgment, I fear not."

Othniel removes the torch light and leaves Shamgar behind in the darkened chancel.

Benjamin returns with the flock to find Evan waiting outside the guild hall. Evan counts the sheep as soon as they're in view; he's surprised and pleased that none were lost.

"Nice to see you too," says Benjamin.

Evan ignores the prompt of his brother's sarcasm and refuses to offer a proper greeting. "I heard rumors from the other shepherds that the watering hole is dry."

"Missed you too," continues Benjamin.

"Answer me!"

Benjamin hesitates, tempted once more to lie.

"The hole is dry," admits Benjamin.

"I told you to watch out for those wolves."

"It wasn't wolves; it was Tinkers."

"You were fooled by Tinkers? You're worthless. How hard is it to push a rock over a hole? What were you doing in the hills while I was gone?"

Benjamin hangs his head and remains silent.

"I know exactly what you were doing, hangin' around that old fanatic again." Evan grabs Benjamin's chin and forcefully lifts his head. "Look at me! I told you to stay away from him. Maybe it's time for me to teach you some obedience."

Benjamin puts his hand on the hilt of his sword as desire for equality with Evan jades his thoughts.

"You want to spar? With me? I taught you everything you know about swords, and nobody in these hills is better with a blade."

Benjamin suppresses his pride and removes his hand from the hilt.

Evan forcefully pokes his chest.

"Stop," says Benjamin, taking a step back.

"Afraid I'll beat you down?"

"For someone who despised Nabal, you sure act a lot like him."

Evan pushes Benjamin. Benjamin shoves back with equal force. The brothers push one another with greater force as the shoving match escalates into a fist fight. Evan plows Benjamin into the dirt, and the brothers roll on the ground, exchanging body blows.

The Baladans rush to watch the feud; they pick sides and cheer.

Benjamin's strength surprises Evan, so he takes it up a notch to fend him off. Evan belts the scraper in the side of the face and presses him to the ground. The crass shepherds root for Benjamin to stay in the fight, but he stops, and the scuffle ends. Bo assigns him the title of *pushover* for quitting so easily.

The brothers stand, breathing heavily. Evan looks upon Benjamin with disgust, "Get cleaned up for the wedding."

Chapter 9

White Roses and Daisies

Judith and Daniel dance a jig to a large ensemble of drums and flutes. A clean-cut shepherd with an earnest face and a proper disposition - Daniel compliments Judith's elegance. Her beauty captures his gaze, for Judith looks like a princess in her wedding gown. Her thick hair intertwines with ribbons of white lace under a tiara of white roses and daises.

Manors and hovels sprawl across a hill that spans the landscape of Tsadi. Families of all trades celebrate the good fortune of their beloved Daniel. Even the townspeople not invited to the ceremony at the guild hall celebrate privately outside their dwellings.

Flowing ribbons of white lace wrap the largest guild hall in Hallowed Hills like a wedding gift. The air smells of white roses and daisies arranged about the tables. The same decorations grace the adjacent shops circling the guild hall.

The setting sun in the west turns the white roses a soft shade of orange.

Evan sips a mug of wheat ale alongside Ardon Tsadi and his sons. Ardon Tsadi's presence commands the respect of the Evan. The veteran guild master scratches his full grey head down to his graying beard with one hand, while sipping ale with the other. Admiring his charming son and beautiful daughter-in-law, his old eyes smile brightly.

Jael leans on Evan and tries to fit in with the shepherds by throwing back a mug of wheat ale - the stout brew turning the whites of her eyes red.

Jacob Tsadi squeezes between Evan and Jael; he sidles up to her and awkwardly inhales her scent. Short and plump in stature, he sticks out among his fit brothers. Ale dribbles from his bucked-teeth underneath his bowl haircut.

Jael grabs Evan by the arm, "Dance with me." Evan doesn't have a choice as she drags him away from the Tsadi boys, leaving Jacob behind with disappointment.

Benjamin sits alone and stares into his wooden cup of ale. The encounter with the nephesh haunts his conscience, and the beating from his brother taunts his pride. He tries to muster happiness for Judith's sake, but watching her dance with Daniel makes him miss his parents.

A circle of smitten girls eye Benjamin, but he refuses to flirt so they whisper gossip about him. He struggles to enjoy the party for it reveals his social awkwardness. Even worse, it makes him feel more isolated for he always finds it difficult to breathe in a crowd.

Jael runs in from behind and startles him. "I hate being tracked by that creepy slob, but at least I'm acting like I'm having a good time."

Her humor fails to liven her brother.

"Evan beat you up again. You'll take him next time." She ducks lower to look into his eyes. "Fine, don't talk to me."

"Jael! Come dance with Jacob," yells Evan from a distance. Jacob wears a smirk on his flabby face, impressed with himself for outwitting Jael by going through Evan to get a dance.

Jael shoots Benjamin an all-too-familiar look as she drags herself to the dance floor.

Jacob and Jael join hands and unfortunately feet as the clumsy shepherd clogs atop her toes. They make for an awkward couple set in stark contrast to Daniel and Judith, the prince and princess of Hallowed Hills.

Prince Aden forges his way through the cornfields of The Heartland as the setting sun sprinkles golden rays across the green stalks; the smell of corn and dirt welcome him to rural life as he leaves the bustle of Tizra behind.

"We have a good pace, we'll make Bera's Bridge before the half moon shines," says Ishem, a loyal childhood friend of the prince. He accompanies the prince and two faithful rangers as they make their way south to find Aden's uncle, Lord Emmerick Tizra of The Southern Kingdom.

"Once we reach Bera's Tavern, you can reconsider going south with me. My father will hunt you down if he finds out that you're with me."

The two rangers stomp with resolve to assure Aden that he will not travel alone.

Ishem's nerves tingle as he looks over each shoulder, flinging the hood of his black cape over his wavy black hair. A frightful scarecrow atop a dirt mound stops the men dead in their tracks. Its zipper scowl runs diagonal underneath spikes of hay that stick out of its sackcloth head. The prince and his rangers move in for a closer look while Ishem holds his ground.

A faint scream ripples through the cornfield.

Aden and his men draw bows and spring to action. The fearful cry gets muffled by the cornfield, and the rangers lose their sense of direction. They wait quietly hoping to track another cry of desperation.

A call for help goes out to the dusk, and Aden and his men answer, sprinting to a farmstead hidden within the fields. Upon their arrival, they see a burly man shred a wedding dress from a bride. He yanks her blonde hair in one fist and rips her clothing with the other. The groom lies bludgeoned to death next to a blood-stained rock.

"Melek makes you mine!" shouts the assailant terrorizing the woman.

Aden lets loose a black-feather arrow that plants itself into the man's hand. His punctured hand drops the shreds of torn white clothe. He then releases his fist full of hair to pull the arrow from his punctured hand.

"Face justice in the courts or in the fields. Your next move will give me your answer," says the prince with another arrow ready to fly. Ishem and the two rangers stand poised to administer judgment.

The burly man swipes at the woman with both arms in hopes of using her for a shield, but the slender woman slips through his arms and falls to the dirt when four arrows slam into the man's chest, rendering justice for the bride and groom.

She runs to Aden and sinks her face into his black-leather cuirass. He allows her time to grieve and reclaim her wits.

"His name was Rorrick. He was our farmhand; he worked these fields since I was six. My mother died when I was a little girl, my father in the revolt. Rorrick refused to fight King Zimri. I realized why, when I stumbled across a Melek shrine in his hovel.

He changed over night and began to obsess over my day-to-day routines. He tried to shame me out of my wedding ceremony, said it was wrong to get married so soon after losing my father. I thought it was his love for my father and me that drove his jealousy. I was wrong… When we retuned from the wedding, Rorrick saw me wrapped in my husband's arms and went mad. He picked up that rock…"

The terrorized bride spills more anguish onto Aden as her chest convulses.

"When will Melek worship end?" cries the bride.

As the prince plays precept for the bride, the scouts search the farmstead. Ishem continues his ritual of looking over his shoulders.

Three henchmen in black longcoats leap from a stable-loft to engage Aden and the two scouts. The henchmen whirl about with a hatchet in each hand, so the rangers close ranks with their prince and place the bride at the center of their protection.

Ishem draws an arrow as his nervous hand shakes his bow. He fires into the mayhem and drops one of the rangers. Aden runs through a ruffian while shooting a worrisome look at Ishem.

The other scout ends his attacker with an exact slice of his blade, before escorting the bride to safety.

Another arrow from Ishem's quiver lets loose, again off target. To avoid getting slammed in the chest with the bolt, Aden shoves the remaining henchman into the line of fire. The arrow sails high, nicking the henchman's shoulder.

Another arrow from Ishem glides above Aden, ducking the bolt.

The wounded henchman flees into the cornfield.

Ishem ends his escape with a shot through the heart.

Ishem offers Aden and his ranger a nervous grin as an apology for his inconsistent aim.

As Aden surveys the carnage, his mind perceives an image that captures the vile nature of Melek worship- a bouquet of white roses stained in scarlet.

✦ ✦ ✦

Benjamin lightly steps through a once boisterous Tsadi and takes in the calm offered by silence; he walks around empty drinking cups and over wilted wedding decorations. He looks to the west with his longbow in hand – a sword strapped to his side and a backpack strapped across his shoulders.

Benjamin fires an arrow high into the night sky as Jael approaches with soft steps.

"I wish I was that arrow, free to fly."

"Me too," offers Jael, watching the arrow vanish into the moonlight.

"Sorry about the cold shoulder. You were right, Evan got to me. He always gets to me," says Benjamin, even though Evan's beating still unsettles his mind and the call of Neshama continues to disturb his soul.

"You can't let Evan affect you like this."

"It's more than Evan… You wouldn't believe me if I told you."

"I'm your sister. More than that, I'm your best friend."

It's a sincere enough opening for Benjamin to enter, but he fears the rejection that might follow. If Jael thinks him a lunatic, then maybe he's becoming one.

"I saw a nephesh. He said that I've been called to overthrow Zimri. To complicate matters, Othniel told me that my calling is the same as our parents."

"A nephesh of Neshama… Told you to overthrow Zimri?"

"Yes, an actual nephesh."

She reduces her giggle to a squeak of disbelief.

"Forget it."

"Benjamin. A nephesh…"

"You think I'm crazy."

"No, but it's one thing to hear about fairytale creatures from Othniel, not you too."

Jael's skepticism lessens when an unexpected sensation warms her heart. The mysterious warmth brings her to reconsider Benjamin's account. "Sorry… It's not right for me to doubt you. Go on."

"Othniel told me how our parents died in battle."

"So the story is true."

"Yes, have no doubts about their valor."

"What are you going to do now?"

"If I don't answer the call, I feel like I dishonor our parents. Maybe there's freedom at the end of this call."

"Let's find out together," suggests Jael.

The answer pinches his brotherly instincts. The thought of sharing the load of his call offers comfort, but what perils await, he knows not. He dare not compromise his little sister's well-being.

"No. Evan would kill me if anything happened to you, this is my calling."

"Mother went along with father when he was called."

"I'm not our father."

"Fine," says Jael, walking away. Benjamin feels terrible, but he knows that Evan would never forgive him for leading their little sister away from Hallowed Hills, and he would never forgive himself if death were to claim her.

Benjamin makes his way west.

He reaches outskirts of Tsadi when Jael catches him with her bow in hand, sword on her hip, and backpack in tow − her dress stuffed into a pair of shepherd trousers.

"I'm sick of being treated like a little girl. Tell Evan I'm too much like our mother." Jael pushes Benjamin aside and marches west. He shakes his head to rattle out the voice of caution and can only smile at her determination.

Chapter 10

The Columns of Kings

Are we close?" asks Jael.

"I guess. I've never been there. I've never left Hallowed Hills."

"You sure Othniel will be there?"

"That's what he told me," says Benjamin with an annoyed exhale, hoping to repel more inquiries.

They wade through the high grass of the Pony Pasture. Jael's excitement sets the pace, her ponytail whipping back and forth, her curls flopping around like the tails on the wild ponies frolicking across the horizon. Benjamin draws from her positive energy, which allows him to suppress his thoughts of Evan's retribution for leaving the hills.

Benjamin and Jael stop in their tracks when they catch the first glimpse of the Columns of Kings. The memorial was completed by Josiah Tizra the Second 'The Wise' in honor of his father - white columns soar into the bright-blue sky as if they touch the clouds. A family of bald eagles circles high above sending up screams into the heavens.

"We made it!" yells Jael picking up the pace.

Her enthusiasm carries her legs into a jog and then a sprint as she races Benjamin to the landmark. The setting sun shoots purple and orange blasts through the clouds. The white columns reflect the ginger tones of the sunset.

Benjamin and Jael double over with aching ribs and tight stomachs. Raising up, they feel the stares of the imposing kings peering down on them. Gigantic stone statues immortalize all of the kings after Josiah Tizra the First. Long rows of columns enclose the nearly thirty statues.

At the far end of the memorial is a statue of Josiah Tizra the First 'The Shepherd King' slaying the rogue prophet, High Magi Zithri 'The Invincible.' His statue surpasses all others in height and width. King Josiah is a plain man with woolly hair; he's dressed in his simple shepherd's clothing with no armor or adornments. He runs his sword through the chest of the haggard prophet draped in a thick robe lying on the ground.

Weeds grow up through the floor of the poorly maintained memorial, and the statues are in need of a scrubbing. Unlike every king who ruled Issur before the tyrant, preserving the Columns is not a concern of the Zimri kingship.

"My prayer is answered," says Othniel, standing up from his meal. Ezekiel jumps up, pinched by awe at Benjamin and Jael's arrival.

The mentor wraps his arm around Benjamin and whispers into his ear, "You've taken your first step toward freedom."

Othniel hugs Jael and whispers into her ear, "Child, you have the boldness of your mother."

Jael joins Ezekiel for supper while Othniel and Benjamin make their way toward the statue of Josiah.

"Is that the Shepherd King from Tav?" asks Benjamin obsessed with the guild icon.

"The one."

"My father told us his story so many times, but I was too little to understand it; he defeated that evil prophet is what I remember most."

"Zithri and his magi betrayed the Order of the Prophets to follow the false god Melek. Zithri was the first to introduce Melek worship to Issur. He initiated The Book of Blight, a work of dark magic. Zithri killed the master of our order. When the Order of the Prophets couldn't defeat him, Issur lost faith in the prophets, so the nation cried out to Neshama for a king.

Josiah marched his army on Zithri's fortress called Blight; the ruins lie just across the basin. Josiah triumphed and ushered in the second age, the age of justice."

Othniel pauses and grinds his teeth. Benjamin takes note of the prophet's frustration with the age of justice.

"Josiah did what the prophets could not… he protected the Covenant."

"Remind me, what's a covenant?"

"It's only natural that Neshama works through covenants. As the ancient stories teach, the Goddess is a relational being. When two people make an agreement, they create a covenant. If the agreement is upheld, both sides prosper; if the agreement is ignored, both sides suffer."

"Why would Neshama create one with Issur?"

"Neshama created a covenant with Miriam because the world was in danger of forgetting the Goddess. Miriam was a desolate woman, an outcast for believing in Neshama. She didn't want to live a desolate existence, and the Goddess didn't want to be forgotten. It was a perfect union."

Benjamin removes the stone statuette from his pocket and holds it up in front of the teacher.

"That's her. Who gave you that blasphemous idol?" questions the prophet with a scowl of disapproval.

"Shamgar Ram."

"Ah! The Synod believes in veneration; they teach that these blessed relics bring believers closer to Neshama - another foolish scam to pull coins from the pockets of the poor."

Benjamin promptly returns the statuette to his pocket before asking his next question, "When we were in Hallowed Hills before Zimri's men chased us, Ezekiel told us the story where Miriam came back from the ether world. How is that possible for a human?"

"When one tells the story as long as the prophets have, one learns to appreciate the mystery that exists in the Goddess."

"What does Neshama require of us?"

"To remember the Covenant. To first extend grace to the condemned, then execute justice when grace is scorned by the condemned. Miriam extended grace; Josiah executed justice."

"So what's better, grace or justice?"

"Don't look at it that way. The key to freeing the spirit exists in the depths of grace and justice, both of which are rooted in sacrifice."

Benjamin's blank stare reveals his disconnect from Othniel's lesson.

"In order to experience freedom, one must learn the meaning of sacrifice - the ultimate act of selflessness. This is what Zidon could never understand. It's why he left the prophets, deceived Zimri, and reestablished the worship of Melek."

Zidon's decision haunts Othniel, weakening him to the point where he leans heavy on his staff. Benjamin slides into his old mentor to prop him up.

After Othniel regains his composure, he leads Benjamin behind the statue of Josiah and triggers a mechanism that reveals a secret passageway into a dark room beneath the statue. Othniel invites Benjamin to enter by directing him with an open hand; the shepherd hesitantly enters, and the prophet follows.

Othniel triggers another mechanism from inside the passage that seals them in the chamber. Benjamin feels anxious as he breathes in the stale air while they stand in the darkness for a few moments.

"Benjamin, remember these words that I am about to speak, hide them in your heart, for this ancient truth is about the power of the human soul. On these words hinge the fate of Issur."

Othniel breathes deep and exhales the ancient truth, "Darkness can only exist in the absence of light."

Othniel lights the dark room with a torch. Benjamin jumps back frightened by a statue of a nephesh holding a sword.

"Meet Kurion," introduces Othniel.

"The nephesh or the sword?" asks Benjamin, his heart still thumping.

"Both. Kurion forged the sword in the ether world and therefore it bears his name. He presented the Lord of Swords to Josiah when he received the call of Neshama."

Benjamin reluctantly removes the blade from the statue and marvels at the craftsmanship of the sword.

Kurion is unlike any sword he'd ever laid eyes upon. The long blade glistens from the a smooth sheen of silver that runs all the way from the tip down to the burnished-gold cross; the grip is polished in the same golden tones, and engraved in the rounded-pommel - a sun face with a hallowed appearance.

Benjamin senses the divine substance sealed within the blade. "What exactly is ether?"

"Ether is what the prophets call spirit. The nephesh that you met is mostly ether, whereas humans are mostly matter, but the human soul is composed of ether. The sword has a powerful affect on nephesh and human souls."

"Why would Josiah need such a sword?"

"As a reward for remembering Neshama, she endowed Miriam with the knowledge to manipulate ether. A prophet can manipulate ether to protect themselves and others so long as there is an ether source. A prophet can also banish ether that has been corrupted within a human soul. Miriam called this pure magic.

Zithri twisted this knowledge and turned it into a destructive craft, which he called dark magic. Kurion aided Josiah when he used it to ward off dark magic and kill Zithri in battle."

"Why do I need such a sword?"

"If we are going to dethrone Zimri, then we will have to have to face his high councilor - the High Magi Zidon. Kurion can protect you from his evil arts."

Othniel triggers the mechanism and the stone door slides open. Benjamin walks up the stairs and gazes into the clear night sky of a thousand stars, his body strengthened with confidence, his faith empowered by expectation.

"What else can prophets do with ether?"

"You are your father's son, Benjamin Tav, never ceasing in your questions... Animals have untamed ether, and it's possible for a capable prophet to manipulate their actions."

Benjamin has a flashback that produces an epiphany.

"Hallowed Hills, the wolf that bowed to me, you did that?"

Othniel flashes his mischievous smile.

The master prophet looks at the bashful Ezekiel listening to Jael ramble on about Judith and Evan. He identifies a spotted-grey night lizard lurking in the corner of a statue. Othniel quietly chants a mystical language, and the frantic lizard dashes at Ezekiel. It runs under his robe and the understudy leaps to his feet while the lizard races up his body like a tree, popping out the top of his robe before escaping down his back.

Jael and Benjamin laugh hysterically.

"That stopped being funny about a hundred lizards ago!" yells the frustrated student stomping away from his tricky teacher.

"He's too impatient," laments Othniel. "I wonder if the Order of the Prophets will die with me."

Othniel and Ezekiel sleep snugly, curled up in their robes. Benjamin and Jael stretch out next to one another on their grey wool blankets. Adrenaline no longer torments the wild-eyed darling, but her restless brother tosses about his blanket in search of comfort.

Benjamin presses the grass into a pattern that pleases him. That's when it stirs within his spirit for the first time. His newfound hope is under attack, assaulted by raging waves of doubt and one horrific thought after the other - his parents' funeral, Nabal's boot in his ribs, spiders spilling out of Jael's hair, wolves ripping his flesh, glowing Melek runes searing his limbs, Zimri's sword piercing his back.

Benjamin clenches the Miriam statuette to escape the uneasiness in his soul.

"What's wrong?" whispers Jael.

"Sorry, can't get comfortable."

"You're a terrible liar… So what's next?"

"Othniel said we need to find Korah, the man Azor seeks… Let's hope we find Korah before Evan finds us."

Chapter 11 | The Inn Of Encouragement

Othniel leads the way into a rickety inn near Abilla's Orchard, "This place has seen better days."

Ezekiel trembles at the scraggly buck heads mounted to the rotten-wood walls, and he gags on the stink of body odor stifling the smell of fresh peaches. A blind bard deafens Jael's pointed ears with thunderous snores from the corner.

Benjamin surveys the sketchy clientele of unemployed orchard pickers, ruffians, and veterans who wear their battle scars from the Farmers Revolt. Ever since Zimri seized the Farmers Guild and took control of The Heartland and Abilla's Orchard, the farming industry in Issur had been depleted.

"This is no place for my little sister."

Jael feels the stares of the drunken farmers undressing her and grips her brother's bicep to draw closer to him.

Ezekiel does likewise, only to release after an awkward look from Benjamin.

"Rubbish. These poor souls are the salt of the earth. Besides, Barnabas brews the finest peach ale that you'll ever taste. Find a table, I'll fetch the ale," says Othniel, thinking with his thirsty palate. He hands the understudy his staff and heads for the bar.

The three travelers settle into a table in the far corner near the blind bard asleep with a lute across his lap. Out of pity, Benjamin drops his only coin in the bard's tin cup. The ring awakens the blind musician.

"Thank you, kind sir. Name your guild."

"Shepherds."

The blind bard tunes his lute and plays a familiar jig, the hometown music providing Benjamin and Jael a sense of comfort.

Othniel approaches the barkeep, a short and portly man- the stubble on his face grows atop his emotionless facial expressions.

"You again," says Barnabas with a lisp.

"I'll take four pints of your peach ale."

Barnabas thinks on the order before pouring the ale, "I thought I told you not to come back here."

"Barney, I've been coming here for years."

"You make me nervous. Nothing good comes of your visits."

"Are you referring to the foxes? The fool had it coming."

"I can't make wine this season," complains Barnabas with a whimper.

"I didn't know they'd go for your vines."

"What's done is done, I suppose," says Barnabas, handing Othniel the tray of ale.

As the prophet receives the tray, he leans into the barkeep. "Have you ever heard of a man named Korah?" whispers Othniel.

Barnabas scratches his stubble while processing a long list of names in his head.

"I've got nothin'."

"Most unfortunate… Put these on my tab."

Barnabas lets out a regretful sigh as Othniel carries the tray to the table, tarrying for a second when he recognizes the jig. "Tussle in Tav. Good tune Gomer, good tune."

After Othniel praises the bard, he settles in with the group.

"You seem to know your way around this place quite well," observes Benjamin, breathing in the peach ale to alleviate his nose from the stink of the famers.

"Nothing wrong with a drink or two."

"Or nine or ten," corrects Ezekiel. "Please, Master… It'd be a welcomed change not to have another one of your bar room brawls."

"Wow! This ale is delicious!" interrupts Jael.

"Don't encourage him," says Ezekiel.

"Peach ale puts me in the mood to dance," offers Othniel. Jael shakes her head in agreement as the ale tickles her toes.

"Don't you think it's a bad idea to draw attention to ourselves?" says Benjamin with Ezekiel nodding his head in agreement.

"Nonsense," says Othniel, reaching out to tap the bard's shoulder. "Gomer, drop your lute and pick up your drum, there's a pint in it for you."

Othniel gives Ezekiel's pint to Gomer, who delightfully receives it - the backwards prophet feeling slighted by the gesture. "What? Not like you'd drink it all, show some charity."

The shy apprentice shrugs his shoulder in concession.

"How about Pella Moved South, old friend?"

Gomer downs his pint and cracks his knuckles.

The ballad begins and immediately draws the attention of the rest of the patrons in the tavern. Within a few beats, the patrons start tapping their feet and then their wooden mugs. The taps turn to thumps, and the rickety inn begins to shake.

Othniel guides Jael's hand to an open spot on the floor, and the two begin to dance. Once Gomer reaches the chorus of the song, the farmers belt out the words and pound their mugs to their guild's most revered tune.

> *Pella came down from the mountains,*
> *Pella came down with his till.*
> *Abilla came down with her blossoms,*
> *Abilla came down from the hills.*
> *Pella fell in love with the soil*
> *and Pella fell in love with his ale.*
> *Abilla fell in love with his toil*
> *but Abilla nagged about his pale.*
> *And that's when Pella left Abilla,*
> *that's when Pella moved south.*
> *Yeah, that's when Pella moved south.*

Othniel, quite thirsty after a spirited dance, chugs his remaining ale. Ezekiel shakes his head in disapproval. Benjamin drops his cautious attitude and enjoys the happy moment with his free-spirited sister.

"How about another round?" asks Othniel, heading back to the bar. Pella Moved South puts Barnabas in a good mood, and he pours the ale without mentioning the prophet's bar tab.

As Othniel gathers the tray, the door slams open and the music stops. The cheerful chatter ceases when a massive orchard farmer enters.

Othniel turns around and nearly spills the ale onto the large farmer with a bull-like head; fruit and alcohol stains tint his shirt, and bite marks cover his face and arms.

"I thought fox bites would heal quicker," says Othniel, swerving around the bitter farmer while keeping the tray perfectly balanced.

The joyful mood dampens as the farmers move on from their past happiness and reflect on their present misery. The imposing orchard-picker makes matters worse by pressing the patrons for ale.

Benjamin's attention abandons the brute disturbing the peace when intuition churns within his stomach. The door opens, and in walks Rezon Scar with two of his henchmen. His mangled face scans the inn and instantly recognizes Othniel.

"The king will pay a thousand gold pieces for that man's head!" offers Rezon.

The troublemakers amongst the patrons turn their faces in unison toward the wanted prophet. The maligned farmer looks ready for some payback and approaches Othniel.

A bar stool crashes across the back of the farmer's bull-like skull and knocks him unconscious; the aggressive act agitates the belligerent clients and a brawl breaks out.

Othniel and Ezekiel crawl on the floor to avoid flying mugs and chairs. The thirsty prophet is careful not to spill his ale and decides to down his pint mid crawl. He offers Ezekiel a pint, only to be met with a confused stare, so Othniel downs his disciple's ale as well. Othniel shows his gratitude with a loud belch in Ezekiel's face.

Barnabas stands motionless with regret, empty bottles whizzing by his head and shattering behind him.

Benjamin grabs Jael and heads for the door; the two henchmen grab Benjamin, and Rezon squeezes Jael into his arms. Making a pass at Jael, she picks up an empty wine bottle and smashes it across the smooth side of his face. He drops to the floor in pain.

Benjamin frees himself of the strongman and uses a mounted buck head to repel one of the attackers over a table. The other henchman runs out the door.

The four travelers leave Barnabas, Gomer, and the brawling orchard farmers behind.

The rider mounts his horse and darts off.

Benjamin draws his bow and lets loose an arrow. The fortunate henchman cuts left to avoid an arrow into the back of the head.

"Into the orchard!" shouts Othniel directing them into Abilla's Orchard to the south.

The travelers unwittingly separate in the maze of the orchard. The types of fruit trees organize the grove from north to south - peaches, apples, pears. Sections of the orchard are well-manicured creating perfectly straight paths; other sections have not been maintained and the trees grow wildly intertwining with one another. The varied tree grooming creates a perplexing maze to navigate.

Othniel scurries along with his staff in one hand and a peach in the other. Ezekiel scoots alongside his teacher.

Benjamin scans the orchard for his sister.

Jael unknowingly moves away from her brother.

Thundering horses and barking dogs rove about the orchard, so the siblings fear yelling out to one another.

A horseman gallops down a straight path, lowers his sword, and nearly decapitates Ezekiel - Othniel briskly pushes the lucky novice out of harm's way as the steed zips by.

At the same time, a soldier with a shaggy black dog appears in the distance and releases his mangy dog. As the hound charges the prophets, Othniel tosses his peach to Ezekiel and chants in his mystical language.

The dog reverses course with unnatural speed and swiftly lunges at the soldier, allowing him no time to draw his sword. The soldier attempts to fend off the dog with his forearms, but it's no use - the content beast feasts on his dead master.

A soldier, gripping the chain of the second black dog, barrels down a different path toward Benjamin. The shepherd draws his bow and connects his arrow with the soldier's chest. The fallen soldier releases the shaggy mutt, and it charges the shepherd.

Benjamin lines up another arrow. Before he lets loose, the dog reverses course to chase a rabbit. Benjamin lowers his bow with a sigh of relief.

Suddenly, a horseman executes an ambush and his steed plows Benjamin to the ground. The standard bearer gallops off, his purple banner with the black wolf head fluttering behind him.

Two foot soldiers press the ambush against Benjamin, and he's unable to get to his feet and draw Kurion. The infantrymen try to cut him open with their swords.

Rezon spots Jael from atop his horse and gallops toward her. She fires too quickly at him, and the arrow misses high.

Jael breathes deep and calms her adrenaline before ripping another arrow. The shot nicks the horse's ear and grazes Rezon's neck.

The dart frightens the horse, and it rears up, throwing Rezon face first into the ground. The frazzled horse taps in a circle atop Rezon's face.

Hidden from Jael's vision, Zimri watches his misfortunate captain from atop his mount. Rezon curses Jael, which lets the tyrant know that his captain is alive. Zimri dismounts and stealthily moves through the orchard.

The horseman returns for another run at the prophets. Othniel chants once more, this time to the horse. The beast throws his master and tramples him before fleeing the orchard.

The horseman sits up in a daze, favoring his ribs. Othniel chants one final time. A handful of foxes break cover to gnaw the dazed horsemen. Ezekiel tosses the peach back to Othniel, who takes another bite.

Benjamin rolls across the orchard floor, avoiding the vicious swings of the two swordsmen. The relentless soldiers stay aggressive keeping him from unleashing Kurion. The ambushers force him into a cluster of peach trees and move in for the kill.

The soles of Evan Tav's boots graze the top of Benjamin's head as his brother leaps from the trees above with his longsword aimed at the swordsmen.

Evan overpowers the swordsmen with his longsword, splitting the black and purple armor of a soldier with a powerful strike. After watching the swift demise of his comrade, the other attacker flees.

Evan pursues him and pegs his longsword into the back of the cowardly soldier.

The standard bearer refuses another pass at the Tav Brothers and opts to escape. Benjamin gets to his feet, draws bow, and lines his arrow.

The yellow-feather arrow pierces the spine of the rider. The horseman drops his banner and falls to the ground as his steed gallops out of the orchard.

Jael seizes the initiative in her duel with Rezon. Zimri watches the challenge as he sneaks through the orchard, slowly drawing his sword from the sheath.

Rezon's frightened horse trots into the duel and distracts Jael, allowing the captain to regain his footing. Rezon drives Jael into a cluster of peach trees. He raises his sword high above his head to deliver a death blow.

Jael slides to the ground and the mighty sword swing lodges into a tree trunk.

Jael swipes at Rezon, forcing him to let go off his weapon.

The captain throws desperate punches at her. Jael slashes his face and reopens his recent wound from the wine bottle. He falls to the ground and rolls in agony.

Jael raises her sword to finish Rezon when Zimri emerges behind her. 'The Backstabber' stabs her through the back, his steel blade turning crimson as it exits her stomach.

Jael's bloodcurdling shriek summons her brothers.

Zimri and Rezon mount their horses and flee the orchard.

"Get ready for war!" declares Zimri, disappearing into the trees.

Evan falls to the ground and gathers his lifeless sister into his arms. The wind gusts swirl peach tree blossoms around Evan and Jael.

Benjamin keels over, his limbs paralyzed by grief. Memories of chasing Jael as a little girl enter his mind - her dark-blonde ponytail bounces as she dashes through the alleyways of Tav. The memory fails to comfort him, and fiery tears fester in his eye when a burning vengeance wells in his soul.

Evan looks upon his brother with a scorching gaze that consumes Benjamin's anger. Jael's death and Evan's judgment force Benjamin's face into the peach blossoms on the ground.

The prophets stand silently with misty eyes. Ezekiel breathes heavy trying to make sense of the tragedy. Othniel bows his head and silently prays to Neshama, "Receive this child as she begins her journey through the ether world. Welcome her soul upon her arrival at the Great Throne.

Evan stands, holding Jael's corpse in his arms - his eyes glassy, knees weak.

"I'm taking my little sister home."

Chapter 12

Lavender & Black Lace

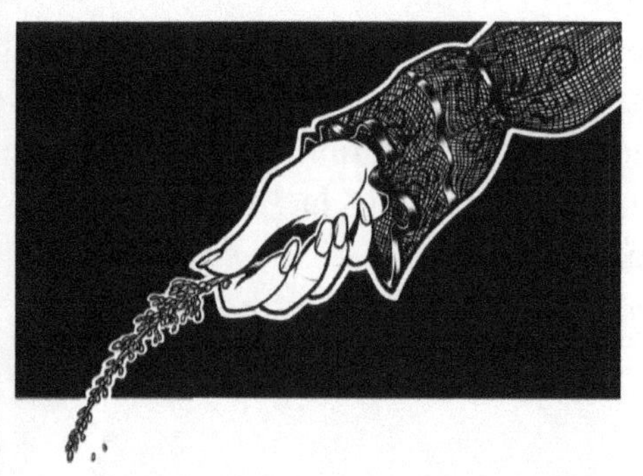

Evan smoothes the dirt atop Jael's burial mound; his fingertips graze the loose earth in the same motion that once soothed the child at bedtime. Benjamin presses his forehead against her tombstone and the grey slab cools his blood.

Judith kneels at the foot of the mound, gripping a stem of lavender. Her tears soak the purple petals. Daniel consoles his bride, kneeling beside her - his hands secure on her shoulders.

Seth Keros stoically stands next to Ashira with his hulking arm draped over her shoulder; she hugs his arm, tears gliding down her cheeks.

Othniel and Ezekiel observe in silence from a grassy knoll overlooking the crowds.

Hundreds of shepherds and their families gather from all over Hallowed Hills. They peer over the waist-high rock wall that edges the memorial garden. Ardon Tsadi and Jether Resh, the revered guild masters, and their families bundle inside the garden under the ivy-trimmed gate.

Ardon pats his youngest offspring, Jacob, on his bowl-shaped hair - his bucked-teeth quivering with emotion.

Dressed in black lace, the women carry a solitary stem of lavender. They form a single-file line that leads to the graveside. Each mourner places a stem of lavender on Jael's grave.

After the last stem falls, Benjamin reaches out to Evan by placing his hand on his shoulder.

"I don't know how to say this…"

Evan removes Benjamin's hand, stands, and walks around him. Benjamin hangs his head in shame as if he'd lost a lamb.

As the quiet day drags on, Benjamin remains in seclusion-sealed within the boulder-maze. He sits in the exact spot where his father felled the wolf that nearly claimed him in his childhood.

Torn to death by wolves or watching Jael die, Benjamin's worst nightmare is reality and far dire than the fangs of a wolf. Yet, a deeper query lingers about the boulders. Do the prophets speak the truth? Is Jael in the ether world on her way to Neshama, or is it all a lie conjured for fools with false hope?

Judith seeks Benjamin in his not-so-secret hiding place. He anticipates the same anger that he received from Evan for Jael's death was by far his worst mistake. Regardless, Benjamin stands as Judith approaches and readies his apology.

Before he can speak, she engages him with a warm embrace. His tears stream an apology that soaks his sister's thick hair, "I'm so sorry."

"I'm not sure you have anything to be sorry about."

The siblings climb atop a boulder and look at the cloudy horizon for a moment while Benjamin tries to process Judith's exoneration.

"Do you remember how excited Jael got when she found out that mother used to take the occasional rotation with father?" asks Judith.

"Evan was so mad at you for letting that cat out of the bag."

"Do you remember how many cats Jael bagged?"

"Six? There was Pepper, Smoke's mom. The Pe's cat. A skinny black one. A fat white one… And a couple of orange tabbies," answers Benjamin, lifting his fingers one by one.

"Seven… You forgot Nabal's cat, Muffin," corrects Judith.

"How did I forget that hideous thing? It was missing the fur on its face, had a snaggle tooth, and a coat like a wire brush. Father hated that cat. It would make bread on the flock in the middle of the night, and scare them awake. The sheep would rattle the stalls and wake him from a good sleep. I never heard father curse, except at Muffin."

"Jael was devastated when Evan told her that women couldn't shepherd, so she decided to herd cats instead. When they wouldn't cooperate, she sacked them together."

The siblings chuckle at the thought of the unfortunate nitwit who yanked the bag from her little hands.

"Nabal had red marks head to toe. Muffin crawled into his pants, clawed his crotch!" laughs Judith, lifting off her seat and bumping hips with Benjamin.

Their giddiness fades with the memory, and reality reminds them of their dark clothes and the smell of lavender in the breeze.

"Jael was my only connection to our mother. I thought I'd always have that connection through her, she was so much like mother."

Judith looks upon Benjamin in a way that makes him feel uncomfortable as if she can sense his concealed angst.

"What? Why are you lookin' at me like that?"

"You were called, weren't you? You have that same troubled look as father and mother."

Benjamin wears his troubled look.

"I was called and look what happened. I led Jael to her death."

"I remember the day our parents shared their calling with me and Evan. I didn't want them to fight, but deep within me faith affirmed that they had to go. Evan resented the revolt. You and Jael were too little to understand."

Judith slides her silky hands down Benjamin's cheeks to grasp his focus.

"Jael died free, so did our parents, and that's something worth celebrating. Don't let her death keep you from your calling. You must not forget Miriam's stuggle to remember the Covenant. Listen to Neshama's call. Don't go through life with regret."

Judith's forgiveness and wisdom humbles Benjamin, and a warmth glows within him that reminds him of his days as an unruly boy stumbling into trouble. Judith was always there to offer grace, never shame.

Inside the guild hall, Evan and Ashira cuddle next to the fireplace. Her comfort allows his mind to escape the misery.

"Thanks for being here, your presence makes this pain easier to bear."

"Seth and I wanted to attend the wedding, but that request was denied. At least our bosses had enough compassion to let us come to the funeral... I wouldn't have been able to make it without Seth. We ran into some bandits near Pella, but they took one look at Peacemaker and fled."

"I'm indebted to your brother's loyalty. Having you here in this hall helps me make sense of my life."

"It's nice to take a break from the city. I love how the smell of manure hits me when I near these hills, love petting those wool coats out there in the stalls."

Evan tries to enjoy Ashira's presence, but his anger keeps cycling Benjamin's decision to leave Tsadi and follow Othniel, a decision that he believes doomed Jael.

"I can sense the torment within you, Evan. I'm not sure we get over losing family."

"It's more than that; I'll never forgive Othniel for deceiving Benjamin. How could my brother be so reckless?"

"Don't blame Othniel or Benjamin, so few remain who remember the Covenant."

"If they would stay to themselves and pray, I wouldn't care, but Othniel agitates and my brother blindly follows."

"Benjamin can grow from this, but you have to give him space."

"He needs structure," says Evan, pulling away from Ashira's embrace, not too fond of her opinion about Benjamin.

"Evan. Can't you see he's still struggling with the deaths of Oren and Rachel? And now, Jael. He needs time to find himself."

"Nonsense. He needs structure and you could use some too. We have an arranged marriage, yet that master bedroom stays empty. I won't live in this hall until you reside here with me. Please, Ashira. I beg of you. Allow me to settle your account."

"I'm not going over this again, Evan."

"You just said how much you enjoy coming up here. Let me pay your debt so we can wed."

"You have more pressing concerns. Aren't you worried about Zimri? He'll use this incident to incite a war."

"I'm being counseled by Ardon Tsadi and Jether Resh along with some of the elder shepherds. I'll heed their plans."

"I can help you, Seth too."

"No, both of you are so close to paying your debts. Don't worry. I'm working out a plan with the guild masters. We'll take care of the prophets."

Evan calms himself and pulls Ashira back to his chest.

"I love you and I won't lose you."

Evan Tav, Ardon Tsadi, and Jether Resh along with a handful of elder shepherds sit around a campfire outside the guild hall and discuss how to deal with Zimri's army.

Benjamin, Othniel, and Ezekiel eavesdrop on the conversation from among the sheep in the stables.

"Zimri has clamored for revenge on the Shepherds Guild since Oren led the resistance," says Ardon.

"Zimri's brought ruin upon other guilds. We'll be next if we don't deal shrewdly with the tyrant," says Jether.

A young shepherd with heavy breath arrives at the meeting interrupting Evan's deep thoughts. Once his breath returns, he delivers his message, "The Foresters Guild won't commit to fight. Erez Elk claims that he paid good money for the Pact of Zimri. He said we should ante up, do likewise, and stop this constant warmongering."

The elder shepherds grumble, but do not act surprised for the Foresters Guild isolated themselves from the affairs of Issur centuries ago.

Evan stands and the chatter settles.

"I know I've said some things, done some things that upset the people in this town. For that, I ask your forgiveness… I need all the help I can get, even if that means going into battle with prophets. War is upon us. My father faced Zimri with a show of strength and we must do likewise."

"Evan's right. We can't allow Zimri to ravage our hills.

Let's keep thinking on a diplomatic end, but in the meantime we will muster the shepherds for war," says Ardon Tsadi, receiving an affirmative nod from Jether Resh.

After hearing Evan's declaration of forgiveness and unity, Benjamin, Othniel, and Ezekiel look upon one another with encouraged eyes.

Nearly three thousand shepherds form ranks across Ephah's Field under an overcast sky. They're divided into three companies armed with a mix of axes, swords, bows, and clubs. Their banners wave their ancestral colors of black and yellow.

Evan, Benjamin, Othniel, and Ezekiel peer across the horizon to watch King Zimri and Captain Scar arrogantly gallop in front of a grand army of fifteen thousand that dons the colors of purple and black. They're divided into three sections - the halberdiers clad in black iron cuirasses form the battle line, the swordsmen dressed in black leather armor stand behind the halberdiers in reserve, the archers in purple tunics hastily form ranks out front.

The wind whips the numerous purple banners with black moons, but the shepherds show no fear at the sight of Zimri's ominous army.

Evan emerges from the ranks of the shepherds and walks across the field to offer terms to Zimri. Benjamin sends Othniel a look of confusion, but the prophet remains silent, never taking his old eyes off Evan.

As the guild master approaches the king, Zimri offers Evan the Signet Ring of Issur as he lords over him from atop his horse. Evan swallows big and kisses the ring.

Zimri smiles at Evan and throws down a solitary stem of lavender, the flower landing softly on his boot. The shepherd's composure hangs in the balance, but remains in tact.

Rezon hands Zimri a scroll that he unrolls and scans.

"Rezon said that he received your terms yesterday. Did you pen these terms?"

Evan nods.

"All of the guild masters stand behind these terms?"

"They make their stand on this battlefield."

Zimri surveys the shepherd army with disdain, "So be it. I will withdraw my army and the guild masters will keep their halls."

"What about the terms concerning my brother?"

"I will remove his bounty, but if he takes one step out of Hallowed Hills, he will die."

Evan walks back to the battle line. Benjamin, Othniel, and Ezekiel anticipate the news.

As Evan draws near, Ardon Tsadi and Jether Resh approach Othniel and Ezekiel from behind. They swiftly sling burlap sacks over their heads to muffle the prophets while other shepherds bind them in rope.

Evan, with the assistance of some muscular shepherds, restrains Benjamin. He flails his arms and tries to get free. He nearly breaks their hold, but the forceful shepherds strengthen their resolve and wrestle him to the ground.

Terror and tears flood his eyes when he watches Ardon and Jether hand over Othniel and Ezekiel to Zimri's soldiers. They string the prophets on posts attached to a cart that's pulled by two horses.

Benjamin's tears mix with dirt as he watches Othniel and Ezekiel disappear into the horizon.

Citizens line the streets of Tizra to cheer the return of the army. Women rain down purple petals from the taller buildings as victory bells ring.

Ashira breaks from her meal preparation to view the jubilee from the tiny kitchen window.

Zimri's ego inflates from the image of raised hands that praise him and from the chimes of tower bells that extol him. A vast crowd gathers and desires to know the identity of the two men masked by sacks.

Zimri dismounts and climbs atop the cart.

"Glory be to Melek, god of the dark, god of the moon! He foretold of this divine day. We're one step closer to ridding Issur of Neshama and her false promise."

The crowd approves with a blast of cheers.

Zimri rips the sacks from the heads of Othniel and Ezekiel, the crowd gasping in disbelief.

Tears form in Ashira's eyes at the sight of the helpless prophets.

"Ezekiel will face Seth Keros in The Pit!"

The crowd laughs at the disciple's impending doom.

"Othniel 'Wayfarer' will burn alive!"

The crowd scorns the prophet with venomous insults.

"The burning of the great prophet will commence the coming moon festival… None of this would have been possible without my prowess as a prophet hunter. Hail your king, get on your knees, kiss my feet."

The crowd kneels and lauds their king. Those close to the cart begrudgingly place their lips on his filthy boots.

Chapter 13

The Tekoa Question

Torches guide cautious steps as Aden, Ishem, and a ranger navigate their way through the swamps of Tekoa Bottom; the croaks of bullfrogs drown out all of the insects and reptiles straining to be heard in the humid night. Sweat slides down Aden's cheeks as he grabs his animal skin canteen and downs the remaining water, pausing mid chug when a red-bellied swamp snake slithers across his black boots. The snake plops into a trench of green water and swims off after a small brown frog. The adventurers reposition their cloaks across their faces to protect their lungs from the noxious fumes seeping from a decayed mank tree.

The men arrive at Lord Emmerick's command tent. A guard wearing black leather armor trimmed in yellow stops them at the entrance. His sense of duty stiffens him straight.

"Lord Emmerick is not to be disturbed."

"This matter is of grave importance. He will see me, I'm his nephew," exhales Aden with desperate breath.

"Lord Emmerick is not to be disturbed, especially by family."

"Maybe me and my men should disturb you instead."

Aden's threat coupled with his intense sweaty face intimidates the guard's sense of duty.

"You are his nephew," says the guard, stepping aside.

Aden and his men enter the spacious tent. It looks less like a war room and more like a laboratory with flasks, beakers, and ceramic mortars with pestles spread about. Emmerick twists his slick handlebar mustache as he examines numerous insects, snakes, and frogs splayed out on a table. His dull armor collects dust in the corner, reminding Aden of his uncle's true passion.

Emmerick smoothes his thin oily hair before lifting his magnifying monocle to his blue iris. He licks his cracked lips while scanning the data in his research journal. Engrossed in his work, Emmerick doesn't acknowledge his guests.

"Greetings, Uncle Emmerick. Sorry to disturb your siege… and your research."

Aden's voice pulls Emmerick's long nose from his journal, and one glance at his nephew sends his memory to the past.

His nephew's face was cut in the image of Emmerick's father, Aden the Fourth 'The Deerstalker.' The memories of his father were bittersweet. He encouraged Emmerick in his academic endeavors. Realizing that being the younger son, it was highly unlikely that he would ever sit on the throne.

Emmerick appreciated the encouragement to discover his true passion, but he always sensed that his lack of military prowess disappointed his father. Maybe it had to do more with Deerstalker's fear of his older son's ambition, for Zimri kept a constant eye on the Signet Ring of Issur.

"Does your father know you're here?" questions Emmerick.

"My father's gone mad, Melek worship makes him so. He

no longer claims me as his son. If he stays in power, he'll destroy Issur. I've come here to ask you to lead your army north and put an end to his reign."

"The people of The Southern Kingdom have entrusted me with their lands. I vowed to protect them and will take no action until Tekoa is free of the Calcedonian raiders. I and my men are hard at work designing siege plans."

Tobi Tamar, Emmerick's captain, glares at his lord for such a response, annoyed by the professor's deeper interest in the wildlife of Tekoa Bottom than the campaign to free the citizens of the raiders from Calcedon. Tobi strokes his full red beard with one hand while wiping the sweat from his freckled bald head with the other.

Aden recognizes Tobi's frustrated body language so he walks over to the table and scans the campaign map. "What troubles you, old friend?"

"The main force camps here, north of Tamar, prepared to counter an invasion from The Northern Kingdom. Our small force camped here in Tekoa lacks the fortitude to push the raiders from the land bridge leading into the city. And these raiders, they're driven by an urge, an urge much deeper than greed."

Aden absorbs every word from Tobi as he studies the campaign map.

"I have an idea. This will take a little time, but the raiders will never expect it."

With his research once again captivating his attention, Emmerick ignores the battle plans of Aden and Tobi.

"Go on," implores Tobi.

"A few lengths north of here is Mara's Woods. Take some troops and fetch me a good amount of lumber. I'll visit the commissary for rope and locate an engineer."

"Yes, Sir," says Tobi, happily obliged to follow the order before exiting the tent.

Aden wipes thick amounts of sweat from his brow. He feels nauseous from the smell of the dead amphibians and chemicals in the tent; he grabs his canteen, but quickly realizes that he drained it.

"Ishem, do you mind pouring us a round of wine?"

Ishem pours a round of chardonnay into three metal goblets atop the dinner table. Aden receives the first goblet but politely passes it to the ranger, "Here, you look like you need this as much as I do."

The ranger gladly receives the libation and siphons it down his throat.

Aden is about to drink from his goblet when Emmerick halts his wrist. The professor sniffs the wine. He then strikes Ishem in the temple with his index and middle fingers.

Ishem drops unconscious.

The ranger's face greys. His eyes bulge while he clutches his throat. The ranger drops dead next to the unconscious Ishem.

Emmerick takes the chardonnay to his chemistry set and pours the wine into a flask. He adds some chemicals that turn the wine different colors. He filters the wine though some tubes flowing into a beaker and stares at the solution for a few blinks.

The liquid turns black.

Emmerick sniffs it from arm's length. "Citrullus Colocynthis, a poison found in rare fruits, blends perfectly with wine."

Emmerick reaches down and pulls a vial of that same poison from Ishem. The biologist holds it up like a prize. "I could smell it. Not to mention, Zimri tried to kill me with it."

Aden looks at his drink in amazement. His vision blurs and the goblet goes in and out of focus. He drops the metal cup and falls to the floor with it. Emmerick scrambles for water while Aden's mind scrambles in his blackout.

Aden hears his grandfather's voice on the other side of

the blackness; the words come from the final conversation with his mentor.

"I've failed as a father with Zimri, for I stood idly by and let Melek worship ruin him. This false god will demand that Zimri seek first the signet ring. After taking the throne, he will trample Miriam's Covenant. Issur will perish one soul at a time.

I'm too weak to stop Zimri. You are my only chance at redemption, Aden. You bear my name and I pray that Neshama vindicates my namesake for her glory. I sharpened your battle skills. Better yet, I strengthened your character. The Tizra line will either live or die with you. Issur's fate is linked to your hope. No matter how black Melek's darkness looms, your hope will be a lantern for Issur."

Cold water rushes across Aden's face, and he sits up gasping for air. The initial shock of the cold water quickly changes to a refreshing sensation assisting Aden's return to reality.

It may have been the humidity, the boredom, or both that made three sunsets feel like three seasons while Aden recovered from his weakened condition. The prince's thoughts remained fixed on the two slain rangers.

The warning signs of Ishem's betrayal were evident in the cornfield, yet he missed the warning signs, from the traitor's skittish behavior to his errant shots. The conspiracy was an easy one to figure - Zimri got to Ishem, it was that simple. It was the why that nagged him. Aden planned to confront his childhood friend once Tekoa was back under the protection of Emmerick.

Aden wipes sweat from his flush face and swigs water from his canteen to relieve the affects of the muggy swamp as he surveys the area. The hearty bullfrogs of Tekoa Bottom bellow at the bright moon that covers the water around the port city with a yellow sheen.

A narrow land-bridge cuts the marshland and connects Tekoa to the King's Highway, which leads north. The city has four walls but no gates - the south wall shields the port city from the Strait of Mara as rickety docks jot out from the wall; the eastern and western walls keep the Bottom from swamping the city. The beige mud-brick shops and houses are built to survive the raging sea storms that assault the coast in the winter season.

Emmerick's force divides into two regiments. The larger regiment numbers over three hundred men and women armed with halberds and clad in iron cuirasses. The smaller regiment numbers over one hundred men and women armed with bows and short swords, and dressed in black leather armor.

Captain Tamar divides the smaller regiment into units, and they await their orders on rafts that have been constructed from Mara's Woods.

Aden waits for Emmerick to give the orders, but the professor buries his nose in a book underneath his tan pith helmet, his loyal guard providing light from a lantern.

The regiments on the rafts look uncertain about what's going to happen. Tobi gives Aden a familiar look of desperation in hopes that the prince will provide leadership to the regiments.

"Shall we pray before going off to battle?" asks Aden.

"Who shall pray?" asks Tobi.

"The paladin precept, of course."

"There's no precept among the ranks. They're all locked away in the Grand Chancel... Prayin'."

"The Synod's duty is to their king," complains Aden, the new direction of the once-volatile precepts unsettling him.

"True. But there's no king on this battlefield, no general either. All I see is a biologist and a lost prince."

The blunt captain motivates Aden to action. "Captain Tamar will lead the halberdiers to the land bridge, where they'll stop and show themselves to the raiders. I'll join the regiment on rafts, and we'll float our rafts through the swamp around their flank. We'll trap them in the city."

Tobi grabs his heavy halberd and takes his place in the front rank.

The prince's plan impresses the troops, but Emmerick didn't hear a word of Aden's instruction. "I was unaware that swamp fungus can reproduce asexually." He pulls his nose from his book, surprised to see the regiments in good order. "Did I miss something?"

"No. Nothing at all, Uncle."

Aden drifts away on his raft, Tobi marches his company to the land bridge, and Emmerick returns to his research.

The soldiers on the rafts use large poles to propel the transports through the swamp, never losing sight of the city walls as they stealthily navigate their way to the harbor. They dock their rafts and sneak into the city.

The Calcedonian raiders don a mix of furs, raggedy clothes, and scraps of armor. They relentlessly hound the townspeople for food.

A handful of bandits yell that troops have assembled at the land bridge. The marauders cease their harassment of the townspeople and move toward the front wall. The rustlers number more than five hundred strong and go into battle with an assortment of crude weapons. The Calcedonian raiders form ranks in the mouth of the front wall connecting to the land bridge.

Aden waves a group of relieved townspeople into cover. Once safe, he quietly leads his regiment through the cobblestone streets of Tekoa. He marks the raiders and readies his troops. The front rank kneels while the back rank takes aim over their shoulders.

They draw strings and fire into the regiment of raiders blocking the front entrance. Their fast arrows stick into the backs of the raiders.

The marauders turn face and abandon the opening. Aden's regiment lets loose again, and the volley of arrows shreds another rank of brutes before they charge Aden's regiment.

With the entrance now abandoned, Captain Tamar marches the regiment of halberdiers across the land bridge.

Aden's unit lets fly one more round of arrows before preparing for close combat. The volley slays another rank, but the raiders keep coming.

The Calcedonians surge into swordsmen. They strike vicious blows, and Aden's regiment fails to match their animosity. They break and flee.

The wave of raiders nearly tramples Aden, but he keeps his footing and narrowly escapes with his troops.

Aden catches up with his regiment and rallies them on the docks, "Stand firm, for Tekoa!"

His regiment turns to reengage their aggressors, but the enemy surges harder than before removing Aden along with his regiment from the rickety docks and pushing them into the water.

Aden loses his sword in the murky water.

Before the raiders can finish off Aden and his regiment flailing about in the water, Tobi's troops arrive at the south entrance overlooking the docks.

The raiders reverse course and charge back into the city.

The iron-clad regiment withstands the charge from the exhausted Calcedonian raiders, for the raiders struggle to land the powerful blows necessary to penetrate the defensive weapons of the halberdiers. Tobi releases a season of pent-up aggression cutting down one foe after the other with his heavy halberd.

Aden rallies his unit once more, and they crawl back onto the docks. After his troops regain their composure, he barks out his orders, "Draw bows, arrows ready, on my command!"

Tobi's regiment breaks the raiders, and they flee to their boats. As soon as the raiders set foot on the docks, Aden shouts his command, "Fire!"

The hail of arrows decimates the fleeing raiders from Calcedon.

Once the city is secure, Aden walks about the dead pillagers. A closer look reveals that many of them are peasants. He feels sick to his stomach when he rolls over a dead lad clutching a loaf of bread. The troublesome revelation puzzles the prince.

Empowered by the thrill of victory, the battle-hardened captain approaches Aden with a confident countenance, "Well fought, good Prince!"

Tobi puts his arm around Aden's shoulders when the liberated citizens of Tekoa swarm them with celebratory dancing.

Chapter 14 | Going South

The morning sun brightens the Tav ether chancel with a warm glow. Benjamin feels the warmth of the sun and opens his eyes to sparrows fluttering about in the rafters.

Shamgar Ram's rugged mug enters his line of vision.

Benjamin sits up on the pew and the precept sits next to him.

"It has been a trying season for you. I know how much you loved your sister, and Othniel's pending execution must be taking a toll on your faith."

"Not at all. It's only strengthened my resolve. I didn't come here to pray last night; I came here hoping I'd wake to see you this morning."

"What do you want with me?" asks Shamgar, confused by Benjamin's boldness.

"I want you to join me on a quest."

"To where?"

"Tizra. Help me rescue Othniel and Ezekiel. Help me fulfill my call to dethrone Zimri and end Melek worship."

"Benjamin… I know I've questioned your doubt, but going into Tizra to prove your faith is a foolish notion."

"You were once High Precept, your faith was unrivaled in all Issur. Come with me."

"I can't."

"Why not?"

"I'm going to my hometown, Sapphire. I'll make the trek up Serpents Stream tomorrow. My time has passed."

"You'll head north tomorrow, and I'm going south today."

Benjamin stands and moves toward the exit.

"I wish you would've stayed under this chancel to rot. I regret ever meeting you, and now I'm going to forget about you. I can't believe you had the nerve to question my faith… Hypocrite."

Shamgar smiles at the insult as Benjamin slams the heavy doors of the chancel.

Benjamin enters the guild hall to Evan, Judith, and Daniel eating at the breakfast table. Evan greets him with a suspicious glare. Judith hops up and scoops him a warm bowl of oatmeal. "Good morning, Benjamin."

He nods in gratitude, pulling up a chair at the far end of the table away from Evan.

"Now that Benjamin has decided to join us, I can explain how we'll survive this drought. Of course we wouldn't be in this mess if someone knew how to follow simple instructions."

"Evan," interjects Judith. "Just tell us your plans."

"I'm going to replenish the mountain flock with the coin I earned from the sheep for moon festival. I'm buying three hundred head from Jether Resh. He granted me permission to water the new flock at Lake Resh until the fall rains come. I hired Bo and his brothers to move the flock in the stalls out to the mountain glade until the drought ends.

Daniel and Benjamin, I need you to come with me and tend the new flock at Lake Resh. Can you handle this?"

"Definitely," affirms Daniel.

Benjamin refuses to answer.

"Well…," prompts Evan.

"I'm not going."

Judith stops eating and sends a worrisome look down the table to her defiant brother. Daniel spoons his oatmeal to keep the moment from becoming awkward for him.

"Are you ill?" asks Evan.

"I feel fine. For the first time in a long time, I feel alive. I'm going to Tizra to free Othniel and Ezekiel."

Benjamin's defiance sends Evan to his feet.

"You know Zimri's terms! You're dead if you leave these hills!"

"Then, I guess I'm a dead man."

Benjamin leaves his oatmeal and exits the guild hall.

Daniel keeps his head down and doesn't insert himself in the feud. Judith stands and gently takes Evan's hands, "You're practically his father. Benjamin needs you now more than ever."

Evan tries to leave, but she squeezes his hand, "Do you remember our parent's call? Does it trouble you still?"

"They abandoned us for a lost cause. Benjamin follows in their footsteps."

Evan turns his back on her and exits the guild hall. Daniel moves to Judith's side to offer comfort.

Evan runs in front of Benjamin to block his exit from the village, "I refuse to let you go."

"You're not my father."

"I know that, Benjamin. You've reminded me of that every day since I became your guardian at fifteen. Do you think I wanted that responsibility? Judith was only thirteen, what about her? We were kids raising kids.

You're bitter because I never prayed with you or took you to the chancel like father. I didn't stay up all night answering your questions like he did. I had no time for Neshama then, and I have no time for her now. Father's faith profited him nothing. I have his work ethic, not his faith. All this Neshama garbage has poisoned your mind like it did his."

"I'm not going to listen to this," says Benjamin, trying to slide around Evan.

"The truth hurts."

"I don't know if what Othniel told me is true, but if I stay in these hills I'll never know the truth."

"You would choose that fanatic over your own blood."

"Othniel wants what our parents died for, what Jael died for… Freedom."

Evan backhands Benjamin across the mouth.

Benjamin shakes off the strike and looks upon Evan with resentment as he dabs his tongue on the bitter blood that trickles from his lip. He grabs his backpack from the ground, slings it over his shoulders, and marches by Evan.

Benjamin travels south across Josiah's Path. The steep inclines level out at the rolling hill where the manors and hovels of Tsadi reside. He's tempted to seek shelter in the guild hall. With Daniel Tsadi as his brother-in-law, he's certain that he'd be denied nothing.

He fears, however, that Ardon Tsadi may feel disrespected by his decision to leave Hallowed Hills in defiance of Zimri's decree - a deal that Ardon helped negotiate. The risk of being forced home is too great.

The setting sun and the cry of a wolf compel Benjamin to enter Tsadi. Instead of enjoying the comforts of a guild hall, he sneaks into a crowded stable for a safe night's sleep with plenty of sheep to count.

Benjamin wakes at the sound of a crowing rooster atop the stable. He sits up to see a radiant vision of a young girl with a pail of water staring down at him. The moment would have been awkward, but the curious girl with locks of blonde curls pulled into a ponytail reminds him of Jael.

"Have a drink before I pour it in the trough," offers the saintly-faced darling, handing him the pail.

Benjamin accepts her kind offer. He splashes some water on his face, and slicks back his wavy hair before taking a long drink. After refilling his canteen, he feels a little guilty that her pail is empty.

"Sorry, I wish I could offer you something in return for your kindness."

"The prophetess Miriam wants us to help others. Neshama will reward me."

Benjamin feels blessed by the little girl's faith and thanks her with his humble smile.

"I've never seen you around here, you're a cute one. You should meet my sister; she's not spoken for," says the charitable child, before running toward her sister.

Benjamin stands to see a woman in the distance approaching with two large water buckets dangling from a yoke on her shoulders. The buxom lass stomps across the hill like an ox.

A little too much woman for me.

Benjamin maintains his anonymity and passes on the meeting; he jaunts down the hill toward The King's Highway.

Another long day of travel lands Benjamin at the outskirts of Abilla; he's physically exhausted, but the day has taken a greater toll on his emotions. The little girl from the stables makes him ponder his fond childhood memories with Jael, and Abilla's Orchard to the west is a constant reminder of her death. As much as he wants to focus on his mission to rescue the prophets, all he can do is channel an all-too-familiar pain for his deceased sister.

The pain cycles down from Benjamin's chest to the depths of his stomach; it shortens his breath and rips his gut in two. He has yet to find a remedy to this misery. He can't reason it away or pray it away.

If only he could be as black and white as Evan. The deaths of Oren and Rachel Tav were their fault, lives wasted on a revolt that profited nothing. Jael's death was Othniel's fault, a life wasted on a fool's faith. But he can't rationalize an equation that doesn't factor Zimri. His childhood psyche was no doubt molded by Evan, and there was always a part of him that blamed his parents like his brother did, but seeing the tyranny of Zimri first hand changed everything.

Vengeance kicks in the gate to Benjamin's soul, and surprisingly, he finds solace in his hatred of Zimri. Vengeance restores his breath and calms the acids in his stomach. He's hesitant to accept the remedy for it goes against his upbringing, but he longs for release from the torment of Jael's death unsettling his soul.

Benjamin approaches a sign at the mouth of The Dark Road leading into The Forest of Elah that reads: *By Order Of Erez Elk, All Trespassers Will Be Executed.*

He, like most shepherd folk, held a strong distrust for the Foresters Guild because of their reclusive existence. Over the course of their history, they never welcomed outsiders, only those interested in buying their timbers. They never intervened in the perils of Issur dating all the way back to the Vilekin invasions. While other guilds intermarried, the foresters forbid it. They were the first to outlaw prophets and denied the paladin precepts land to construct chancels. Hallowed Hills always extended a hand of friendship to the foresters, but the reclusive woodsmen refused to leave the Forest of Elah to accept it.

Benjamin runs low on water, and not only will his deer jerky fail to sustain him for another day, he's sick of eating it. He'd rather avoid crowds, but he realizes that he must enter Abilla. This is his price to pay for trusting that Shamgar Ram would accompany him, and for leaving Tav in haste.

The town square settles down as the sun in the western sky dims over the forest. Benjamin admires a gigantic oak that fills the town square. Exhausted farmers cool off against the rock wall circling the majestic tree, while children dance around a quaint wooden statue of Abilla with her hand in a basket of blossoms.

Benjamin pulls a wolf skin from his knapsack and hands it to the tanner. The balding man with a smooth face and beady eyes inspects the skin.

"I tagged that wolf earlier this season," explains Benjamin.

The tanner reaches into his pocket and offers the shepherd three copper pieces; he accepts the fair offer and shakes the tanner's hand.

Benjamin enjoys a juicy pork chop and corn on the cob while sipping on some barley ale. The smell of melted butter drips off the corncob and the bite of cracked pepper pops off his pork chop to delight his senses. A foamy sip of the barley ale tickles his tongue.

He stuffs carrots and potatoes into his bag, plenty enough to sustain him on his remaining journey to Tizra.

The tavern hosts a handful of tables filled with tired farm hands; some complain about Zimri's mismanagement of The Heartland while others chew quietly, thankful for the day's wage provided by the crown.

Benjamin sits at the bar next to an overstuffed pig-farmer, who loudly jeers the shortcomings of each farm hand. The tavern patrons ignore the boasts puffing out of the obnoxious farmer.

"That's a good cut," admires the chubby farmer, looking over Benjamin's chop. The pig-farmer chugs his pint of ale and belches in Benjamin's food. He disregards the slob's poor manners and finishes his final bites.

Benjamin slides his bar stool when the pig-farmer slams his flabby hand into his back. "Leaving so soon, shepherd?" The slob pushes Benjamin's stool back toward the bar. "Give this outsider another pint."

The bartender refills Benjamin's wooden cup.

"Let me sing you a song about Abilla, matriarch of our guild and Pella, patriarch of our guild."

Benjamin recalls the song and the brawl that ensued after it, "I already know that tune."

"Don't get smart with me, shepherd," scolds the oaf, starting to feel the affects of his fifth pint of ale. "You've been sitting there all night acting sheepish. You come in here and don't offer your name."

Benjamin fears that word of Zimri's decree about him staying in Hallowed Hills may have spread throughout Issur and therefore protects the secrecy of his name.

"Well, out with it!"

Benjamin rises from his stool fed up with the loudmouth.

The pig-farmer slides his stool to block Benjamin's path. Using the momentum of the slide, Benjamin kicks the stool out from under the tubby farmer, who crashes onto the floor boards.

The tavern patrons assume that the unconscious oaf has consumed too much beverage yet again, and tipped his stool. After a brief glance, the farmers return to their meals and appreciate the quiet. Benjamin downs his ale, steps over the unconscious farmer, and exits.

Day three of Benjamin's journey south brings him to the outskirts of Pella. Thankfully, it's a quiet day of cutting through corn fields to avoid traffic along The King's Highway.

Despair devours Benjamin's confidence as he moves closer to the walls of Pella. Crows peck scraps of flesh from the skeletons that hang from posts lining the road into Pella - the remains of adolescents and adults, of men and women, serve as Zimri's trophies from the Farmers Revolt. Benjamin looks to the setting sun and considers the city for shelter, but the stench of ashes and rotting corpses repel that notion.

Benjamin ventures away from the walls of Pella. His mouth gapes at the ungodly statue commemorating Zimri's victory over the Farmers Guild. The king points his sword to the sky, triumphing atop a heap of starving farmers with pitchforks.

The flickering stars remind Benjamin of home, so he unfastens his effects and decides to sleep under the stars. He finds a grassy spot, untucks his shirt, and removes his boots. Benjamin nears the monument once more to admire the craftsmanship, but thoughts of knocking Zimri's head off the statue enter his mind. As he contemplates defacing the heinous monument, his foolish notions of vandalism vanish when the mayhem caused by the vile king injects a dose of grief into his veins.

The soul sick shepherd heals himself with his new cure named vengeance. A vision of Zimri falling from a castle tower calms his blood. The long hair of the tyrant dangles in the wind as he plummets from the heights, an explosion of shattering bones booms on the cobblestone streets of Tizra.

The sounds of boots tromping through grass interrupt his thoughts. Benjamin turns to see five filthy bandits eyeing his belongings, their hands sooty from rummaging through the charred debris of Pella. One of the bandits picks up his longbow and quiver of arrows to admire the balance of the bow. The leader of the bandits takes notice of Kurion. Benjamin feels insecure separated from his sword and bow.

"That's a unique looking sword, shepherd. You're a long way from home, aren't ya?"

Benjamin stays silent.

"You're foolish to travel The King's Highway alone. Do you have the coin to pay our toll?"

"I have no coin."

"This sword will do."

"You'll have to kill me for that sword," threatens Benjamin, jealousy throbbing within his soul while he watches the head highwayman put his filthy hands around the hilt of Kurion.

"How about I kill you with it?" threatens the bandit as he and his cronies advance towards Benjamin.

Azor appears as if a watchtower guarded Benjamin.

The bandits flee immediately leaving their chief behind.

"My bow!" complains Benjamin.

The head highwayman, caught up in a moment of delusion, points Kurion at the nephesh. Azor unsheathes his ether sword and gets into his fighting stance. The movement of aggression intimidates the highwayman. He drops Kurion and flees in terror.

Benjamin turns to find a dimmer version of Azor, "You've faded."

"I've been away from Neshama for a while now." Azor takes notice of the shepherd's down body language. "How different our second encounter begins. Lost your sense of wonder already?"

"No, but I wanted to make it Tizra by myself to prove my brother wrong."

"Selfishness. The root of the evil that plagues Issur, and in my experience, the most disgraceful quality of humans."

"Sorry… Thanks for helping me out, but aren't nephesh selfish?"

"There are a couple major differences between humans and nephesh. Neshama is pure spirit. Nephesh are mostly spirit and possess little matter. Humans are mostly matter and possess little spirit. We were created to serve Neshama, so by nature we are less selfish. Initially, the nephesh thought humans were created for the same purpose, but selfishness jades our understanding of your kind."

"Why did Neshama create the world?"

"That's what she does, she creates."

Azor kneels and draws a circle about the size of a small coin in diameter on the ground, and the curious shepherd peers over his shoulder.

"Look at this circle, now look to the heavens. That circle is the size of your world when compared to the entire cosmos. The Goddess can't help herself, she's an artist. Neshama not only creates, but she's interdependent with what she creates."

"That's why she forged the Covenant with Miriam, she's relational," says Benjamin, grateful of his lesson with Othniel.

"Correct. The nephesh travel the ether world observing and protecting her masterpieces. Though your world is not among the ether realms; it still remains one of her greatest masterpieces."

"Are other humans out there in the cosmos?"

"No. That's what makes humans so mysterious to the nephesh."

"It doesn't seem fair that she forces the nephesh to serve her."

"We're not forced. Like humans, we have free will, but unlike humans, nephesh will rarely misuse their free will. Serving the Goddess is not an obligation. It's an honor to fulfill this call to find Korah."

"My mentor once told me that freedom is found in sacrifice."

Benjamin loses his thoughts in grief for his imprisoned mentor. Then, a revelation snaps him back to the conversation.

"Korah, the man you seek. He's not a man, he's a nephesh."

"Neshama has called me to bring him back to her. I hope to see this through by peaceful means."

"Can a nephesh be killed?"

"Yes, but a human would have a difficult time accomplishing such a feat with mortal weapons." Azor picks up Kurion and returns the sword. "Ether swords, however, have a lethal affect on my kind."

"Have you ever killed a nephesh?"

"Unfortunately, but you must understand that a nephesh would rather converse than kill."

"Then why did you?"

"It was the Great War of Rayah… I will not speak of such matters to a human. I must continue my call."

Azor's purple eyes dim underneath his silvery hair, and Benjamin senses that the mysterious war vexes the nephesh.

"Will I see you again?"

"Our paths may meet again."

Azor walks away, looking back on Benjamin with fondness.

"Do you know Neshama's favorite quality of humans?"

Benjamin shrugs his shoulders.

"They ask a lot of questions."

Azor places his hand underneath his robe to slip a disc from behind his back. He motions his hand across the top of the circle to activate the ether within. Wind currents swirl underneath the disc allowing it hover over the ground.

Azor leaps onto the vessel, drops to one knee, and clutches the sides with his fists. He vanishes like a shooting star into the night sky, leaving Benjamin to conjure one more question that will have to wait for the answer.

The Lost Shepherd

The sight of Tizra steals Benjamin's breath as he marvels at the grand palace peering over the thick walls. The ominous tower guarding the north gate warns Benjamin to stay out by taunting him with its purple banner embroidered with spooky yellow moons.

Benjamin ignores the taunts and enters the north gate by blending in with the citizens of Tizra. The bustle surrounding the merchant stands pulls his attention in a hundred directions. Prostitutes ruffle his hair and gamblers attempt to seduce his lucky eye. The lost shepherd recalls his brother's words about Tizra eating him whole.

Maybe Evan was right, ponders Benjamin, pushing through the ranks of prostitutes and gamblers.

As Benjamin meanders through the market, he notices that most Tizrites engage the same topic of conversation- the disappearance of Queen Rizpah. His mind wanders in the troublesome revelation making his way through the crowd.

WHAM! A misfortunate turn plows him smack into Rezon Scar's grotesque face.

"Watch where you're walkin', shepherd trash!"

Interfaced with the captain, his memory soars back fifteen years to the boulder-maze behind the guild hall. Visions of Oren Tav berating the attacks of a hooded assassin emerge in the present collision. One distinct scar on the side of his face remains, a signature from Oren Tav's blade.

"It was you!" blurts Benjamin.

A heroic inkling to finish his father's fight is short lived when an innate nudge shoves Benjamin down an alleyway.

The fearful shepherd moves about the alleyways of the residential sections in the north plaza, turning every corner anticipating Rezon Scar. After Benjamin successfully navigates a few alleyways, he finds himself at a side entrance leading into Zimri's palace.

The guard on post harasses a little girl for her basket of fruit. Rezon approaches and gives the guard an order to search for the rogue shepherd. Benjamin watches the guard move cautiously down an adjacent alleyway.

Once the watchman clears the area, he scans the streets for the captain. The area clears, and Benjamin dashes for the side entrance, swiftly climbing a flight of stairs that leads into the palace.

Suddenly, Rezon appears at the top of the stairs with an evil smirk. He lunges his sword at Benjamin, narrowly side-stepping the blade.

The shepherd grabs Rezon's forearm to pull him toward the street below. Zimri's overlord plummets off the flight of stairs and lands face first onto a horse drawn wagon with a nasty CRACK!

The brown beast spooks and dashes through the city streets, taking the shocked merchant at the reins and Rezon Scar for a wild ride through Tizra.

Benjamin picks up a trace of apple tarts warming in an oven. He follows his nose to the source and peaks his head into the hectic palace kitchen to see all the baking, stirring, and roasting. He picks up a plump purple grape from a dirty plate in the dish pit and tosses it at Ashira.

The grape hits her in the back of the head; she turns around with a scowl and knife drawn in no mood for horseplay. The frown transforms into a smile at the appearance of Benjamin.

Ashira slips out of the kitchen to talk with him in the dish pit, and immediately notices his shaken demeanor, "What's wrong?"

"I ran into Zimri's captain on my way into the city. I was hoping to go unnoticed. Now all the guards will be after me."

"Did you come alone?"

Benjamin answers with his naïve eyes.

"What were you thinking?"

"I've no one to help me. I came here to rescue Othniel and Ezekiel."

"Evan has no interest in helping the prophets?" asks Ashira with fears that he may have betrayed the prophets.

"Why would he?"

Benjamin's response taints the memory of her fireside chat with Evan. "I can't believe your brother. He told me that he'd take care of the prophets. He did just that, didn't he? How could he lie to me like that?"

Ashira thrusts her knife into a wooden cutting board, and Benjamin's eyes begin to water.

"You don't have to cry about it."

"It's not that. Your perfume, jasmine. I'm allergic to it." The light-hearted moment calms Ashira's rushing blood.

"I hate to tell you this, but I have awful news."

Benjamin prepares his faith to respond to the news with a hero's resolve.

"Zimri plans to burn Othniel at the stake. Ezekiel will face Seth in The Pit."

The overwhelming news shatters Benjamin's faith, and he scrambles for ideas.

"Maybe I can talk Seth out of killing Ezekiel."

"Good luck. Unlike me, Seth doesn't believe in Neshama."

Seth strains his muscles to lift a grey stone column above his head. He drops the column to the ground, rattling the racks of weapons and armor in the training room. Benjamin enters in time to witness the raw display of power and questions his decision to talk Seth out of killing Ezekiel, *What are you doing here?*

Benjamin ruffles his hair while mustering the courage to approach the pitfighter. He lightly taps the giant on the shoulder, and Seth turns to tower over him. Benjamin freezes and fails to produce a greeting.

"Aren't you Evan Tav's little brother? What are you doin' down here in The Pit?"

"You can't kill him, it's not right. Let Ezekiel live," blurts Benjamin.

"I'm gonna smash him."

"He's a prophet of Neshama, and your sister keeps the Covenant. Ashira doesn't approve."

"I don't care, I don't subscribe to that nonsense. This is my last fight and I'm a free man."

Benjamin was certain he could convince Seth with Ashira's desire to save Ezekiel, but once again he finds himself at a loss for words. With his thoughts locked on Seth and Ashira, he suddenly recalls the grimmest moment in Keros family history.

"If you kill Ezekiel, you honor the wishes of the man who killed your parents."

Benjamin's words weigh heavy on Seth, heavier than the stone column at his feet.

King Zimri and the High Magi Zidon pass through the torch-lit hallway of the palace dungeon, the barred windows of the cells providing a narrow glimpse of the moon and stars.

Ezekiel sits shackled to a bench in a cell across from Othniel. 'Wayfarer' stands chained to the wall of his cell, his face bearing the marks of persecution at the hands of the prison guards.

Zidon eyes Ezekiel through the cell bars for a moment.

"That monster's gonna rip your arms off," taunts Zimri, before entering the chamber of his prized prisoner.

"Tomorrow we bid farewell to this troubler of Issur. I dreamed about your death for decades. I can't wait to watch you burn."

A cloth-gag muffles Othniel, blocking any response.

Zimri grabs his face to force eye contact. "Neshama is a liar, she's the false god! She leaves her followers for dead! Melek has delivered on every promise, and soon I will deliver you to my god."

Zimri retreats from the cell and exits the dungeon, leaving Zidon to lecture Othniel.

"Greetings, most excellent prophet. The last time we met

was on the battlefield with the shepherds all those years ago. You always had a soft spot for lost causes." The magi looks over the prophet's shackles. "I hate to see you in chains; it will be bittersweet to watch you burn alive. I had hoped for one last showdown with the master prophet."

Zidon grimaces at the deep bruises embedded in Othniel's face. "You look pathetic, but you do worship a pathetic goddess. I can't believe that I ever bought into that grace garbage. Melek is a god of freedom, a god of results, a god of opportunity. Freedom is taking what I want when I want it. Melek empowers me to consume resources and use people to claim the power that I deserve.

Look at where our allegiances have gotten us. I manipulate a king, the same king that is going to burn you alive. I guess this is the sacrifice that you have longed for all these years."

Zidon unties the cloth-gag from the prophet's mouth.

"There's nothing in your magical words that I can't silence."

Othniel swallows deep and tries to siphon enough air to speak. Zidon tilts his head and listens intently for the prophet's response.

Othniel strains his voice to whisper his words, "I still love you and nothing that you do, not even burning me alive, will destroy this love."

Tears flow from Othniel's bruised eyes as he watches a bewildered Zidon exit the cell.

Zidon stands at the entrance of the throne room and gazes at the seat of power with deep longing. Zimri prays on bended knee in the circle of candles. The magi gather round him, and Korah takes his place next to the imposing statue.

"Melek is most pleased with your capture of the great prophet. The Covenant is on the verge of annihilation. He sends warning that the shepherd from Tav is at your doorstep. His faith in Neshama has increased. You made a vow to kill this shepherd, and your god expects you to honor it. If he's not eliminated, then you risk Melek's retribution."

"In the name of Melek, he will die," proclaims Zimri, the candles flickering wildly to match the rage in his possessed eyes.

Chapter 16 | Another Conspiracy

Moonbeams shine through the thick incense that hovers above The Pit, and lanterns glow across the arena to allow the vast crowd to witness the judgment of Ezekiel. Benjamin blends in with the sea of Tizra citizens, and senses the rich anticipation for blood.

"Neshama is a distant and forgetful goddess," taunts a scoffer causing laughter to pour out of those around him.

Seth enters The Pit with Peacemaker over his shoulder; the crowd offers up a thunderous applause and chants, "Seth, Seth, Seth."

King Zimri watches from his box seat with Rezon and Zidon by his side. The captain's mangled face makes the magi cringe, so he switches positions to avoid seeing the deformed flesh.

Ashira stands expressionless alongside the rowdy kitchen staff, her soul trembling with dread for what her brother is about to do to his victim.

Seth walks slowly toward Ezekiel.

He towers over his victim. The martyr shrinks, tormented by the caress of death. Seth raises his warhammer high above his head to deliver a death blow.

Ezekiel's faith rejects death's caress and emboldens the fearful prophet. He steps toward Seth, who lowers Peacemaker, baffled by the change in Ezekiel's disposition.

The crowd jeers the prophet with thoughts that the pitfighter taunts his victim.

As the crowd intensifies their jeers, Ezekiel swells with a righteous anger. He prays the mystical language of the prophets, the same language that Othniel prayed in Hallowed Hills and Abilla's Orchard.

A faint hope floating on his magical words blesses the souls of Benjamin and Ashira.

Readying his warhammer in a defensive posture, Seth takes a step back intrigued by the unique language.

Zidon moves to the edge of the box seat - surprised that such a young prophet can utter the mystical tongue. As Ezekiel's voice deepens, the crowd quiets. Zimri and Rezon look upon one another puzzled by the foreign dialect. Zidon's eyes grow large while tension settles on the crowd watching with curios anticipation.

A small black object appears in the night sky. It swoops down from the sky and through The Pit lanterns. It zeroes in on Seth like a dart falling from the sky. The lanterns reveal the small black object.

A sparrow.

The sullen bird lands on Seth's shoulder and viciously pecks his armor. The rapid pecks ping the armor and relieves the crowd's misplaced curiosity.

The onlookers erupt in laughter.

Ezekiel lowers his face in embarrassment.

Seth shakes his head for entertaining the prophet's religious hype. With the bird still pecking on his shoulder, he makes his way back toward the martyr.

He raises Peacemaker high above his head. Ezekiel tenses his shoulders awaiting the death blow.

Seth peers down on the defenseless prophet. A wave of somber emotions unexpectedly washes over him, and he lowers his weapon. Benjamin's words rush through his memory.

You honor the wishes of the man who killed your parents.

Seth's pacifism stuns Ashira and relieves Benjamin's worry.

The crowd gets restless, and the scoffer urges Seth, "Finish him!"

Feeling disrespected, Zimri arrogantly moves to the edge of his seat.

"Seth Keros, I command you to execute him!"

Peacemaker weighs heavy on Seth's shoulder, but the burden of his moral dilemma crushes his conscience.

"Do it now or sacrifice your freedom!" demands Zimri with such force that spit flings from his teeth.

"No," says Seth, staring Zimri in the eyes.

Ezekiel lifts his head in awe while the crowd directs noises of discontent at Seth's defiance. Guards flood The Pit, and the pitfighter surrenders.

"If you're not against the prophets, then you'll burn with the prophets!" declares Zimri, his guards cuffing Seth and Ezekiel and leading them out of the arena. The vile crowd boos and hurls rotten food down upon the merciful pitfighter and condemned prophet.

Og collects Peacemaker and Seth's armor and locks them in a stone chest within the training room.

Benjamin sneaks under the cover of dark through the alleyways of Tizra, returning to the side entrance with hopes to reenter the palace and make his way to Ashira's living quarters. He identifies Zimri and Rezon, their attention occupied by randy temple prostitutes and greedy gamblers shooting dice. He takes advantage of the carnal distractions and dashes out of his cover.

Benjamin flies up the stairway that leads into the side entrance, but a misstep on the last stair dislodges a brick that shatters on the street below. He jumps into the entryway with thoughts that he's entered unnoticed.

Rezon catches a flash of his white shirt.

The captain stops flirting with his prostitute and pushes her to the ground, drawing Zimri's mind from his dice game. "Your shepherd came back."

Dying candles from the last feast dimly light the palace hall as Zimri and Rezon track Benjamin through the hallways. The taps of their boots alert him, so he quickly slides behind a tapestry in hopes of going unnoticed. He glides along the wall under the tapestries and recognizes an open closet. Benjamin picks up a metal tray and whirls it into the closet. The tray makes a clanging sound when colliding with a stack of metal platters.

Zimri and Rezon draw swords and rush into the closet. Benjamin slams the door on them. He grabs a spear from the weapons rack next to the frame and bars the door shut.

With the sounds of pounding fists behind him, Benjamin attempts a quick exit when a swift breeze rushes through the hall and extinguishes the candles. The lost shepherd has trouble feeling his way out of the space.

His heart stops as he nearly collides with a dark figure in a black robe. He slides behind a thick tapestry and ceases his breath. The dark figure senses a presence and stops, his head slowly motioning to the left then to the right. The dark figure doesn't tarry.

Benjamin's curiosity overcomes his better judgment, which warns him not to track this man.

In short time, he spots the tall figure moving down a long palace hallway that leads to the throne room. Benjamin marvels at the vision of such a large man, a man larger than Seth.

Benjamin tracks the figure into the throne room that sits empty. He nestles into a dark corner to observe.

Shockingly, the circle within the candles morphs into an ether vortex that hovers above the stone floor. The vortex swirls shades of grey - the swirls whipping the ether in a hypnotic flow.

The figure lingers above the vortex and vanishes from the throne room though the portal. The swirls fade from light to dark greys, and the stone reappears.

Benjamin's mind travels to his encounters with Azor; the experience feels similar but in an eerie way. He recalls the height, the mystery, the majesty of a nephesh before putting the clues together.

Korah.

Benjamin delays another moment for one more scan, hoping to see Azor, when the shouts of frustration echo down the hallway. He recognizes the raspy voice of Rezon Scar calling for guards, so he flees the throne room.

Benjamin skirts around the kitchen area and moves down the hallway to the servants' quarters. He scans the doors looking for any hints of Ashira when he hears the faint sound of a woman singing. The melody sneaks out of the last door on the right; he puts his head to the door and listens to the voice, which he easily identifies as hers. He takes note of the lullaby and lets it soothe his anxiety.

Benjamin sneaks into the quaint chamber. Her small bed rests in the corner under a window, and a wooden chest fits snugly against the bed frame. The bathing area hides behind a white linen screen. A large candle atop a tiny table provides the room with a warm glow.

"Ashira?" calls Benjamin. His light voice fails to overpower her lullaby that lifts from behind the screen where she washes for bed.

He catches a glimpse of her bare back, and the image steals his breath. A rabble of butterflies blossom in his stomach like a bouquet of wild flowers; the foreign feeling reminds the awkward shepherd of the only time that romantic notions fluttered about his stomach.

Her name was Sarah Nun. He was sixteen; she was fourteen. It was her flawless skin that first demanded his attention as she emerged from the swimming hole. Next were her pearl teeth, then her pure eyes. Spying on Sarah and her sisters at the swimming hole made the summer of 3011 his favorite to date, but it took him the entire season to muster the courage to ask for a dance at the summer bazaar. He overcame a bad case of indigestion that skittered about his throat and stepped on beat, sparing Sarah's nostrils and her toes.

Benjamin only saw her once during the fall season when they bumped heads at a yarn stand. He wasn't so crossed by Judith's errand after the encounter.

He spent many frigid winter nights warming Sarah's lips behind the Nun Hovel, their passionate breath billowing into the frosty air like the smoke from the fire pit within. It didn't take her father long to figure out his daughter's newfound fondness for gathering fire wood. All it took was one conversation with Mr. Nun holding a hatchet to keep Benjamin away.

The restless shepherd eagerly waited to graze his flocks near the swimming hole the following summer, but Sarah and her sisters were nowhere to be found. The longing to set free the butterflies became far greater than his fear of a father's hatchet, so he sneaked over to the Nun Hovel in search of Sarah.

There he encountered Mr. Nun weeping atop a mound of dirt.

Benjamin never learned the name of the disease that claimed her life, only that she got sick in the spring and died suddenly while asleep.

Benjamin always wondered if Judith sanitized the sickness to lighten his remorse, but he accepted her version of the tragedy as truth.

The miserable memory prompts an oppressive revelation that settles the infatuation bubbling within. The ones he draws near, death draws near. Oren and Rachel Tav, Sarah Nun, Jael Tav… Ashira Keros? Maybe he was cursed, maybe he should've embraced his isolation and stayed in Hallowed Hills like his brother desired. He now threatens the security of Evan's bride to be, the woman he expects to birth his legacy.

Benjamin second-guesses his decision and regrets ever involving Ashira, but before he can retreat from the quarters, she emerges from behind the screen in a white nightgown- her wet, black hair dangling around her face.

Ashira clutches her heart at the unexpected sight of the voyeur, "I was unaware that someone was stalking me. You could've knocked, you're worse than the cooks… I figured you'd return, but not tonight."

Her allure enraptures his thoughts, and leaves him speechless.

"Come over here, sit down," orders Ashira, grabbing some jasmine perfume from the wooden chest. As she's about to uncork the bottle, she notices a tear forming in his eye. Ashira promptly returns the perfume bottle to the chest.

"Almost forgot."

"Thanks," says Benjamin, hoping that the dim light will hide his red cheeks.

"Are you blushing? You're so sweet."

"I've never been around a woman as beautiful as you. Well, there was this one girl, but she was fourteen."

The babbling shepherd draws an odd vibe from Ashira.

"What I'm trying to say… Evan's a lucky man."

"I'm in no mood to talk about your brother," warns the scorned fiancé.

His inner-voice curses his poor choice of words that kill the innocent moment.

"I came here to plan the rescue of your brother and the prophets. You know the palace so I figure you could help me out."

Ashira picks up a pair of cook's garments from the edge of her bed and tosses them on his lap. "The plan's already done. I take dinner to the prisoners on occasion. I'll be sure to take it tomorrow. You can pose as a new cook. We go into the prison, free my brother and the prophets."

"How will you get the key?"

Ashira dangles the key in front of him, "Never underestimate the love between a guard and a steak."

"How do we get out?"

"Have you seen my brother? He'll rip the head off any guard that gets in our way… You've been trained by Evan, I'm sure you got some fight in you."

Her words agitate him more than encourage.

Once the conversation dies down, Benjamin realizes his awkward predicament- spend the night in her quarters or sleep elsewhere.

"See you at dinner, then?"

Ashira's question assists him with his decision.

Ashira serves the handful of guards a plate of seasoned steaks smothered in onions with a side of steaming potatoes speckled with chives. They receive the steaks like begging pups. The distracted guards fail to interrogate Benjamin, abandoning their posts for a more comfortable location to enjoy their meal.

Benjamin and Ashira continue to the cells. They open Seth's chamber and exchange perplexed looks once they realize that he's no longer in the assigned block.

"According to the guard blotter, he's supposed to be here," says Ashira, fearful that her rescue attempt may unravel.

Benjamin and Ashira twist around to the sound of drawn swords. Zimri, Rezon, Zidon, and Aden's spy, Caleb, move to the front of the guards.

Zimri steps forward, "Melek delivers my enemy into my hands once again. Your plan to rescue the prophets has failed; now give me your sword."

Benjamin draws Kurion from behind his baggy chef's coat. Taking the ether sword from the sheath strapped to his back, he contemplates a bold move. Afraid of putting Ashira in harms way, he reluctantly hands Kurion to his nemesis.

Zimri admires the craftsmanship of the weapon before handing it over to Zidon. The magi's eyes widen as he receives the legendary sword.

"I will consecrate this instrument on the Altar of Melek," says Zidon, before exiting the prison.

Zimri puffs himself up to fill the empty space that Zidon leaves behind. "Foolish shepherd, how your soul must rage with hatred for me. I most enjoyed backstabbing your little sister; I'd give anything to hear that brat squeal again. Though I must confess that putting my blade into your father's back was much more gratifying."

Ashira grabs Benjamin's arm and pulls him to her side. The human touch of a friend redirects his absurd notion of assaulting Zimri. His desire to protect her erases the absurd notion to lash out.

Rezon rips a steak from the mouth of a guard and sinks his fangs into the meat.

"This steak tastes like trash!"

Before Benjamin can grab Ashira's arm and redirect her irrational thoughts, she forcefully wraps her hands around the captain's throat.

Zimri knocks her on the crown of her head with his clenched fist, and she falls out cold into Benjamin's arms. Zimri slams the cell door and locks it with the stolen key still in the lock. He removes the key and exits with Rezon, Caleb, and the guards following behind.

Benjamin sits on the cold hard floor and guides Ashira's head to his lap.

Slivers of moonlight slip through the barred windows of the prison holding room. Othniel, Ezekiel, and Seth sit on a bench covered head to toe in shackles and chains.

"Why do you think they moved us in here?" asks Seth.

The prophets remain silent.

Seth taps his feet against the stone floor. He rakes his fingers across his knees, rhythmically jingling his chains. The boredom of imprisonment stresses his muscles.

"Fine, don't answer me. You two are nothing but frauds. Why don't you use your magical powers to free us?"

The prophets maintain their silence.

"Weak… Why did I have to be so weak? I should've ignored Benjamin. I would have my freedom; instead I'm locked up with two fools."

"What did Benjamin say to you?" asks Ezekiel.

Seth hesitates to expose his weakness, but his boredom drives him to answer Ezekiel.

"My parents were members of the Merchants Guild and

part of a plot to remove Zimri. He found out about the plot and seized the Merchants Guild in Tizra. He demanded that my parents sell out everyone involved. When they refused, he burned down our pottery store with my father and mother inside."

Seth masks his misery from the prophets as he did with everyone. For pitfighters find no value in tears, no solace in sorrow.

"Zimri blamed the fire on my parents, said that they were trying to get back at him. Since he controlled the Merchants Guild in Tizra and owned the business, he handed me and Ashira a bill for the damages. When we couldn't pay, we were forced to become indentured servants; we would serve until the debt was paid. Ashira was sent to the kitchen, and I was sent to The Pit."

"I'm so sorry for your loss," says Ezekiel.

"What would you know about it?" asks Seth, unaware of the prophet's childhood tragedy.

"I know enough. I also believe that the Goddess feels your pain."

"You see, that's the kind of garbage I don't need. It's not helpful. Sayings like that are as false as your religion, and your so-called powers."

Seth senses that his words agitate Ezekiel, "Why don't you conjure up some vermin to retrieve the keys from the guards?"

Ezekiel loses his temper and whispers the mystical language.

"Please stop, you're getting angry like the brute wants," warns Othniel.

The defiant prophet increases the volume of his chant.

"Now you're embarrassing yourself."

Ezekiel's temper won't allow him to heed his master's advice to cease his chant, which boldly echoes off the stone walls. The resolute chant demands Seth's attention and peaks Othniel's interest in his disciple's command of the language.

A moment of tension fills the room before Ezekiel's sparrow returns. She pecks at the iron bars in the window, her tiny beak rapidly pinging the metal bars.

"That's the future of the Order," says Othniel with a smile.

Seth laughs, and the master prophet joins him while Ezekiel burns hot with impatience.

Their laughs quickly quell when Zimri, Rezon, and Zidon enter the room. Caleb blends in with the guards in the background.

"I bring good tidings. I captured your shepherd friend, and I'm pleased to announce that he's going to burn with the rest of you," boasts Zimri, walking over to Seth and ducking into his face. "Your sister was captured in the conspiracy as well; looks like conspiracies run in the family."

"What are you going to do with her?"

"I have plans to make her feel special," says Zimri while grinning at Rezon.

Seth rattles his shackles with such force that the room quakes.

"The line of Tav and the line of Keros, two thorns soon to be removed from my side."

The dank cell makes Benjamin long for the fresh night air of Hallowed Hills, as Ashira's head rests on a pillow of chef's clothes bunched in his lap. Her peaceful face keeps his mind off his predicament and offers him a sense of security that he's never felt before.

Ashira's face also makes him think of Evan and his prediction, *Tizra will swallow you whole.* The precise prediction taunts the little brother's pride as Ashira opens her eyes to see the shepherd watching over her, his busy fingers lost in her thick hair.

"Am I bothering you?" asks Benjamin.

"I think your conscience is the one being bothered."

Benjamin knows that caressing Ashira's hair would anger Evan so he stops. The uncomfortable moment forces her to sit up.

"This is my first time in a jail cell. Odd, but my life has the same feel."

"You could've left your life a long time ago; Evan's willing to pay your debt."

Ashira stands in protest.

"When are you gonna grow up and be your own person? Maybe you should stop relying on Evan, or maybe you're too weak to get out from under your brother's thumb."

Her accusation forces Benjamin to his feet, the very thought of being controlled by Evan inflames his ego.

"Me? You're the one who won't stand up to him."

"That's not true. I refuse his offer every time he throws it in my face."

"I'm not talking about money."

"Then what are you talking about?"

"Love."

A twitch in Ashira's face reveals the answer stings a nerve, "Love? What does love have to do with any of this?"

"Admit it, you don't love him. If you did, you'd marry him. Instead, you stay locked away in that kitchen because it's safe."

"That kitchen's no different than this prison cell."

"Do you love him?"

"I don't know. I don't know what to think or feel. Why do you care?"

As one accusation piles on top of the other, Benjamin and Ashira find themselves interfaced. Their breath wisps across each others lips and he feels compelled to kiss her. As his lips draw near to hers, a guard appears at the cell door.

"I'm Caleb Glade. I serve Prince Aden. He planted me in the palace guard as a spy."

"Release us," says Benjamin.

"I can't, I don't have a key. Zimri took all the dungeon keys."

"Why'd you come down here, then?" asks Ashira.

"To be the harbinger of bad news… Benjamin, Zimri plans to burn you alive with Seth and the prophets."

The omen crushes Ashira's spirit, and she retreats to the far corner of the cell.

"Will Ashira burn too?"

"No. Zimri has other plans for her. I assume whatever he does to her will be heinous, for he desires to trample Evan Tav's honor. The offense will provoke a war with Evan, with Tav, maybe with all of Hallowed Hills. When your brother gets word of Zimri's plans for her, I suspect that the shepherds will march on Tizra.

I'm leaving the palace to alert Prince Aden. A messenger informed me that he's among the ranks of The Southern Kingdom army encamped outside of Tamar. He avoided an assassination plot devised by his father and recently returned from a successful military campaign in Tekoa.

Aden went to his uncle to convince him to march his army north. If Lord Emmerick's troops and the shepherd army siege Tizra at the same time, there's a chance that we overthrow Zimri."

"Could you free us first?" asks Ashira, returning from her retreat.

"You know of Zimri's paranoid ways. I guarantee there's one key to your cell, which can only be found in his clenched fist. He has a nose for sniffing out conspiracies."

Caleb immediately regrets his poor choice of words, "Sorry… I must be on my way."

Ashira latches onto Benjamin's arm. His impending execution weighs on his soul, making his body numb to her embrace.

Chapter 17 | Mustering Two Fronts

The northern lights shine down upon the gathering of elder shepherds in Tav's town square, the ranks of their brethren swelling to three thousand. Murmurs puff out of the shepherds like the smoke from the hundreds of campfires scattered about the outskirts of Tav. Some question Evan's age and leadership while others don't find merit in going to battle over a woman.

Evan pretends to ignore the criticism about his age and his honor. The shepherds from Tsadi and Resh wait for Zimri's decree to be read before they either join Evan's cause or return home.

Judith and Daniel stand side by side listening to the hum of the crowd. She leaves his side and pulls Evan to a quiet corner. He nervously taps Zimri's unsealed scroll across his thigh with a fury festering in his eyes.

"I can't pretend to know what you must be feeling. You're the only one to have read that scroll. Only you know what terror Zimri has planned for Ashira, but I can assure you that these shepherds won't go to battle for the sake of honor. The only way these shepherds stay is for you to convince them to fight for freedom. Invoke the names of the shepherds of old who followed Josiah into battle, invoke the name of our father."

Evan invests in Judith's advice and stops tapping the scroll against his thigh. She takes a moment to read the rage that smolders in his eyes. His reaction to her encouragement disheartens her. She firmly grasps both of his hands, her desperate eyes connecting with his fiery eyes. She speaks no more words, yet Evan perceives exactly what Judith wants him to proclaim to his kinsmen.

Evan releases Judith's hands and returns to the herdsmen; the indifferent shepherds cease their grumbling to hear what the guild master has to share.

"Zimri has charged my betrothed, Ashira Keros, with conspiring against the crown. She'll be publically branded with runes before she's sacrificed on an altar of Melek."

Judith exhales her disappointment and lowers her head. Daniel wraps his arms around his wife with remorseful thoughts concerning Ashira's fate.

"My honor has been wronged. Follow me to Tizra, help me avenge my honor," pleads Evan.

The indifferent shepherds mutter words of dissension. Within a few moments of bickering, a mass of noncommittal shepherds return to their homes, leaving the insulted fiancé with a thousand countrymen ready to take up his cause.

Judith hides her face in the palm of her hands to catch her tears and runs up the stairs of the guild hall. Daniel readies his feet to follow his wife, but his duty to his guild master keeps him at Evan's side.

"Daniel, look after my hall."

"But I can fight for you, Evan."

"No. You're the only one I trust with my hall. You must stay."

Daniel nods in agreement. He returns to his wife and gently wipes her cheeks. Smoke brushes his bushy fur against Judith's ankles, she cradles Jael's cat in the crook of her arm and holds Daniel's hand.

They watch Evan and the shepherd army march under a black and yellow banner adorned with an embroidered ram. The men are struck with a jolt of patriotism as they march down Josiah's path toward Tizra, recalling the heroic feats of the shepherds of old.

Prince Aden walks among the ranks of The Southern Kingdom army camped about a lengths travel from the city of Tamar. The soldiers laud his Tekeo heroics as he passes by, and he humbly nods in gratitude.

He never cared much for being the center of attention, but the only prince in Issur understands full well what it means to be in the public eye for he could never escape it.

Aden finds seclusion in a supply tent and scans the space for a crate of swords. He sits on the crate where he feels an unexpected longing for the palace and his mother.

A clanging noise interrupts his longing, and out stumbles Lord Emmerick with a beige stuffed rock badger wearing a mean face. The stiff creature in Emmerick's arms baffles the prince.

"Oh… Hello, Aden. Seems I've misplaced my badger. Allow me to introduce you to Rodger, Rodger the Badger."

Emmerick sits down on an adjacent crate and places Rodger on his lap. Producing a pipe, he strikes a match across the badger's nose to light the dry tobacco leaves. He calmly puffs rings in a rhythmic pattern.

"I can see you're in a bit of a tiff."

"I hoped to confront Ishem about his betrayal, and I would've liked to try him in court. He has innocent blood on his hands."

"It's my fault that he escaped. I should've searched him better. Ishem had another vial of poison hidden on him some way. How he got the guard to ingest it is a mystery."

"Still, I would've liked to see him face justice."

"Ishem will have to give an account to Zimri. There will be no mercy for him."

"Did he ever reveal his motive?"

"Sorry, Nephew," offers Emmerick, mouthing another smoke ring. He lets out a chuckle, "Navigating the swamps with rafts, brilliant."

The uncle puffs a halo above his nephew's head.

"Not sure how I missed the invasion, though." Emmerick jogs his memory to figure out how he missed the invasion, but all he can recall from Tekoa Bottom are reptiles and amphibians.

"I don't want to diminish what our troops accomplished, but the enemy looked a lot more like refugees than raiders."

"And this troubles you?"

"You mentioned that the King of Calcedon is your friend."

"That's my understanding. We've been at peace with one another for sixteen years ever since King Lars and I reinstated the Calcedon Accord of 555."

"Why would your ally attack Issur? It doesn't make sense, and those refugees fought for food not for gold."

"My father once told me that bees tend to stay in their hive until they get dislodged by a honey bear." Aden livens up to receive the wisdom of his iconic grandfather. "A honey bear dislodged those raiders from Calcedon. I'm worried about my old friend Lars."

Emmerick disconnects his sheathed sword from his belt. "Speaking of your grandfather, I've been meaning to give you this. 'Deerstalker' called the blade, Royal-Blue."

He hands the ancestral broadsword to Aden, who receives it with honor like the treasured family heirloom he remembers it to be.

"Are you sure you want me to wield this?" asks Aden, looking over the steel blade with a blue tint and a steel hilt adorned with a large rounded sapphire - signature markings of the smiths who worked Founders Forge in the town of Sapphire.

"Your grandfather would want you to."

A man entirely devoted to libraries and laboratories, he never took the time to settle down with a wife and raise children. Emmerick always took pleasure in making Aden happy because he realized that his nephew was the closest that he would ever come to having a son.

"Thank you, Uncle," offers Aden, reminiscent of his childhood birthdays where he'd unwrap unique gifts that only Uncle Emmerick could give.

Tobi Tamar interrupts the Tizra family moment when he lunges his shiny bald head into the tent, "Aden, Caleb Glade has arrived in the camp."

"Send him in at once."

Caleb enters the supply tent, and Aden offers him an empty crate. Emmerick sticks out his nose to try to get a whiff of the ranger.

"Don't worry, he's on our side," says Aden.

Once Emmerick feels secure, he returns to puffing his pipe. Tobi stands guard inside the tent's entrance keeping a watchful eye on the visitor.

"What's happened in Tizra that you would break your cover?" asks Aden behind fearful eyes.

"Zimri provoked a war with Evan Tav, son of legendary

guild master Oren Tav, by using his betrothed as bait. I suspect that he's marching a shepherd army on Tizra as we speak. Zimri's also captured Othniel 'Wayfarer,' his understudy, Evan's brother, and the famous pitfighter Seth Keros. He's going to burn them alive at the next moon festival."

Caleb's countenance dampens quickly, realizing that he glossed over the tragedy of Aden's mother. He ceases his report, unable to verbalize the awful news.

Aden reads the anguish on his best friend's face, "What else?"

Aden's intuition prepares his heart to receive the devastating news about his mother. The ranger stammers, and the prince grows impatient, "Caleb Glade!"

"Your mother… She's no longer with us."

Aden's coutenence dims. Rizpah's only child hangs his head, and tears streak down his face to wet the ground. Emmerick extinguishes his pipe and extends his hand to grip his nephew's shoulder.

"How did she die?"

"She drowned. A hunter found her and her dog floating among some mallards near a water tunnel flowing from under Tizra. I had him bury her on the riverbank, had him plant opal orchids on her grave. Zimri and Zidon know nothing of the burial."

The remorseful moment is short lived as Aden's rancor scorches away his pain, "That monster drowned my mother! We must march the southern army on Tizra!"

"Revenge is not a reason to go to war," says Emmerick.

"It's not about revenge, it's about justice. We must overthrow that tyrant."

"That tyrant is my brother, and your father."

"You don't think it pains me that his blood flows through my veins? How many innocents have to suffer?"

"There's no guarantee that we'll win," cautions Emmerick.

"This could end in defeat, but at least we show courage. We are the only hope for this nation; we must stand up to Zimri."

The sage twists his handlebar mustache and reignites his tobacco. He ventures so deep into his thoughts that the ashes overflow his pipe and float down to his lap.

Emmerick makes his decision while looking at Tobi, "We'll take our declaration of war to the city council of Tamar, and seek their approval."

"Oh Goddess, help us," sighs Tobi Tamar, throwing his arms up.

"We don't have time, Uncle. You're the lord of this land, your word is final."

"I'm an academic, not a monarch, and I refuse to operate as such. We'll consult the council."

"Can't be but so bad," says Caleb.

"It can, trust me," says Tobi.

"That's why you'll plead our case, Captain Tamar. You're their hero and besides, the council's not too fond of me after my resolution presented at the last meeting."

"What happened?" asks Aden.

"No worries, Nephew.

Tobi, why don't you take this horse faced fellow with you? Aden and I have some unfinished work to attend too."

Caleb feels his face as to question Emmerick's description. Tobi nods in acceptance of the mission with dejection weighing on his shoulders.

"You made it to the scarecrow, so what went wrong?" asks the raspy voice of Rezon Scar.

Ishem trembles while a constant stream of sweat flows

from his dark-haired scalp. The captain hands the traitor a goblet of white, and he drains it without coming up for air. The libation calms his tongue and enables him to form words, "Aden would've walked into the trap, but he had to play the hero for some damsel. We ran to her rescue, executed her attacker."

"So that's why my men were out of position?"

"Yes. Still, they gave me enough time to get a couple shots off. My first arrow missed Aden, but I killed one of his rangers. Aden dodged the second shot and it hit one of your men instead."

"Who killed the wounded one?"

"I did," admits Ishem.

Rezon's mangled jaw gapes at his soldier's slayer.

"He had to, couldn't blow his cover," says Zimri, entering Ishem's chamber and taking a seat at the round table. He guzzles the chardonnay straight from the bottle.

"Why so surprised, Rezon? Let's face it. When it comes to assassination plots, you're the worst."

Rezon attempts to read Zimri's gambler-face when the king erupts with laughter. His loyal bodyguard finds humor in the insult, "Guess who trained this twit!"

Rezon's retort causes Zimri to spit a swig of wine across the room. The merriment from the king and captain puts Ishem at ease allowing him to make eye contact with Zimri.

"What went wrong with the poisoning?" questions Zimri.

"I handed the first glass to Aden, but he passed it to his ranger. Aden was about to drink the second glass when Emmerick smelled the poison."

Zimri squeezes his brow with his thumb and index finger when he realizes how close he came to ending his son's life.

"While the separatists liberated Tekoa, I poisoned the night watchman's food and escaped."

"Does Aden still think he can convince my brother to lead The Southern Kingdom into war with me?"

"Yes, Sire."

"It'll never happen. Emmerick is weak. He's afraid of me just like the masses in Issur."

Ishem rings his hands as he musters a suggestion, "They could come against you if they get wind of another shepherds revolt. Maybe you should prepare your army."

"You speak to me as if you are my sentinel," mocks Zimri.

"I thought this was Melek's will for my life. If I betrayed Aden, you promised to train me as your sentinel."

The king stares through the empty wine bottle, "You have more?"

"Yes, Sire," says Ishem, walking to the cupboard to retrieve more chardonnay.

Zimri and Rezon rise together. The king motions his captain to take care of the wine service. Zimri puts his arm around Ishem's shoulders and guides him to a window overlooking Tizra.

"I've always liked you, liked your family. In fact, your father was one of my first converts to Melek. Trickery runs in your bloodline. I've always admired that about you ever since you and Aden were little boys. I can think of no one better to be my sentinel."

Rezon serves the two goblets. Zimri lifts his high, "A toast! To Ishem, whom I love as my own son!"

The flattering words enter the sentinel's soul as smoothly as the wine that enters his stomach.

Zimri's gambler-face forces Ishem to reinterpret the toast.

The blessing becomes a curse when his face greys. Ishem clutches his throat and thrashes about his chamber before falling headlong across his bed.

Zimri offers a eulogy while Ishem gasps his dying breaths, "Citrullus Colocynthis, a poison found in rare fruits, blends perfectly with wine… Ishem, your lack of faith in Melek makes you mortal."

"Pisser! Bit my hand, bit it good," announces Aden.

"Yes. Yes, indeed. Look at those marvelous puncture wounds," analyzes Emmerick in the torchlight.

"Why are we doing this? It's a complete waste of time."

"I told you; we wait on word from Tobi... Now, you'll have to go deeper into the rock face to get him."

"Why me?"

"I can't fit through that crack." Emmerick takes Aden's torch and tosses it into the cavern. "That'll give you enough light."

Aden slips through the opening, cobwebs netting his face as his stomach scrapes the stone.

"Can you hear them?"

"Yes, Uncle. It's like they're talkin' to one another about me."

Aden lifts his torch to expose the colony of about fifty rock badgers lined up like a choir. They warble at the intrusion of Aden. The naïve prince becomes immersed in his serenade.

"The friend of my mate is my mate," says Emmerick.

"That's the name of this song?"

"No, you fool. It's a warning."

Suddenly, the dominant male leaps onto Aden's head and gnaws at his scalp. He gets a firm grip of the badger's pelt and rips it from his hair. The frazzled prince tosses it into a sack. The badger boxes the sack with a combo of jabs.

"Got him, Uncle!"

"Just wait."

The melody of the badgers dies down, and soon the entire colony swarms the intruder. Emmerick hears the rush of critters and the angst in Aden's call for help. "Uncle?"

"Throw their man back!"

Aden frees their leader, and the entire family funnels deeper into the rocky crag.

"We're done here. Meet me outside."

Aden crawls out of the rock face with heavy breath, shedding beads of sweat, "I thought our goal was to get the leader."

"And we did."

"You weren't planning to dissect him or something of the sort."

"No, don't be silly. Such a foolish notion, dissecting an alpha badger. I simply wanted to hear their song. Beautiful, was it not?"

"What did you say to me in the cave about mates?"

"The friend of my mate is my mate. The lesson is not lost on you is it, Nephew?"

"No, Uncle."

"Nature is our classroom. Besides, you needed to calm your blood. If we go to war, we must go with our wits unfettered from passion, and we must go as mates. I've never been in a battle, but I bet it's similar to what you saw in that cave."

As Emmerick finishes his lesson, Tobi and Caleb arrive with a sense of accomplishment.

"They gave their consent, the army musters for war," boasts Tobi with the pride of his Tamar bloodline. "They remembered the compassion of Queen Rizpah; many poor children in Tamar were fed by her hand. The news of her death aggravated the council."

"The tower proposal worked, I presume?"

"Finished," says Tobi.

"You should see it. A heap of brush built next to a smaller heap of brush. And talk about a gaggle of imbeciles honking over rules and orders. How anything gets done is beyond comprehension," adds Caleb.

"You prefer to be dictated to?" asks Emmerick, insulted

by Caleb's assessment of a free-thinking council.

"No time for debates, Uncle. Just give the marching orders."

"Fine. Captain Tamar, order more rafts be built, ready the catapults and send them to the front lines. Aden and I will break the camp and march the army north. Ranger, hurry by horse. Find this shepherd army, and let them know we make our stand with them."

The Moon Festival

A tight black leather outfit etched with Melek runes encases Ashira's body, her hands bound behind her back. Zimri smiles perversely running his hands down Ashira's slender frame. Rezon rubs her shoulders and presses his mutilated face against her cheek. Quivers ripple down her legs to her heels.

"I'm getting the brands nice and hot, my lady," says Rezon as Zimri turns his attention to The Pit arena.

Benjamin, Othniel, Ezekiel, and Seth hang from posts with logs drenched in oil underneath their feet. Four executioners stand poised with long poles topped with jagged axe heads, torches occupying their other hand. Their merciless eyes brood beneath their purple hooded-robes as they await their command.

"Glory be to Melek, god of the dark, god of the moon!" roars Zimri.

Stirring with a serpentine energy, the crowd raves at

Zimri's proclamation of faith. The king breathes in the glory of the moment.

Korah and Zidon secretively enter the box seat and lurk behind Zimri. Their stealthy entrance goes unnoticed by the crowd. Ashira senses Korah's dreadful presence and slowly turns to see the ominous being, but Zimri grabs her head and forcefully twists it back to the arena. "I want you to see this."

The tyrant puffs himself up and announces the execution, "Burn them!"

The full moon glows brightly above the arena and casts dark shadows over the executioners. Their gigantic shadows march lockstep in a ritualistic rhythm while devotees in the crowd thunder their palms across bongo drums.

Benjamin reflects on his life as the executioners approach. He recalls the stars above Tav on the last night with his father, and the warmth of his mother's final embrace. Thoughts of chasing Jael as a child race through his mind, her lively ponytail bouncing on the breeze. The elegance of Judith's soul and the taste her cornbread warm his thoughts. He recalls sparing with Evan and feels the sting in his hand from the vibrations of his sword; even though death is near, disappointing Evan is nearer still in his heart. His thoughts pause on Ashira. He recalls her dark brown eyes and mischievous smile, left to wonder what might have been.

In the midst of his final reflections, a soothing peace floats on the night breeze and flutters down upon him - a peace that he hasn't felt since the night he fell asleep on his father's lap. In the serenity of the moment, he whispers his common prayer, "Neshama. Are you there? Are you listening?"

Othniel's eyes grow wide. His fingertips come to life, and he stretches them as far as his shackled wrists will allow. The master prophet senses a presence of ether coming from the box seat. He opens his hands as wide as possible and begins to channel Korah's ether; the substance gradually morphs from black to grey to white the closer it gets to his fingertips.

The channeling is subtle at first, but the more Othniel draws the thicker the ether gets. Zimri looks down at the bottom of Korah's robe to see ether flowing out from beneath, "What's happening to you?"

Zimri watches in disbelief as Othniel threads the ether through the shackles of all the prisoners. The ether unlocks the shackles and the prisoners drop to the ground.

The phenomenon subdues the savage crowd.

Zimri, Rezon, and Ashira watch the ether magic with amazement, but Zidon stirs with purpose. "Korah, let's put an end to this right now. Sacrifice your ether and let me finish them."

Korah rebukes the demeaning request by leaving the scene, the swift nephesh promptly removing his ether as a potential source for Othniel or Zidon.

The dejected magi drags his feet from the box seat and follows Korah, hoping for another shot to end Othniel.

The executioners drop their torches, break lockstep, and charge with their jagged axes.

As the axe heads fall, Othniel manipulates the ether to form a protective ether wall around himself, Benjamin, Ezekiel, and Seth.

The protective wall wards off the deathblows. The axes recoil as the ether dissipates into thin air.

Seth throws a punch with such force that it caves in an executioner's face. He picks up the axe and tosses it to Benjamin.

He blocks his killer's second blow with the axe handle; the wooden shaft splinters in two, but he's able to keep his grip on the handle. Benjamin evades another strike and plants his axe into the executioner's foot, pinning him to the ground.

The two remaining executioners bear down on the prophets. Othniel thrusts out his arms as if he were reaching for something deep within the killers. He leeches onto their corrupted souls and bellows his mystical chant, commanding their dark souls to come out of their bodies.

The master prophet banishes their black souls.

The souls howl ghastly noises as they disappear into the night sky, leaving the fallen executioners dead on the arena floor.

Upon seeing the banished souls vanish into the darkness, the crowd frantically scatters in all directions, trampling one another to escape The Pit.

Zimri contemplates taking Ashira with him, but his innate desire for self-preservation decides against it. He flees, leaving her alone with his sinister captain.

Rezon removes one of the white-hot brands from the fire pit underneath the box. Holding the brand like a spear, he marches toward Ashira. He lines up his lunge so that the full-moon rune will sear into her cheek.

Ashira ducks the poke and rolls into Rezon's knees. His knees buckle and he falls on the brand. The rune melts into the flesh of his forehead.

In a fit of rage, Rezon hurls Ashira into the frenzied mob and departs the panicked scene.

Ashira struggles to stay upright in the mayhem.

Benjamin and Seth rush to her aid. The shepherd scales the arena wall and dives into the crowd. He wades through the mob, knocking aside any roadblocks. Benjamin wraps his arms around Ashira, leads her to the edge of the wall, and tosses her down to Seth. He catches her, and then breaks her bindings.

The heroes congregate in the center of the arena.

"How do we get out of here?" asks Othniel.

"Through the training room, follow me," orders Seth.

Seth dashes into the training room and quickly equips his armor. Pit Boss Og returns Peacemaker, the weapon pumps Seth's adrenaline.

Benjamin and Ashira ransack the weapons rack in search of quality blades. The prophets scan the room for Othniel's staff and book; they locate the sacred items locked in a stone-column cabinet with engraved Melek runes.

"Sir, do you have a key?" questions Ezekiel of Og.

"Nope. The magi from the temple locked that chest."

"We'll never get them now," complains Ezekiel.

Seth approaches with Peacemaker and explodes the stone cabinet.

"Let's move," orders the warrior waving them out of the training room. Othniel gathers his belongings, yanks Ezekiel from his shock, and exits behind the group.

Seth plows through the frantic mob to create a pathway for his followers. The guards struggle to restore order in the north plaza as The Pit crowd stampedes across the cobblestone.

A harem of prostitutes, dressed in the same black leather outfit as Ashira, pour out of the Temple of Melek. The Queen Mother emerges on the pinnacle of the temple steps.

An alluring woman with dark features and flowing black hair, her beauty is unrivaled in Issur. Terror ices Othniel's soul, and the prophet freezes - his mind tormented by a tragedy from the past.

Isavel was a terror to prophets and precepts, and the scribes dreadfully called her 'The Whore of Issur.'

Only a handful of scribes remained, hidden in the sewers under Tizra. According to their works that survived, it was Isavel not Zimri that lusted for their blood - that craved the destruction of the Hall of Knowledge.

Queen Rizpah despised Isavel. Though no confession was ever offered by her husband, Rizpah's intuition warned of a hidden evil concealed within Zimri's affair with Isavel.

Othniel knew their dark secret. It was birthed in an act he failed to prevent - the night Isavel sacrificed her infant daughter on the Altar of Melek. Othniel tried to rescue the child in the midst of the violent storm, but the winds were too harsh, the harem too many, and the altar too distant.

The daughter's sin was not being born a son. Isavel wanted to raise Zimri's prince, a Melek devotee who would take Aden Tizra's place at the table.

The unshakable image could not be remedied by prayer, though Othniel tried. Instead, he turned to his vice, a toxic way to forget. It may have been the secret that Zimri hunted more than the prophet, but Isavel refused to birth his heir until Othniel was dead.

Othniel's eyes shed tears for the innocent infant-girl.

Isavel glares at the prophet with a hunger to devour the secret, "Rip out that troubler's heart! Claim Melek's sacrifice!"

The harem of a hundred prostitutes swarms the group and rips at their clothes, trying to penetrate flesh with their razor-sharp fingernails. The heroes cover their faces while fending off the attack of the prostitutes.

Seth hesitates, reluctant to harm the unarmed women. A vicious swipe across his chest changes his mind. He winds back his warhammer and swings with such might that he catapults a tramp into the harem with such force that she topples twenty witches.

Othniel keeps Ezekiel close to his side while repelling the harlots with his staff.

Restrained by the multitude of hands, Benjamin and Ashira are unable to free their swords from their sheaths. Benjamin notices that the harem is more interested in Ashira's capture than they are in fighting him.

They tug and pull on his clothes. Grip by grip, they separate him from Ashira. Isavel strokes her headdress of twisted antlers and smirks with approval as her harem surfs Ashira to the temple steps.

Within moments, Benjamin finds himself swamped under a pile of prostitutes. They tear at his clothes and the fumes of their fragrance sting his eyes.

One swift swing of Peacemaker clears the pile.

"They want Ashira!" warns Benjamin. Seth sweeps the scene for his sister but can't locate her because her black outfit blends in with the sea of prostitutes.

"Othniel, help!" implores Benjamin, watching Ashira arrive onto the steps of Melek's temple.

The prophet hears Benjamin's prompt and turns to face the temple. The Queen Mother produces a silver dagger while four attendants grab Ashira's arms and legs to pin her to the altar. The hag kneels over Ashira and seductively scratches her nails across her prey's stomach. Isavel puts both hands on the dagger and raises it high above her head.

"Melek, receive now your daughter, your festal sacrifice. For the honor of Zimri, your chosen!" proclaims Isavel, her dagger glistening in the moonlight.

Othniel hands Ezekiel his staff before stretching out his arms. His apprentice pushes away some witches, but more flock to the prophets. They latch onto Othniel's arms and weigh them down.

Benjamin and Seth rush to the prophets and clear a perimeter for Othniel to begin his banishment. As the dagger falls, 'Wayfarer' connects with Isavel's corrupted ether and attempts to pull her soul from her body.

The force of the mystical energy parts the sea of prostitutes, including the attendants pinning Ashira. She jumps to her feet and dashes for Benjamin.

Othniel latches onto Isavel's soul and rips it cleanly from her frame. Her youthful appearance withers as her corpse bounces down the temple steps.

Othniel violently whips the wailing soul through the harem, scattering the temple prostitutes into the crowd. The frantic citizens rage in the mayhem as he releases Isavel's corrupt soul into the black of night.

"Kurion is in the temple!" shouts Benjamin.

"We can't risk it! I'll reclaim Kurion when the time is right. I promise," assures Othniel.

The hesitant shepherd joins his friends and escapes out the north gate.

Chapter 19

The Ashes of Pella

The morning mist lifts off the unkempt crops in the fields spread about The Heartland. The charred town of Pella distracts from an otherwise charming Issurian sunrise. As Benjamin nears the crumbled walls, the rows of skeletons nailed to posts warn him not to enter.

"Are you sure we should go in there?" asks Benjamin of Othniel.

"We must find Nebo Korse 'The Pig,' master of the Farmers Guild. We need him to have any chance of recruiting farmers to our cause," says Othniel, pressing onward with Ezekiel at his side.

Ashira agrees with her feet and keeps pace. Seth grinds to a halt. "Wait. You want to form an alliance with a guy named 'The Pig.' Are you crazy, old man?"

"Yes, I'm crazy, most prophets are. And yes, we must search for him. We must rally as many men to our cause as possible. Who knows, maybe the miners, foresters, and farmers will join the shepherds. Maybe the guilds will unite to confront Zimri."

"I stand corrected. You're beyond crazy, old man."

"Seth, we're tired and hungry. We're going into the city to find food. A man with the surname of 'Pig' must have some food to spare," says Benjamin, pushing his way to the front of the pack and marching toward the city.

Ashira follows. Her boldness shames her brother, and he falls in line as the group enters Pella.

Benjamin scans the city for survivors when a boy approaches the visitors. He's sooty and malnourished, but his eyes light up at the site of Othniel. "Welcome back to Pella, Prophet. Follow me to Lord Nebo's manor, your companions too."

"How do you know we seek Nebo?" asks Benjamin.

"Lord Nebo and my father are the only ones left. Our master has given no instructions on moving the guild north to Abilla, so we stay."

"Sounds like a swell plan," says Benjamin, following the filthy child through the burnt streets.

Any possession of value has been either burned or looted from the city; the dreadful scenery forces Benjamin's head to the ground.

"Keep your head up. Take a look at the ruination of this once proud town. This is what Issur will look like if Zimri stays in power, if Melek worship continues," says Othniel.

The group comes upon the only secure structure fortunate enough to survive the burring of Pella - a manor house formed mostly of stone. Not entirely unscathed, the fire took a full bite out of the roof and second floor of the house.

"Father!" shouts the little boy and within seconds, the Steward of the House of Korse appears in the front entrance.

"You seek council with my lord?" asks Steward Bradstock, wearing a velvety green jacket with large silver buttons and velvety green pants to match.

"And his table, if your lord would be so generous," requests Othniel.

The moppy-haired steward squints his bushy eyebrows at the suspicious outsiders. "The prophet returns. I recall how Lord Nebo 'The Bovine,' Goddess guide his soul, used to speak of your legend and of your unyielding tolerance."

"Such flattering words, Master," says Ezekiel.

"Tolerance for alcohol," informs Steward Bradstock, reminding Ezekiel of his teacher's vice. "Lord Nebo may approve of you, but I'm not sure he'd approve of your friends."

"I promise no harm will come to your lord. My companions are sustained by the same zeal as 'Bovine' was in wanting to dethrone Zimri."

"Lord Nebo still sleeps, but he's generous with his food if you have the stomach for it."

Bradstock motions them into the large dining room and seats them at a long table already set for breakfast. "Come to me, Buz. Help me serve our guests."

His son runs into the kitchen and returns with a pot of goulash. He jumps onto the table and slings the goulash into the wooden bowls. The smell of the ingredients forces everyone back in their chairs.

"That's a most interesting aroma. What are the ingredients?" inquires Ashira.

"Some seed-corn, scraps of cabbage, onion skins, and some other blends of farm foods. Goulash stuff, the way Lord Nebo likes it," says Bradstock.

"I'm really more thirsty than hungry," says Othniel, tingling for a drop of alcohol.

"Here, try this," offers Bradstock, handing Othniel a dirty jar filled with grain alcohol.

"Master, no. Show some self-control," cautions Ezekiel.

Othniel sips the bitter drink and turns a deep shade of purple. "I warned you." His grey head shakes out his bulging eyes before he takes another sip and returns the jar back to Bradstock.

"That'll do… That'll do."

The guests take a few bites of the goulash, enough to quiet their stomachs. Seth shows no remorse by eating his entire bowl.

"Have you no shame?" asks Ezekiel.

The behemoth ignores the insult and licks out the bottom of the bowl. "You gonna eat that?" asks Seth of Ezekiel's half-eaten bowl. The prophet gives him a look of disapproval, hesitantly sliding his bowl. "What? I'm hungry."

The clanging of a large metal spoon against the goulash pot gets everyone's attention. "All stand, Lord Nebo Korse the Second awakens," announces Bradstock. The group stands as Buz brings out a trough and places it at the head of the table. He dumps the remaining goulash in the trough, and the pungent fumes from the slop make the breakfast guests nauseous. Out of respect, they don't verbalize their disgust, but all collectively question, *"How can any man eat that much slop?"*

Bradstock pulls back the curtain to the living quarters to reveal Lord Nebo Korse 'The Pig.' The steward picks up Nebo, a chubby, adorable, pink pig donning a fashionable velvety green vest. Bradstock straps a felt green bycoket on Nebo's head.

The stunned guests watch Bradstock place Nebo on the table in front of his trough. The pig lunges his snout into the slop and chows down.

"That's the guild master? He's a pig… Literally," says Benjamin.

"His surname is 'The Pig,' so I fail to understand your surprise…

Nebo Korse 'The Bovine' was mortally wounded in the Farmers Revolt. As he perished in the blood-soaked soil, his final request was to appoint his best friend as the new guild master. He had no human heir, just his pig that he treated like a son. Nebo gave me his final decree before he died, and I gave my word," says Bradstock with a tear in his eye.

Othniel rolls his eyes at the historic recreation, "Farmers Guild."

"That slop wasn't nearly enough to fill me up. Ashira makes some tasty bacon. Let's fry that pig," suggests Seth.

BAM! Bradstock slams his fist on the table in protest. "You will not eat my lord!"

Benjamin raises his hand and waves it to protest the request, "We will do no such thing. All we want is for the farmers to commit what men they can to fight."

"The only farmers who might join you live in Abilla. But Nebo refuses to go north, south. He only travels east, west. Maybe you should head north to Abilla to recruit farmers."

Benjamin recalls the unfortunate incident with the pig farmer. Moreover, the suggestion brings to mind his most horrifying memory from when he, Jael, Othniel, and Ezekiel were driven out of the Inn of Encouragement near Abilla's Orchard.

"What would it take for Nebo to travel to Abilla?" asks Othniel, clearly sharing the same disastrous memory.

"A miracle. I already told you, Lord Nebo doesn't travel north, south."

"I happen to believe in miracles," says the prophet before lowering his tone to a light chant under his breath. He connects with Nebo's ether and commands the pig to go north.

Nebo's little legs carry him off the table, and he scurries onto the city street outside the manor. Within moments, Nebo heads north with Steward Bradstock and Buz running after their lord.

The following day, Evan marches his army of a thousand shepherds into Pella under the midday heat. The charred remains of the city and rows of skeletons serve as a harsh reminder to the shepherds of Zimri's resolve against those who oppose his kingship.

The thunder of footsteps draws Benjamin out from the Korse Manor. A mix of emotions turns in Benjamin's gut when he sees Evan in the front rank. His accomplishment may appear daring to Evan, and may even draw praise. However, his accomplishment is grounded in a cause that Evan deems unworthy, and may drawn scorn.

Benjamin approaches his brother, hoping for the best.

Before Evan and Benjamin have time to greet one another, Ashira runs out of the house and clings to Evan. She embraces him so hard that her fingernails sink into his shoulders.

The affectionate greeting dampens Benjamin's feelings for her. Ashira's short memory bothers him, for she appears to have forgotten her disappointment in how Evan dealt cruelly with the prophets.

Evan's jaw cringes awkwardly when he notices her obscene leather outfit.

"I'm not going to explain this," warns Ashira.

Benjamin approaches his brother and extends his hand. Evan ignores it; instead, he offers a suspect look for being the only one to appear with Ashira.

"What are you doing in this trash heap with Ashira?" Benjamin attempts an explanation, but Evan fires off another question, "How'd you free her?"

"Angry that I stole your glory," says Benjamin while Ashira positions herself between the brothers.

"Come on, boys." She tames the two brothers and moves on to more pressing matters. "We need to know, on your way south did you see a pig, a man, and a boy?"

"Some fool in a green jacket and a boy were chasing a pig, heading north. We let 'em by, made for a good laugh. Why?"

"They're with the Farmers Guild on their way to Abilla, hopefully for reinforcements," says Benjamin.

"We don't need that farmer scum. Where's your shepherd's pride?"

Seth and Ezekiel exit the manor house to welcome Evan and the shepherds. Ezekiel hides behind Seth, distrustful of Evan's intentions.

Othniel makes his way to Benjamin's side. The sight of the shepherd army invigorates his faith and his grace overrides the resentment of Evan's betrayal at Ephah's Field.

"Thank you for marching this army to Tizra. I must admit that I had some bitter thoughts about you while shackled in Zimri's dungeon, but I held my tongue and never cursed your name, Evan Tav.

Let's put the past behind us. Let's allow grace to prevail in this circumstance for the hands of the Goddess are at work shaping the Remnant. Neshama will reward your faithfulness to the Covenant, for you come to us ahead of the changing of the tide."

"Get away from me, you fanatic. This is all your fault. You deceived my brother, you got my sister killed. Now you've entangled Ashira in your underhanded ways."

The insult summons Benjamin to defend his mentor, "Othniel's an honorable man. He stands in the open when everyone else hides. Besides, he's the one responsible for saving Ashira; you owe him your gratitude."

"I owe no man… You got what you wanted. The old fool is free; isn't that why you're down here? Stop pretending to be a hero. You're not. You're a shepherd. Now stop embarrassing our family name and come home."

"Benjamin's only doing what he feels is right," interrupts Ashira.

"I'm tired of your indecision, it's time that you swallow your pride and marry me. You're coming to Tav."

"That's not possible. Zimri will never allow us to live in peace, not after what just happened in Tizra."

Evan's curiosity to know what happened gets purged by searing anger at her defiance. "I don't want to hear about it. Come! Now!"

Caleb Glade rides in on a horse and interrupts Evan's doglike commands to Ashira. His mount lifts to a stop, sniffing out the tension. Caleb looks over the ranks of the shepherds shielding his disappointment at the low turnout.

Benjamin approaches Caleb, eager to hear the news that will seal either his or Zimri's fate.

"Lord Emmerick's army is but a few lengths away making siege preparations on the other side of the river. He wants to know if he can count on the shepherds to stand with him."

"Yes," says Benjamin. Before the affirmation exits his tongue, Evan interjects, "No! No way that happens. These men are going back to Hallowed Hills."

"This is our best chance to defeat Zimri," says Benjamin.

"It's just that, a chance. If you go to war with Zimri, you'll end up like our parents, like our sister. Dead."

"No matter what happens, my end will be the same as our parents, as our sister. Free."

"What good is freedom to the dead?"

Benjamin's face warms hotter than the summer sun above. A boldness swelters within his soul, and an unfamiliar confidence rushes through him as if Neshama herself prods him to speak.

Benjamin's ardent words spill out for every shepherd to hear.

"Death may wait for us inside the walls of Tizra. I guarantee you that death will find us in Hallowed Hills. Zimri will stop at nothing to destroy our way of life as he did the Farmers Guild. Neshama did not create us to live as slaves;

we were created to live free. Are your souls truly free?

If you're afraid of Zimri, go back home. If you're afraid of losing your liberty, follow me into the gates of Tizra and into the jaws of tyranny. We may be devoured by the wolf, but at the least we kick his teeth in, the only way a shepherd can."

Othniel glows with pride at Benjamin's bold words.

Struck with a bolt of faith from the proclamation, the troubled faces of the shepherds transform into confident stares at the son of Oren Tav.

Evan surveys the confident stares and senses that the speech was well received, which embitters him all the more. He forcibly grabs Ashira by the arm and yanks her to his side. "Come on, we're leaving. You people go to your deaths."

Ashira pulls her arm away with equal force. Seth moves to protect her flank, his body language daring Evan to grab his sister again.

"You side with Benjamin?" questions Evan, his cocky ego shrinking to that of a boy with hurt feelings. "Fine then, I don't want any part of this suicide. Who's coming with me?"

Not one shepherd moves.

The guild master feels very much like an amateur when he fails to convince one shepherd to return with him.

His failure to secure Ashira's well-being chokes his pride and he speaks with desperate breath, "This is how you repay me, Brother? A dagger in the back. I sacrificed much to protect father's heritage, but you rush to wreck it. You snuffed out Jael's light, now you seek to do likewise to Ashira. You curse! It's not enough for you to kiss death, but to whore out Ashira to the void… I'll never forgive this."

Evan hangs his head and drags his feet out of Pella.

Pity replaces Benjamin's animosity for his brother, for he's never seen Evan carry himself with such a pathetic presence. He takes a step to follow after his dejected brother, but Ashira squeezes his hand, her eyes telling him no.

"It's not easy to be a brother," whispers Othniel into Benjamin's ear as Evan makes the lonely trudge north, vanishing into the horizon.

Benjamin turns to shake Caleb's hand. "We stand with Lord Emmerick."

An oil lamp streams a line of black smoke into the ceiling of the manor house. The lamplight casts shadows on the household objects used to create a replica of Tizra. Benjamin and Othniel get lost in their thoughts trying to figure out how they will infiltrate the city with no siege equipment.

Ezekiel sits quietly in a dark corner and whispers a chant to connect with the ether of a field mouse. He turns a dark shade of red as the mouse disregards his summons.

Seth becomes obnoxious to Ashira, looking over her shoulder as she cooks. She elbows him in the stomach forcing him to back off.

"Is that enough to feed all the shepherds and still have enough for us?" worries Seth.

"That's all of Nebo's cabbage and potatoes."

"Some corn beef would sure be good."

"Why don't you be of use and serve the stew?"

Seth follows orders like one of the palace cooks. Ezekiel joins him to assist in the meal service.

Othniel takes a break from the makeshift campaign map and focuses his attention on Oren Tav's son. Within a few moments, Benjamin senses the prophet's stare, "Why are you lookin' at me like that?"

"You've come a long way in a short time. That was quite the speech you delivered. I never heard your father give a speech like that."

"Then why did the shepherds follow my father? They

followed him to their deaths."

"Oren led by example. Speeches inspire, but men don't follow speeches; they follow leaders. These shepherds follow your lead. It's time for you to accept the responsibility of your call. The Remnant rises and you must lead us."

Othniel looks upon Neshama's chosen with troublesome eyes, "I do worry about you, Benjamin. I've seen what war looks like - gritty, bloody, unlike anything you've ever experienced."

"I've killed wolves," notes Benjamin. In another thought, he recalls his good aim in Abilla's Orchard, "I've put arrows into a couple of the king's choice hunters."

"Not the same as a wolf. Taking the life from a man, draining his soul from his inward depths is unnatural. Nothing can prepare you for such a torment. And while I admire your archery skills in the orchard, the fray of battle is much more gruesome. Staring your enemy in the eye as they perish on your sword is pure torment."

"Again with torment. I can't wait to look Zimri in the eyes when I run my sword through his guts, I long for such vengeance."

The answer rattles off Benjamin's tongue with such venom that it stings Othniel's convictions. The prophet shrinks in disapproval.

"You feel differently."

"Neshama is a Goddess of grace. Though Zimri deserves death, she would caution you to extend grace. If he rejects grace then let him walk the path of justice."

"But Shamgar Ram would condemn me for such behavior. He says that faith should be fierce and retribution swift."

"Ah, that's the way of their order, all law and no grace. Black or white, wrong or right, faith or doubt. Neshama's grace is more fluid than the precepts care to acknowledge. It flows through us like the ether inside and around us. Grace loves to penetrate the grey areas because she's not black or white, or gets hung up on wrongs or rights. Grace glides with the ebb and flow of faith and doubt."

"I'm not sure if I can live in grace. Zimri is the root of all my pain and he must die."

"Then you will end up like your brother, incapable of forgiving yesterday's pain. Killing Zimri won't bring your parents back, won't bring your sister back. Long after your sword has been removed from Zimri's corpse, you'll still be filled with hate. Justice is swift, grace is longsuffering, but you'll never comprehend either until you unlock the power of sacrifice."

Othniel's words on sacrifice weigh on the shepherd's soul, heavier than the deaths of his parents and sister.

The powerful odor of Nebo's cabbage steams off the stew and brings Benjamin's and Othniel's attention back to the table.

"You two need to eat up," orders Seth. They take a seat at the table, pleasantly surprised by Ashira's savory stew. "What's got you down?"

"We don't have any siege equipment to storm the back gate. If we tried to get some ladders on the wall, the archers would shred us to pieces," says Benjamin.

"Maybe there's some kind of secret passage or weakness in the walls we could exploit," suggests Othniel.

"Zimri's so paranoid that all the passages are sealed off," says Ashira, spilling out the final ounces of stew into her bowl.

"That's not entirely true. Zimri leveled the Hall of Knowledge and built The Pit on top. I found out that the scribes use the sewers to send messages to one another and sneak Neshama worshippers in and out of the city. In his haste to construct The Pit, Zimri's architects decided not to seal off the sewer," says Seth.

"Would you be willing to infiltrate the city through the

sewer and open the north gate?" asks Othniel.

A morbid energy darkens Seth's disposition.

"What's wrong with him?" asks Ezekiel.

"Rats. He's deathly afraid of them," answers Ashira.

"Wait… You filled The Pit with heaps of men and you're afraid of rats? Seriously?" chides Benjamin.

Ashira mouths *stop*, playfully shoving his arm.

"I will send Ezekiel with you. He can control the rats," offers Othniel to his student's surprise.

"These aren't your typical rats, and they're much larger than sparrows," says Seth.

"Can you pull it off?" asks Benjamin.

Seth puts his face into his bowl to ignore the request.

Ezekiel stands and proclaims his commitment to all shepherds in ear shot, "I will not fail the Remnant."

Ezekiel's boldness floors Seth, who fears his manhood might be demeaned by the courage of a scrawny prophet. He lifts his head from his bowl and begrudgingly nods in agreement.

Chapter 20 | The Gates of Tizra

A swarm of a hundred rats chase Seth and Ezekiel through the murky sewer water. The mangy brown vermin unsteadily hop over one another as they pursue their prey. The men gasp for air inhaling the noxious sewer fumes.

"I hate you!" shouts Seth, grabbing Ezekiel by the collar of his robe to insure the prophet keeps pace.

BOOM! The sound of thunder creeps down from the surface to the sewer ceiling - the vibrations scare the rats into the holes of the sewer walls.

"It begins," says Seth, pausing to allow Ezekiel to catch his breath when another thunderous BOOM! rumbles atop the surface.

✦ ✦ ✦

Lord Emmerick, Prince Aden, Caleb Glade, and Tobi Tamar watch the first volley from the catapults slam into the front walls of Tizra. BOOM! Debris from the wall plunges into the waters of the Tizra River below.

The drawbridge tucks tightly into the south gate that's protected by two large towers that bookend the front wall. The towers ready their catapults for a counter strike, and the archers on the front wall prepare fires in metal cauldrons spread about the wall.

"We've obviously caught them by surprise and seized the initiative. We'll have a few rounds of boulders into the walls before they counter attack. Are the rafts ready?" inquires Emmerick.

"They're set for assault," says Aden.

"As soon as the catapults create a breech, send the rafts."
The Tizra towers counter attack with boulders that smash some of the separatist's catapult battery. One boulder strays from the mark and bounces through the ranks of the southern army.

Emmerick's catapults still intact return fire, and their boulders crush the section of the wall between the west tower and the south gate. Zimri's archers scatter through the air and crash into the stone townhomes; others plummet into the river below as the wall crumbles beneath them.

Once Emmerick's troops recognize the breech, they launch their rafts across the Tizra River. The soldiers put muscle into their strokes to fight the strong currents pushing them east.

Zimri's archers shoot their fiery arrows at the rafts, but most vessels drift across unaffected by the missile fire. One unlucky vessel bursts into flames. The soldiers onboard dive into the river; some feverishly swim to safety, while the mighty currents claim others.

The first wave of rafts traverses the river toward the swampland that connects to the firm ground near the breech in the wall. After the units disembark from the rafts, the crews return to the other side for reinforcements.

Zimri awakens from a drunken hibernation holding Isavel's crown. The thunderous blasts from Emmerick's catapults rattle his wits. He springs up from his bed and startles Rezon Scar, preparing himself to fall on his sword. Zimri snatches the blade from the captain's grasp.

"It can't end like this. Zidon and Korah promised us freedom, not death."

He returns Rezon's sword and places Isavel's crown on a small shrine dedicated to the Queen Mother.

Zimri darts into the throne room.

"Zidon! Korah!"

Rezon rushes after his king, sharing in the panic.

Zidon, with his assistants Zur and Zoheth by his side, calmly enters the throne room. Zimri runs to Zidon and grabs hold of his councilor, "Melek must be displeased with the moon festival… I need Korah. Where's Korah?"

Zidon guides Zimri to his throne, "I beg of you. Sit, calm yourself," says Zidon. Rezon agrees with the advice and helps the magi usher his king to the throne.

The feel of the cool marble slightly soothes Zimri, which allows Zidon to offer council.

"Let Zur and Zoheth light the candles. We must summon Korah at once," requests Zimri.

"There's no need to summon Korah, and Melek is not displeased with you, far from it. He likes to surprise us from time to time in order to test our devotion, the Remnant resists much sooner than predicted, that's all."

Zimri digs his long fingernails into his throne, his panic transitioning to frustration.

"Captain, magi, allow me a moment with our king," orders the councilor.

The men obey the dismissal.

"Why does Melek curse me?" asks the haggard king.

"Curse you? Why, he's given you a gift."

"How can you call an unforeseen siege a gift?"

"Melek delivers the shepherd, the prophet, your brother and your son into your hands. All at the same time, and right at your doorstep."

Zimri rips through his scraggly hair with his fingernails. He pulls and tugs his roots trying to make sense of his councilor's rhetoric. He mashes his face into the palms of his hands to blot out the torchlight in the throne room.

Zidon grins as agony has its way with Zimri. He removes the grin when the king lifts his head from his hands.

"What must I do?" asks Zimri with exhausted desperation.

"Kill… Kill them all. Your sword will break open the dam of crimson as you spill the blood of Neshama's faithful and the temple prostitutes will bathe in the blood of the Remnant. Hack, maim, slash."

Zidon's talk of death exhausts Zimri, and the haggard king collapses to the floor.

Zidon lifts the king by the roots of his hair. He cocks his hand then slaps Zimri across the face. "You are King Zimri Tizra 'The Backstabber.' That is a title you earned because you massacre your opposition. You murdered your father and your wife. You will go forth to murder your brother and your son. You backstabbed Oren Tav for his revolt, and you will now go forth and backstab his son for the exact treachery.

You made a pact with Melek because you told me that you wanted nothing more out of this life than to be free. Now draw your sword, march down to the gate, and slaughter such a heap of men that The Southern Kingdom becomes a kingdom of orphans. Do this, and Melek will set you free."

The rage in Zimri's eyes returns, and he storms out of his throne room. Zidon wears a devious smile while stroking the knot of his fuzzy grey beard.

Seth and Ezekiel gasp for air on the floor of The Pit training room. Once they regain their strength, they exit the room and move through the city streets of Tizra.

The deafening roars of the boulders shake the city as they blast the stone sections on the front wall. Ezekiel shudders at the loud explosions of the boulders. Seth's anger from the rat incident overrides all his senses; he aims a spiteful glare at the nervous prophet.

"What's that look for?"

"I should've smashed you when I had the chance," says Seth, pushing Ezekiel in the back to get him moving toward the north plaza.

Seth identifies the entrance into the ominous north gate tower where two guards stand post. He stealthily approaches the guards while the prophet lightly treads behind in the shadow of the colossus. Seth makes a surprisingly quiet effort as he sneaks toward his targets.

SMASH! Peacemaker blasts a racket while clobbering the guards.

The bashes draw the attention of more guards in the tower. Ezekiel barricades himself behind Seth while the warrior wades through the guards, peacemaker smacking them down one after the other.

Seth and Ezekiel reach the top of the north gate. Happily surprised by the absence of a tower master, Seth thoroughly studies the lever system that locks the north gate.

Benjamin, Othniel, Ashira, and the shepherds lie in wait under the cover of night outside the north gate. Benjamin's heart pumps adrenaline all the way to his fingertips. He can sense the tension that emanates from Ashira and the shepherds clustered about him. Some shepherds look upon the woman in their ranks with suspicion; in their patriarchal views, women have no place in the perils of shepherding or battle.

In the moment of high anticipation, Benjamin thinks of Ashira's wellbeing among the ranks of the apprehensive shepherds. "Maybe you should stay near the rear of the army. It could get ugly in the front ranks."

"Maybe you should move beyond your shepherd standards. Your father did. I know of your mother's resolve."

"It's more than that. I worry that you're not ready for battle."

"And you are? Oren Tav was quite the swordsman, and Evan's no slouch with a blade. I'm sure they taught you well. But you don't have Seth Keros for a brother. I have more skill with this sword than you think.

Besides, I wished for this moment every day that I slaved away in that kitchen. I have just as much at stake in this as you. Forgive me for not being flattered by your desire to protect the helpless girl."

Ashira's boldness overwhelms Benjamin. He stammers for a response when suddenly the metal bars of the gate rise.

"Charge!" yells Othniel.

The shepherd regiment breaks cover.

The archers on the walls have little time to react but do their best to launch a volley of arrows at the charging shepherds.

Their aim is off, and only a few shepherds fall.

Seth recognizes the archer-threat, so he rumbles out of the gate and across the walls. He lifts two archers by their throats and tosses them into their regiment, disrupting the second volley of fire. Seth tosses two more archers off the wall, and mauls two more with his paws.

Warning bells ring, alerting Zimri's army of the infiltrators in the north plaza.

King Zimri, with Rezon Scar by his side, withdraws from the breech in the front wall. He orders a fourth of his army that totals twenty thousand to counterattack the invading shepherds.

The ranks of shepherds led by Benjamin, Othniel, and Ashira flow into the north plaza; the king's strike force counter charges as Zimri and Rezon lead their swelled regiment of swordsmen from the back rank.

Zimri's large numbers and the shepherds' aggressiveness make for an even surge; therefore, neither side gains the initiative.

Seth clears the wall of archers and looks across the city to see the separatists struggling in the breech. The levers in the gate tower offer him an epiphany, so he summons Ezekiel.

"Stay close to me; I got an idea."

They leave the north gate and scurry unnoticed along the city walls on their way to the south gate.

Emmerick's soldiers struggle in the main breech because Zimri's troops are too numerous, and the low ground puts them at a disadvantage. To make matters worse, the number of rafts diminishes greatly due to the flaming arrows and vicious river currents.

Emmerick looks upon Aden with unsettled eyes, "This battle could go south in a hurry. If we lose here, we lose The Southern Kingdom."

Emmerick's conviction challenges his skepticism as he watches his soldiers fight valiantly in the breech.

The north plaza battle rages with neither side giving ground. The perils of warfare make the city spin reminding Benjamin of Othniel's wisdom. The encouragement of his mentor prepares him for the sights and sounds of battle.

Benjamin maintains his footing to allow his sword to strike swift and exact. Ashira fights ferociously and displays the tenacity instilled from Seth's tutelage. Othniel uses his staff to ward off an attacker; he takes a stiff poke that connects the butt of his staff with a soldier's jaw, knocking his adversary to the ground.

"Othniel, I must get to the temple! Kurion's in there!" reminds Benjamin.

"Stay with the shepherds, I'll get it!" yells Othniel, retreating into the rear ranks, and moving toward the Temple of Melek.

Othniel pauses at the altar atop the temple steps, a gentle drop forms in his eye as he runs his hand across the cold marble. His thoughts dwell on the infant-girl sacrificed by Isavel when a righteous anger pumps his blood.

Othniel enters the pantheon and the immoral architecture sickens his stomach. The temple is a den of debauchery - the tight black leather outfits of the temple prostitutes line the narthex, thousands of wine bottles line the far wall, cushions of all shapes and sizes row the near wall.

A Melek idol, similar to the one in the throne room, towers over the far end of the sanctuary. An enormous glass window, from which the moon lights the room with bright shades of amber, sparkles behind the head of the idol. A small pit created for duels rests at the foot of the idol; weapons of all shapes and sizes adorn the outer wall of a small pit.

Kurion rests on an altar of black marble with Melek idols masterfully engraved into the four corners of the altar, the altar serving as the centerpiece of the temple. Zalmon and Zatu, two of Zidon's magi, chant over the blade while running their hands over the surface, attempting to connect to the ether within the mythical sword.

"Trouble finding something?" asks Othniel of the frustrated magi. "Kurion doesn't allow us to use the ether locked in the blade... This is bad news for you."

Othniel's lesson befuddles the two magi.

"Have you come here to woo us with your grace

garbage?" asks the flabby-faced Zalmon.

Othniel extends his right arm with his palm wide while balancing himself with his staff in the left hand. He locks onto Zalmon's soul and begins the banishment.

The overweight magi gasps for air as his flesh jiggles under his grey robes. Zatu freezes in terror at Othniel's display of magical might.

Zalmon digs all ten fingers into his robe, and they sink into his chest as he attempts to alleviate the affliction of his gluttony and the banishment.

Othniel launches the tubby magi into the Melek idol and rips his soul from his chest. His black soul swirls over his corpse as the Melek idol topples over. The statue shatters on his corpse and the corrupted soul dissipates.

The blast from the collision snaps Zatu back to reality. It also stirs the harem of prostitutes, who spill out of the darkness and salivate with revenge for the prophet who felled the Queen Mother Isavel.

Zatu arms himself with Kurion and charges Othniel.

Othniel drops his staff, stretches out with both hands, and digs his heels into the stone floor. He leeches onto the magi's corrupted soul and halts the charge. Zatu shows more willpower than his feeble counterpart and attempts to fight through the banishment.

Zatu stumbles a few times but refuses to surrender his soul.

The temple prostitutes mob Othniel, but he continues to extract the corrupted ether.

Zatu edges closer.

The prophet struggles to stay upright as the harlots rip his robe.

With a few willful steps, the magi enters striking distance of the vulnerable prophet. Zatu winds back Kurion and aims for the prophet's grey head.

As the sword swings down, Othniel hurls the vile magi into the wall of wine bottles - Kurion rattles across the floor.

Othniel rips the soul from Zatu's body; the ether force of the extraction is so powerful that it blasts the entire harem into the temple walls.

Zatu's soul is more demented than his vanquished counterpart. Its deafening scream booms throughout the temple bursting the window above. Glass shards shoot out from the temple into the back plaza of Tizra as Zatu's soul shrieks throughout the city disappearing in the night sky.

The terrified prostitutes flee the pantheon through a secret passage leading into the sewers.

The chilling phenomenon momentarily distracts both regiments warring in the north plaza. Benjamin looks back to see Othniel return from the temple with Kurion, so he slips to the back ranks to retrieve the sword.

"Hold the plaza, I must find Zidon," says Othniel, returning the blade to its master.

"I'll come with you; I can defeat him with Kurion."

"No. You must lead the Remnant."

With Benjamin in the far ranks, the shepherds lose some of their impetus and begin to give ground.

"Hold the line. The shepherds need their leader," says Othniel, edging closer to the palace.

Zimri and Rezon notice the wavering ranks and press their attack. They shove their way to the front ranks to bolster the courage of their infantry.

Zimri claims a handful of shepherds while Rezon scavenges the fallen to finish off the wounded.

"Benjamin, the line is breaking!" shouts Ashira.

Rezon hears the desperation in her voice and makes way for his prize.

An invigorated Benjamin returns to the front ranks and plows into Zimri's battle line. The fading shepherds rally to join the surge. Rezon targets Ashira when Benjamin notices his mangled face.

"Scar!" cries Benjamin.

Ashira draws a chef's knife from its sheathe behind her back, and whirls the knife - blade over handle. The sharp metal sinks into Rezon's bicep.

He yanks the blade from his arm and throws it to the ground with fury. His fury immediately turns to worry at the aggressive shepherds.

Zimri howls in anguish as Rezon Scar drowns in the surge of shepherds.

Benjamin claims his first victim with Kurion - a lanky soldier with pale face. He pauses for a moment when the ether sword glistens as if lightning bolts of purple pulse through it. As Kurion connects with more souls - brighter purple bolts appear.

Seth sneaks into the guard tower above the drawbridge; Ezekiel crouches behind him feeling helpless in the throes of battle. Seth slugs the guards posted inside the entrance of the tower and the two run up a flight of stairs that lead to the pinnacle of the tower.

Ezekiel takes post at the top of the stairs and scans the tower for more adversaries while Seth checks the tower for the drawbridge controls in hopes of lowering the bridge for the separatists.

Two guards ambush Ezekiel. He flees the swipes of their halberds as he moves around Seth. The sly guards are no match for the pitfighter, pounding one after the other with Peacemaker.

After the short distraction, Seth locates the drawbridge lever. He must travel a catwalk to access the lever in the control tower; he's hesitant to cross, for the catwalk is narrow and one misstep means certain death. Seth watches the soldiers perishing in the breech below, and their deaths shame his uncertainty.

As Seth steps onto the catwalk, he hears the rustling of chains, and a barred gate slamming behind him, trapping Ezekiel in the tower. He turns and shakes the bars.

"Looks like you're stuck; I bet the release is in the other tower with the drawbridge lever."

Ezekiel's eyes liven as he sees the tower master appear on the other side.

"What?" asks Seth.

Ezekiel points out the threat, and Seth turns to see the tower master armored from head to toe. His steel helmet resembles a dragon's face and matches the dragons etched into his double-sided axe head. The tower master swings the long axe handle swiftly and in a manner that taunts Seth.

Ezekiel grows nervous as he watches the number of shepherds dwindle in the north plaza and Emmerick's soldiers dwindle in the breech. Dismantled from the fiery arrows and raging river, the rafts no longer ferry troops across. Ezekiel finds a bit of hope at the view of Emmerick's main force nearly four thousand strong and eager to fight.

In the midst of the chaos, he gets on his knees to pray for Seth, who faces a heavily armored obstacle guarding the control tower.

Benjamin and the shepherds hold fast in combat with Zimri and his company - a combat so fierce that only death will quell it. Zimri's survival instincts liven when he realizes that he cannot slip to the back rank. Like a threatened animal, he lashes out in rage; his forceful blow maims a shepherd, and the follow up swing is repelled by Kurion.

Benjamin locks eyes with Zimri and pours all of his vengeance into the heart of his nemesis.

Zimri hesitates, Benjamin initiates.

Benjamin storms the killer of his father and sister with an onslaught of attacks from the Lord of Swords. The veteran king draws from his battle experience repelling the flurry, and narrowly escaping the onslaught.

Infantrymen come to their king's aid and allow Zimri to retreat into the ranks and regain his composure. Benjamin tries in vain to fight through the infantry wall.

When the vengeance adrenaline wears off, the eager shepherd finds himself in a vulnerable position. He receives the same dedication from his Tav brethren when they form a wall in front of their champion.

Seth and the tower master clash.

Better suited for the fight, the tower master's axe slices the air in perfect balance. He fails to land a fatal blow, but dismantles Seth's armor. Sparks fly, the tower master's axe glancing off the pitfighter's armor.

Seth struggles to land a fatal strike against his quicker enemy.

Seth swings at the tower master's dragon-faced helmet.

The veteran squats under the swing and swiftly plants the butt of his axe into Seth's sternum, blowing him back into the barred gate next to Ezekiel.

Peacemaker plummets to the cobblestone below.

The fall is so deep that the large hammer dings like a pin when it hits the ground.

Seth lays motionless in a daze. The tower master taunts him once again with axe twirls before pressing the attack.

Ezekiel fears for Seth's life, so he lifts his head to the dark sky and chants in the mystical language. The tower master halts, tilting his dragon-faced helmet, and listening to the peculiar tongue.

The prophet chants with such conviction that his voice echoes throughout the south plaza.

Seth's vision returns, and he looks to the heavens. He spots a black dot descending from the night sky.

The tower master dismisses the prophetic language. He raises his axe head high above his head.

Seth identifies the black dot as the sparrow.

Disappointment darkens his face and the expectation of death dulls his eyes.

Suddenly, hundreds of black dots appear as Ezekiel summons a flock of sparrows.

The sullen sparrows ferociously barrage the tower master; he tries to maintain his balance, but his armor will not allow it.

The tower master dives to a clanging death on the cobblestone below.

After shaking off the shock of the near death experience, Seth looks upon Ezekiel with gratitude.

Seth gets to his feet, dashes across the catwalk, and yanks the huge lever. The metal lever activates a series of pulleys and chains.

CRACK! The enormous drawbridge thunders down across the Tizra River, freeing Ezekiel from his temporary prison tower.

The jaws of Emmerick, Aden, Caleb, and Tobi drop with equal force.

Aden is the first able to form words, "I will lead the charge. Uncle, losing you would be devastating to this campaign."

Aden quickly assumes his place in the front ranks. Caleb dutifully follows. The prince moves so fast with his words and actions that Emmerick has no time to answer. Tobi nods at the plan to keep Emmerick out of battle, though missing out on the action eats at the fearless captain.

Aden addresses ranks with Caleb at his side, "Zimri has numbers, we have hope; one will run out before the other!

Let the rising sun greet us with the blood of tyrants on our swords!"

Aden points Royal Blue at Tizra, and Caleb draws his pair of steel war axes. They race ahead of the regiment with cries of war as they charge across the drawbridge.

Warning bells ring out yet again to alert Tizra that separatists infiltrate the south gate.

The bells are a welcoming sound for Benjamin, Ashira, and the depleted shepherds contemplate defeat.

Zimri realizes that the shepherd army has been subdued, and he motions for his soldiers to reinforce the troops at the south gate. A soldier trumpets his horn to enforce the order. The consumed shepherds are too exhausted to celebrate, and too exhausted to pursue their enemy. Benjamin still itches with revenge and wants more than nothing to have another round with Zimri. At first he's agitated by the shepherds' lack of willpower to stay engaged. Once he refocuses his crimson vision, he sees the anguish in the eyes of his Tav brethren. Pity stills his anger and allows him to reprioritize his mission.

"Ashira, I need you tend to the wounded."

"Where are you going?"

"To help Othniel. I need you to help the shepherds."

Ashira's initial instinct is to assist Benjamin, but the groans of the wounded in the north plaza summon her to their pain.

"Goddess keep you."

Ashira's blessing pierces Benjamin's heart, and in the midst of death he feels the faintest touch of hope.

Benjamin smiles back at her before bolting toward the palace.

Zimri marches his soldiers to the south gate from the rear rank. When he catches a glimpse of Benjamin entering the palace, he stops in his tracks, but his army marches on without him. Melek's mandate to kill the shepherd rages within his mind.

The king digs his fingers into his scalp to quiet the voice of Korah. *If the son of Oren Tav is not eliminated, you risk Melek's retribution.*

Zimri's eyes glaze over as if some unhealthy force possesses his being. He makes for the palace with a vision of his blade in Benjamin's back.

Chapter 21 | Grace or Justice

Othniel enters the throne room to find Zidon standing in front of the Melek idol. An ether vortex swirls shades of grey on the floor, astonishing Othniel. "Did you conjure this phenomenon?"

"It's not couth to reveal one's secrets," answers Zidon, tossing back his hood and lengthening his arm from under his robes. "I've waited a long time for this moment."

"I wished this moment would've never come. I still love you, my Brother."

Zidon's spite wards off Othniel's declaration.

"As the older brother I always looked up to you. When we were boys, I followed you everywhere. When we were young men, I followed you to the Order of the Prophets. That's why it broke my heart when you betrayed the prophets. Not so much that you pursued Melek, but you went to a place that

I could not follow… Come back to Neshama, come back to the Order, walk the way of grace."

"Always grace with you, the way of Neshama. Where was the Goddess when Lilith fell ill? First, she let her husband die, left her unborn child fatherless; then she let Lilith rot on her deathbed with a baby trapped in the casket of her womb."

"Our sister never lost her faith," replies Othniel in a tender tone.

"Well I did! And you're a fool for keeping yours. I didn't betray the prophets. Neshama betrayed me. She refused to answer my prayers for Lilith. And as a prophet, I was charged to remember the Goddess? She didn't remember my sister, she didn't remember me."

"You're wrong, Brother. She did. You went to search for Melek, and you missed the miracle."

"Too much brew again, Othniel."

"Lilith had a son. She weaned him an entire year before the disease claimed her life, before her journey to the ether world."

"You have no evidence of this miracle."

"I most certainly do. Lilith named her son after our grandfather… His name is Ezekiel."

Zidon's mouth gapes at Othniel's evidence, "Your understudy?"

"I know you yearn for my death, but are you so consumed by wrath that you'd kill Lilith's son? Let's be a family again. Let's restore the Order. Let go of the condemnation in your soul. Let grace prevail."

"Lilith's dead. We can never be a family again. I don't want your Goddess or her grace."

"Then you have no choice but to walk the way of justice," laments Othniel.

Zur and Zoheth enter the throne room reciting the mystical tongue. Othniel hastily scans the room for animals. Hidden stone doors on both sides of the Melek idol slowly open.

Suddenly, two gigantic brown bears charge the prophet. Othniel draws ether from the vortex and wraps himself in a milky white ether bubble. The bears claw at the thick bubble, their powerful paws removing shreds of the wrap.

Othniel boldly proclaims the mystical tongue and takes control of one of the bears. It rears up and wraps its massive arms around the other brown beast; the two bears wrestle across the floor slamming into a wall.

Zur and Zoheth utilize corrupt magic to manipulate the ether into dark grey orbs. The magi fire the orbs at the prophet.

As the orbs approach, Othniel channels ether to create a flowing wind that manifests into rings that circulate his being. The spheres of dark grey ether enter Othniel's orbit and get swept into the white ether rings.

The orbs reverse course toward the two magi; the orbs return with such force that they knock the miscreants off their feet.

"My disciples are as inept as yours," mocks Zidon, before boasting the prophetic language to reclaim control of both brown bears.

Zidon sends them thundering back toward his brother.

Othniel bellows verbose tones and wars for control over the untamed ether within the bears.

The erratic manipulation of their ether works the beasts into a frenzy, and the antagonized bears aim to unleash their aggression on Zur and Zoheth.

The magi shake off their ether orb mishaps and return to their feet when the two beasts barrel toward them. They stammer the mystical tongue to no avail.

In a cowardly attempt to spare his own life, Zur pushes Zoheth into the path of predators. The powerful bears maul the betrayed magi and fling his corpse into the air like a rag doll.

The dismemberment of Zoheth horrifies Zur, and he darts for the exit on the far side of the throne room. The sudden movement of the magi annoys the frenzied bears, and they chase the coward down the hall.

Within moments, Zur's high-pitched squeals of misery echo throughout the palace.

The sound of rumbling bears die down, and the throne room goes hush.

Othniel successfully repels the bears, but allows his ether rings to weaken. Zidon capitalizes by shooting an onyx-black ether strand from the vortex. It cuts the ether rings and hurls Othniel onto the floor, his old bones crunching on impact.

Benjamin walks down the open air hallway that leads from the palace hall to the throne room. He pauses at the Well of Rizpah, feeling an uncanny touch of remorse for the deceased Issurian queen. His senses heighten with awareness when he taps into an oppressive energy floating about the hallway.

Korah emerges from the shadows.

"I admire your resolve. Not bad for a mortal."

"My call is to dethrone Zimri and end the worship of Melek. I have no matter to settle with you; Azor has been sent for that."

Benjamin's plea strikes a nerve with the rogue nephesh, causing his golden eyes to glow underneath his black hood, "Neshama sent Azor to reclaim me?"

Benjamin bites his bottom lip, regretting his loose tongue.

"It's a shame that he's not here. I can assure you, any matter that pertains to Zimri and Melek most definitely pertains to me. Your journey ends at the edge of my blade."

"You're not invincible," states Benjamin in a defiant tone.

"True, but killing a nephesh of my quality is a near impossible for your kind. Melek wants you dead, and I must make you so."

Korah draws his ether sword from beneath his robes, and the sudden motion of the drawn sword sends a chill down Benjamin's spine.

Korah charges the intimidated shepherd.

Benjamin does his best to hold his ground, but the nephesh fights unlike anything that he has ever faced. Benjamin figures Korah's timing and takes crisper swings with Kurion.

Divine arrogance underestimates the human's swordplay, and Benjamin rips Kurion across Korah's midsection. The ether sword glimmers bright red, the color of Korah's inner ether, and the black fiend doubles over in pain.

Benjamin's confident that he mortally wounded Korah, but the formidable nephesh stands and the wound slowly regenerates, his black robes swallowing the red glow of ether. "Kurion makes you strong. Melek makes me stronger."

Korah goes back on the offensive and strikes harder blows. The shepherd tightens both hands on his sword to keep control of his weapon. Korah kicks Benjamin in the chest, hammering him into the stone slabs.

Ashira moves about the north plaza in search of wounded shepherds. The acids in her stomach flare while sorting through the carnage. The stench of death makes her feel light-headed, so she lifts her face to the heavens to refresh her vision.

Hearing the groans of a shepherd, she rolls over the injured veteran only to watch his eyes close and life fade from his being.

She moves onto another shepherd atop a heap of dead soldiers to check for any vital signs. Bending over, Ashira checks his bearded neck for a pulse.

Rezon Scar emerges from the pile and grabs Ashira by the throat.

Putting his hand over her mouth, he pulls her to the cobblestone. The captain stays low to the ground as he forcefully drags her out of the plaza.

As soon as his hostage is out of screaming distance, Rezon throws down Ashira near a trash heap in an abandoned alleyway.

Aden's regiment slams into the wall of Zimri's troops that defend the drawbridge. The skilled prince strikes hard and accurate with Royal Blue as he claims the lives of numerous halberdiers. Caleb reveals his quality in battle by equaling the number of casualties with his pair of razor sharp war axes. A pile of bodies begins to mount on the drawbridge, and the northern army shows signs of wavering.

Zimri's army steadies when the reinforcements arrive from the north plaza. The soldiers in the breech vanquish the remaining Southern Issurians, and no rafts remain to ferry more troops.

They leave the wall to reinforce the battle line that now flows into the south plaza. They file in behind their wall of comrades and offer a much-needed push that slows the momentum of Aden and the separatists. The push becomes so powerful that Aden and the separatists give ground, and are forced out of the south gate.

Archers take aim at the prince and pick off soldiers around him.

Seth offers some protection by tossing archers off of the walls and into one another. Ezekiel orders his flock of sparrows to shield his counterpart from the bowmen. Some unfortunate foes lose their eyes to the beaks of the sullen sparrows.

The sergeant of the archers, a man with a wrinkled scowl

and an eye patch, lines up an arrow for Aden's heart. Seth identifies the dead eye and hurls a chunk of debris at the sergeant.

The debris connects as the bolt leaves the bow. The one-eyed archer loses his balance and flies from the wall into the river below.

His arrow stings Aden in the thigh, and he falls to the hard wood of the drawbridge. Caleb steps in front of the prince, wards off some halberd jabs, and pulls the prince from harm.

Othniel gropes about the floor to find his staff. He leans on the rod to get to his feet; his vision readjusts to the dark throne room as he scans the space for Zidon.

The magi manipulates a bigger strand of ether that will crush his brother against the wall.

As Zidon releases the blast, Othniel channels the ether from the vortex and arms himself with an ether shield that swirls in a circle. The white disc repeals the black blast that ricochets throughout the throne room.

Othniel and Zidon avoid the unpredictable path of the blast as it bounces around the room, smashing everything in its path, and gaining more and more steam until it reaches its final destination.

The powerful strand crashes into the Melek idol, causing it to rock back and forth. The idol falls forward and shatters into a thousand pieces of rubble that spray across the throne room.

The cloud of dust settles to reveal the mass destruction of the space - only the gaudy throne remains.

Othniel and Zidon hastily channel ether from the vortex. The magi channels with hatred and manipulates more ether than before. The prophet channels to match the magi's ambitious amount of ether.

"You channel too much!" warns Othniel.

Zidon refuses to heed the warning, and the strand grows larger and larger.

Zidon unloads the bulky amount of ether onto Othniel, who quickly counters with a massive ether disc. The swirling pearl disc repels the stream of the onyx-black strand suspended above the vortex. As the tainted strand grinds against the pure shield, the ether sparks into brilliant colors that illuminate the throne room.

Zidon labors to advance his onyx ether through the pearl ether, but Othniel's resolve keeps the deadly ether strand at bay.

Benjamin winces as he gets to his feet.

Korah scoffs at his pain, "Mortals."

The nephesh resumes his onslaught, and the shepherd adjusts to the aggressive slices. As he resists the relentless attacks, Korah shows signs of impatience and anger.

Zimri stealthily enters the walkway with his sword drawn, but the engaged shepherd has his back to the king.

Korah takes note.

The nephesh holds a defensive stance and allows Benjamin to drive the swordplay. After he goes on the offensive, Zimri moves slowly toward his target. 'The Backstabber' steadies his sword and locates his attack point in the middle of Benjamin's spine.

Zimri steadies his blade for the kill.

Azor flies down from the tower above at a rapid rate of speed. He latches onto Korah, and the two nephesh spiral downward, crashing through the palace infrastructure as they plummet.

Benjamin senses Zimri's presence and dodges his lunge.

It takes both men a moment to regain their nerve after watching the two nephesh blast through a stone wall below.

Rezon Scar lords over Ashira and salivates with anticipation. "I've been waiting a long time to get a bite of you; I hope you taste better than your steak."

He forces himself on her and tries to undo her outfit. His steak insult burns her pride, and her shock transitions to anger. She refuses to let him have his way, and they wrestle on the ground. She reaches for her kitchen knife; the empty sheathe reminds her that the blade had repelled Rezon earlier.

The forceful captain tries to overpower Ashira, but she resists him. Rezon frees one of his arms and back hands her across the face.

The brutal slap stuns her.

Rezon leans in to smell her hair and brushes his mangled cheek across her smooth cheek. His disfigured mug hovers above her pretty face, his deviant smile stretching from ear to ear.

"That's right, my lady. Resist no more."

Ashira's nerves liven within her being, and she can feel the weight of Rezon on her stomach and the hard cobblestone under her back. The hopelessness of the moment weighs heavier than the captain.

Ashira opens her eyes, and the blurry night sky comes into focus. Her vision identifies two distinct piercing-blue stars. After her vision corrects, she recognizes the piercing-blue stars as the eyes of Shamgar Ram.

Rezon's soul quivers in the presence of retribution. He lifts his nose from her hair, and his eyes cower with the dread of his impending judgment.

"How many daughters of Issur have suffered your

injustice? This daughter will not be among them."

Shamgar unloads his mace into Rezon's mutant face with such power that the executed captain lifts off Ashira and crashes into the trash heap in the alleyway.

Aden limps to his feet, throwing an arm around Caleb's shoulders to balance himself. "How bad is it?" asks Aden, looking down at the arrow in his thigh.

"You're lucky. It's barely in your flesh," says Caleb, examining the wound.

"Rip it out."

"Serious?"

"Now!"

Aden immediately regrets his command when Caleb yanks the arrow from his leg.

Caleb takes a yellow banner from a fallen soldier, rips a strand of cloth, and tightly cinches it around Aden's thigh. His regret turns to gratitude as he squeezes the scout's shoulder in approval of the remedy, "Back to the bridge, my friend."

Emmerick nervously slicks his moustache with his index finger and thumb while Aden and his men struggle in the front gate outnumbered four to one.

His look of concern morphs into a look of enlightenment.

Emmerick sorts through his saddle bag and pulls out his book of arms. He thumbs through the pages, stopping on the page about fencing. He scans the page before putting the book down.

Emmerick rummages though a chest of weapons, and pulls out a slightly rusted steel saber. He retrieves the book of arms once more and holds it in his left hand. The antique saber settles in his right hand. Emmerick prances around like a pugilist with a saber as Captain Tamar watches, unsure of the antics of his lord.

Othniel and Zidon move the ether back and forth as brilliant colors continue to spray across the throne room. The ether tide flows like the ocean over a shore. Zidon's ether strand washes over the prophet's ether shield. Othniel's white ether disc remains resilient rejecting the black ether strand.

"If you don't back down, this ether strand will be the end of us," warns 'Wayfarer.'

"As long as it's the end of you… My life for your death!" declares 'The Absolute' as an ether fog begins to cloud the throne room.

Ether flares spark against the palace walls as Azor and Korah continue to smash through stone walls until they crash to a stop. Azor flickers a glittering gold and Korah a radiant red. As the two nephesh grind to a halt, Azor finds himself in a position of strength when he stands over Korah, "It's time for you to come back to Neshama."

"I'm bound to a greater power."

Korah springs to his feet and strikes at his target. The guardian swiftly blocks the attacks with his ether blade. The two exchange blows as they move through a palace hallway. Azor's blade sprays shades of red slashing through Korah's essence; Korah's blade sprays shades of gold.

The two leap palace trappings as they battle through corridors.

Korah moves up a flight of stairs leading to the king's chambers, seizing the high ground and controlling the duel. A violent strike of Korah's sword nearly lands a fatal blow.

Azor realizes that he can fend off the attacks only for a little longer. Korah gets caught off guard when Azor lowers his head and bull rushes him. The guardian puts his shoulder into his nemesis and plows him through a stone wall.

BOOM! The majestic nephesh blast into Zimri's bedchamber.

Empty wine bottles litter the messy bed. Azor picks up Korah and tosses him across the bed, his red ether flickering as the broken glass rips across his back.

Azor pants in exhaustion and frustration at Korah's defiance, "What makes you so tenacious?"

The rogue nephesh stumbles to his feet.

"You put me to the test," says Azor rushing Korah once more.

BOOM! The celestial creatures blast through another wall crashing into the dismantled throne room.

Benjamin feels the effects of his quest when his muscles tighten. His weakened state breeds confidence in Zimri as the two exchange swings. The dreadful king kicks the shepherd's legs out from under him, and lords over with a raised sword.

"Your father gave a better fight."

The insult pumps Benjamin's adrenaline and he rolls to his feet. He goes on the attack as memories of his father slaying the wolf run through his mind.

His newfound aggression evens the duel.

The broad side of Kurion collides with Zimri's head; the hit bursts his eardrum, and he cries out in pain.

Benjamin backs Zimri to the Well of Rizpah. He swings Kurion with such force that he knocks the king's sword from his hands, and the blade rattles down the well.

Zimri reaches for his weapon, loses his balance, and falls into the well.

Zimri dangles by one hand from the mouth of the well. Benjamin sheathes Kurion and grabs the tyrant's right wrist with his left hand.

The interfaced foes face a crisis of conscience.

Two storms rage within Benjamin's soul - vengeance and faith. Violent images flash within his memory - his fallen mother in the throes of battle, Zimri's sword through his father's back, the blood-soaked petals underneath Jael's lifeless body.

Vengeance demands justice, it demands that he loose the tyrant's hand. Vengeance offers a promise. If he follows through with the plea of vengeance, his soul will find rest when death swallows up Zimri at the bottom of the well.

Faith rushes against the tempest of vengeance in a gale of grace. He hears Othniel's wisdom in the whistles of the wind. Zimri's evil deeds have come back on his head, and Benjamin can render judgment with one slip of the grip.

Zimri deserves death, but grace offers him life, and as Othniel instructed, grace is the only way Benjamin will ever forgive the sins of Zimri that destroyed the Tav family.

Grace keeps no record of wrong, and neither will he.

Benjamin's compassionate act defies logic like the words that spring from his mouth, "Take my hand, I'll pull you up. Take the way of grace."

Benjamin extends his right hand, and Zimri locks his wrist. He pulls him up, and the two rivals breathe heavy for a moment before returning to their feet.

"Why did you do that?" asks Zimri with wide eyes.

"I don't know," answers Benjamin, still attempting to process his act of compassion.

"Don't you want me dead?"

"I thought I did. I came here to avenge my parents and my sister. I've wished for your death every day since I was five."

Zimri's mind throbs while he attempts to process Benjamin's goodness. His heart aches as it tries to accept compassion. Zimri reduces himself once more to his haggard state - the mad king rips at his head and chest to alleviate the condemnation that consumes his soul.

"Finish me, release me from this nightmare," begs Zimri.

"Only the Goddess can do that, as she has done for me. I wanted to see you face justice, but Othniel was right. Grace is the path I must walk if I'm ever going to forgive you for the ways you wronged me, if I'm ever going to be free…

Let Neshama's grace restore your soul. Relinquish your throne, and end Melek worship."

Benjamin's words soothe Zimri, and his aches become itches. His fingernails emerge from his flesh and lightly scratch his skin. His eyes reveal an internal attempt to reconcile the dissidence of Neshama's freedom and Melek's freedom.

A solitary teardrop of hope trickles down the side of the king's dazed face before it's consumed by the sinister monster that dwells within the soul of King Zimri Tizra 'The Backstabber.'

"Grace is for the weak," mocks Zimri, drawing a dagger from his boot.

The mad king scorns the shepherd's act of grace by stabbing the dagger into Benjamin's chest.

Benjamin spins and drops face first to the cold stone.

Zimri basks in the moonlight and gloats over his victim as blood drains into a maroon pool, "Melek's will is accomplished."

"Who are you!?" asks Ashira of her righteous rescuer.

"My name is Shamgar Ram. I'm a paladin precept on a crusade to judge those who forsook the Covenant and whored themselves out to Melek. Their fate will be that of the wretched captain."

He offers his hand and pulls her up, his face cringing at the sight of her outfit, "Daughter of Issur, you must remove that filthy garment at once."

"We don't have time for this. We must get your reinforcements to the south gate," commands Ashira, grabbing his hand and pulling him toward his troops.

Ashira runs to a dead stop of disappointment at the first sight of the crusade that waits in the north plaza. "This is your crusade?"

A hundred miners stand at the ready, armed with a variety of mattocks, picks, and axes. Their ages vary as much as their weapons. The miners sweat profusely in their fur raiment; the heavy sweat only worsens the dirty diggers' need for a hot bath.

"These men have marched day and night from the town of Sapphire atop Serpents Peak. Many of them are kinfolk from the House of Ram. They wanted to stand with their Issur brethren in defense of the Covenant."

Shamgar looks upon the wounded shepherds with pity.

"Maybe we can't stand with them, but we can finish what they started."

"With only a hundred men," doubts Ashira. "You never crossed paths with the Farmers Guild on the way south?"

"We did."

"Then we have more than a hundred for reinforcements?"

"Not quite," says Shamgar Ram, pointing his eyes to the ground.

Ashira figures something's gone awry when every miner does likewise, some with devious eyes. "You met Nebo Korse, didn't you?"

"Yes. I met that possessed pig going in all directions as if evil tormented his mind. A ragged steward and his soiled son chasing the pig around like fools."

"You do realize that Lord Nebo is their guild master."

"Was, my dear. He was the guild master."

"He's dead! How?"

"I ate him."

Ashira's mouth drops in disbelief, "You ate Nebo Korse? Well, that takes care of my question, then."

"He was more useful to us as bacon than as a guild master. Sorry that you held this particular pig in such high esteem."

"I could care less about the pig, but we need more troops."

"Why the doubt now, Daughter of Issur? Look at you. Your face, clothes, and sword are covered in the blood of tyrants. Your faith sharp. Your retribution brutal. If we were not in front of you now, and you stood alone, I have no doubts that you would march alone under the banner of Neshama."

Shamgar retrieves a standard from a fallen shepherd, the banner adorned with an embroidered ram head. He places it in her hand.

"You would march with this standard and plunge it deep into the heart of your enemy. You would plant your foot on the neck of your oppressor and proclaim that this night belongs to Neshama."

Ashira feels a current of faith circulate within her soul as Shamgar's fervent words rush over her.

"Do you feel that energy within your depths? That's how this crusade feels right now, every one of us. I don't know how many troops are in the south plaza, and I don't care. It could be five thousand or it could be fifty thousand. All the Goddess needs is one warrior utterly and unabashedly devoted to justice. One such warrior holds the power to judge an entire nation. Lead on, champion of Neshama, and we will follow."

Ashira lifts high her banner and leads the march to the south plaza.

Emmerick removes his eyes from his weaponry book and peers across the carnage. The battlefield becomes clear to him. His battle line erodes soldier by soldier, and it's only a matter of time before his nephew will be lost to Issur.

The cries of war take him back to the cave, to the warbles of the rock badgers. Emmerick desperately desired Aden to be dominant male, the protector of the colony, for he himself was too frightened to face Zimri.

The groans of the fallen summon him like threatened rock badgers calling out for the alpha, and he finally realizes his purpose as if nature herself ordains it.

The friend of my mate is my mate.

Emmerick returns his book to the saddlebag and removes a glass flask filled with a burnt-orange liquid. He swirls the flask, breathes in the elixir, and takes a big swig.

"My Lord, is that some sort of magical potion?" asks Tobi.

"No, but the book recommended it."

"What is it, then?"

"Brandy," says Emmerick, taking another gulp before handing the flask to Tobi. "Let's see if it helps."

Emmerick draws his rusted saber, points it at Tizra, and charges toward the gate.

Tobi smiles, takes a swig of brandy, and charges alongside Emmerick.

Aden feverishly urges a rally, but the shaken army pays no heed to the prince. The purple banners of Zirmi's infantry swirl about Aden and Caleb like a flock of ravens.

The broken troops get a morale boost when they see Lord Emmerick charge into the amethyst flock of banners. Without hesitation, his soldiers reverse course to wager their lives on the Tizra drawbridge alongside their alpha.

Seth dumps the final archer into the river before entering a stairwell in the wall that leads to the south plaza. Ezekiel follows closely behind with his flock of sparrows fluttering about him.

Seth searches the perimeter where Peacemaker fell. The gigantic nature of the weapon makes it easy to locate, and he joyfully reclaims his hammer of death.

A detachment of guards prepare to swarm Seth, but Ezekiel commands his flock of sparrows and they envelop the oncoming soldiers. The men lose their momentum sifting through the angry birds.

Seth capitalizes on the prophet's command of the flock and rushes the detachment. He pummels them one after the other until the bludgeoned troops are ground into the cobblestone streets.

The bull continues his stampede toward the front gate to join the fight when he unexpectedly runs into Ashira, Shamgar, and the crusade of miners.

Seth wraps Ashira in his thick arms, and she kisses him on the cheek. He sets her down and scans the ranks, "Where's Benjamin?"

"Where's Othniel?" asks Ezekiel.

"My guess is that they're in the throne room confronting Zimri and Zidon," answers Ashira.

"We must help them," insists Ezekiel.

"No. Neshama is with them. Our fate lies with Emmerick and Aden," interjects Shamgar.

The crusade of miners readies their weapons for action.

Seth and Ezekiel look to Ashira for leadership.

"Our fate will be determined in the fray," claims Ashira without a hint of doubt in her eyes.

"The instruments in our hands will execute the judgment

of the Goddess!" roars Shamgar, leading the charge into the south plaza.

The sergeant in the back rank of The Nothern Kingdom army struggles to get his soldiers to turn face in a timely fashion to receive the oncoming ambush. His eyes widen with panic as he frantically trumpets a command through his warhorn.

Shamgar runs out in front of the miners. Ashira and Seth sprint to his side. Ashira's banner with the embroidered ram thrashes in the wind of the rushing crusade.

The crusade slams into the back rank of the northern army.

Shamgar's consecrated mace glows purple at the souls he harvests, while he bashes in the skulls of his foes with his thick round shield.

Seth knee caps his first casualty, and Ashira plants the standard in her victim's chest. Ezekiel's flock feasts on more eyeballs.

Without Zimri or Rezon to calm the chaos, the king's troops panic and break ranks.

Ezekiel fans out his arms allowing his sparrows a safe landing spot while he witnesses the enemy troops fade quickly, beset on two fronts and nowhere to escape.

Sparks flare brilliant colors as Othniel and Zidon continue to battle with ether.

Upon entering the throne room, Zimri's eyes sparkle at the magical marvel. His awareness moves beyond the radiance of the ether sparks as he ventures deeper into his throne room.

Zimri cringes at the carnage of Zoheth's mauled corpse, before his gaze drifts deeper into the space. His heart sinks when the torches reveal the silhouettes of two large figures in the far reaches of the throne room.

Korah crawls away from Azor - the compromised nephesh, an omen of Zimri's fading reign.

His attention shifts instantly to the streets below when he hears the sounds of revolution permeate from the streets of Tizra. Zimri runs to a window to witness the celebration. Liberated citizens emerge from their homes to dance with the southern army. The excitement is so lively that citizens and soldiers fail to notice the oddity of two brown bears barreling north to their caves in Miriam's Mountains.

The separatists hoist Emmerick and Aden on their shoulders.

Caleb and Tobi share a moment of relief that their lords survived the battle. Seth engulfs Ashira in a tender hug before returning her feet to the street. Seth approaches Ezekiel with a humble posture of gratitude, before pulling the tiny prophet into a bone crunching embrace.

Ashira looks about the excitement in the streets for Shamgar Ram, but the enigmatic precept slips into a dark alleyway and disappears into the night.

Zimri can no longer stomach the vision of the rebel victory and returns to watch the last hopes of preserving his throne - a struggling magi and a compromised nephesh.

His countenance plummets when Benjamin Tav enters the throne room, his white shirt soaked in crimson flower from the dagger wound. When Zimri realizes that his blade missed the shepherd's heart, he falls to his knees weeping tears of failure.

Benjamin's concern bypasses the nephesh and goes directly to Othniel. The ebb and flow of the ether tide remains constant, and neither Othniel nor Zidon refuse to back down.

Azor maintains his initiative for he's first to his feet. Korah stands slowly, weakened by the onslaught of bull rushes. Instead of assuming a fighter's stance, Korah sheathes his sword underneath his thick robe. Azor relaxes his stance, surprised by Korah's concession.

The rogue nephesh cautiously retreats toward the ether vortex away from Azor.

"Korah, how could you be the author of so much confusion!?"

"You have no idea, do you?"

Azor's clueless face confirms Korah's question.

"This is only the beginning."

The black nephesh dives into the grey ether vortex.

Korah's abrupt exodus sends a surge through the ether that Othniel and Zidon war over. The surge is so strong that they can no longer control the ether. Like a rock plunging into a pond, the ether splashes vertically towards the ceiling.

Time stands still for the prophet and the magi because they're the only two in the throne room who realize what's about to happen.

Zidon and Othniel dispel their ether.

Zidon scrapes Zoheth from the floor to use the dead magi as shelter from the ether backlash.

In the fate of the moment, Othniel's concern is for Benjamin's wellbeing, as Kurion could never absorb an ether backlash of such magnitude. The master prophet also realizes that the nephesh is too far away to assist the shepherd.

The ether plunge forcefully returns to the vortex and rushes horizontally.

Zidon bunkers behind Zoheth's corpse and avoids the brunt of the ether backlash. He lifts off the floor and soars with the ether gust before brutally smacking against a wall.

Zimri crawls behind his throne. The ether backlash shatters his marble throne into a thousand pieces and hurls the tyrant across the stone floor.

Azor's mind emerges from a haze of confusion and quickly perceives that the ether backlash is about to crush him. He extends his blade and digs in his heels as his only defense.

Azor's ether sword absorbs some of the ether, but the ether wave pushes him backward, his heels shredding the stone floor as he tries to keep his footing.

The backlash is so powerful that even the mighty nephesh cannot withstand it. The ether blast lifts him from the floor launching him into a corner.

Benjamin takes notice of Azor's tactic and extends Kurion to receive the ether. Doubt erupts deep within his soul when he witnesses the failure of majestic nephesh to absorb the ether wave.

Othniel fears that the ether backlash will claim Benjamin's life, so he stretches out his arms and funnels the ether to himself.

The blowback blasts him into the air and dashes him against the stone wall - his wooden staff rattles across the floor. The sound of the rattling staff disturbs Benjamin, but not nearly as much as the sound of Othniel's shattered bones.

Benjamin's emotions swirl like the ether vortex while tears flow from his afflicted eyes. As soon as he settles his emotions, he rushes to his mentor's side and scoops him from the floor. Benjamin props Othniel's near-lifeless body against his chest, feeling a slight sense of relief after he detects life inside the prophet's body. The once playful charm vanishes from Othniel's faintly opened eyes.

Azor emerges from the debris, sheathes his ether sword, and watches over Othniel and Benjamin from the far corner of the room.

Othniel swallows deep to deliver his final words. Benjamin sharpens his ears to receive the prophet's final gift of wisdom.

"My time has come. I now make the journey to the Great Judgment Bridge. Make sure that Ezekiel gets my book and staff."

Othniel pulls his book from under his robe and places it in Benjamin's hand.

"Tell him to return to the seminary and seek Imriel for Lilith's Journal, and promise me that you'll remind him to learn patience."

Benjamin nods his head to affirm the promise.

"I'm proud of you, and your parents would be prouder. You are indeed the son of Oren Tav. Promise me this and only this…

Don't reduce yourself to a concept. The same ether that flows in Neshama flows through you. Don't lose your wonder, your imagination, about who you can become - what you can achieve…

Promise me."

Othniel's wisdom cuts through Benjamin's deepest insecurities and brings more tears to his eyes.

"I promise."

Othniel's face turns grave, and his breathing slows as his words become whispers, "The prophets feared that this day might come."

"What do you mean?"

"Remember, Benjamin… Darkness can only exist in the absence of light."

Othniel looks deep into Benjamin's troubled eyes, "You are not yet free; I can see it in your eyes. See you on the other side."

Othniel closes his sleepy eyes and falls peacefully into his final rest.

Azor approaches and kneels over Benjamin, still clinging to Othniel's corpse. "I failed my call, I failed Neshama. I must return to the Goddess."

Benjamin's mind overflows with thoughts too numerous for his tongue to offer a question or a farewell to Azor.

The faded glow of the white nephesh disappears down a palace hallway.

Zidon regains consciousness and crawls along the floor. He lifts his head for a brief moment to confirm his brother's death- his disgraceful eyes dancing with approval. He stealthily crawls to where the Melek idol once stood and removes a stone slab from the floor. He drops into a hidden passage that runs under the throne room and escapes unnoticed.

Zimri creeps across the floor on his hands and knees. He grovels on bended knee with a hunk of stone that once served as the head of the Melek idol. He lifts the chunk of stone in the palm of his hand and gazes deeply into the lidless eyes.

"All is lost, my Master."

The calm currents of the ether vortex hovering above the floor begin to swirl faster and faster. The strands of grey turn to strands of black as the air thickens. Benjamin suspends his sorrow for Othniel and watches the vortex darken. Zimri turns from his self-absorbed sorrow as an eerie wind whips about the throne room.

A nephesh in black robes slowly ascends from the vortex.

Benjamin's initial concern is the return of Korah, but as the nephesh finishes his ascension, he realizes that this dreadful divine being is much more imposing than Korah.

His flowing black robe wisps across the stone floor as he approaches Zimri. His black hood covers his entire face, except for his yellow eyes glowing within the darkness of his hood. Standing ten feet high, he is much taller and much thicker than Korah.

The ominous nephesh towers over Zimri, whose face turns to stone and his joints lock with terror.

Benjamin scans the rubble from the statue scattered about the floor all the way to the head of the idol resting in Zimri's hand. He pieces the idol back together in his mind and figures a dire revelation.

Melek. Melek's not a false god. He's a nephesh.

The divine being looms as a judge over Zimri.

"You failed me!" proclaims Melek in an ominous voice, casting his doom down upon the condemned king.

Melek raises his right foot and stomps Zimri into the floor, executing him instantly.

Melek turns his attention to Benjamin clinging to the corpse of Othniel. Within three steps, the giant nephesh towers above the shepherd.

"The Remnant rises… Darkness will fall."

Melek steps back onto the vortex. He slowly raises both arms and the ether strands weave around his massive frame. He swings his arms down in a fluent motion and vanishes in a cloud of ether.

The stone floor returns to normal, and any trace of ether disappears.

Benjamin feels the presence of Nehsmama when the rising sun scatters her amber rays into the darkened throne room.

Chapter 22
The Sentinal of Issur

Black and yellow streamers dangle from the tops of the apartments that surround the south plaza and green laurel wreathes line the drawbridge that now unites The Isle of Issur. Long flowing banners swirl down from the palace walls to the stage beneath.

Emmerick stands in front of a humble wooden throne with Rodger the Badger tucked securely underneath. The professor offers a kind smile to acknowledge the grateful hearts of the multitude gathered to commemorate his triumph over Zimri.

The Signet Ring of Issur on Emmerick's hand glistens in the sun as the citizens of Tizra and the townspeople from across Issur, with the exception of foresters, assemble to celebrate the coronation of King Emmerick Tizra I 'The Learned.'

Captain Tobi Tamar stands next to his lord with five black and yellow warrior's belts drapped across his arm. Emmerick motions to Aden, Seth, Ashira, and Ezekiel in the front row to join him on the stage. Tobi steps forward with the belts- an image of King Josiah engraved in the silver buckles.

Emmerick and Tobi move down the line of heroes to place belts around their waists. After Emmerick tries in vain to fasten the belt around Seth's waist, the new king gives up and hands the victor his belt. Seth proudly slings it over his shoulder.

Benjamin watches the ceremony from the shadows of a palace entryway behind the stage. Soon he'll be honored as sentinel, bound to the new king, a new mentor, an unknown, who from the outset seems like a very odd fellow.

Benjamin's happy for his friends to receive their hard-fought accolades, but in the moment all he can do is think of what has gone before him - the final night with his father, Jael's death, his rift with Evan, Othniel's sacrifice, Zimri's judgment.

He's blazing a trail of graves and only in his twentieth year. How much more death lurks in the future? Even worse, will he deliver Ashira into the reaper's caress?

Still, a more oppressive nightmare torments his soul.

Melek.

He was called to end the worship of a false god. Ending falsehood with truth seemed simple enough. At first it appeared to be the lesser of the two mountains of his calling, smaller than the larger mountain of dethroning a tyrant.

The knowledge of Melek's existence frightens him to his core. Melek is a nephesh, a monstrous nephesh at that, and if he couldn't fell Korah, how can he possibly defeat Melek?

Awareness of divine mysteries carries with it more questions than answers. Benjamin finally understands why his father made him promise to never stop asking questions, and he realizes in full what Azor spoke in mystery. Questions are the vessels that transport humans from this realm of matter to the realm of the divine.

Benjamin finally comes to grips with being the son of Oren Tav, and for the first time in his life he misses shepherding his flock. Living with a call of Neshama has become a more problematic matter; he's unsure if he can ever come to grips with being a son of Neshama.

In the midst of his pending moment to receive a great honor, cascading streams of doubt pour over his faith. In hopes of balancing the ebb and flow of faith and doubt, Benjamin exhales his familiar prayer, "Neshama. Are you there? Are you listening?"

He pauses for a moment, desperate for an answer.

There's no response from the Goddess but no more anxiety either. For the moment of serenity, he's grateful.

His call to end Melek worship looms large, and though he can conjure a hundred reasons to quit his call, there's one good reason to stay the course.

Ashira beams a bright smile that warms his soul.

Caleb Glade steps into the entryway and watches him stare at Ashira before elbowing Benjamin in the ribs. The voyeur shepherd feels awkward that he's been caught, and Caleb thickens the embarrassment by raising his eyebrows.

"Why aren't you out there?" asks Benjamin.

"Never been much for attention," answers Caleb.

"Me neither."

"Better get used to it. You're about to be proclaimed the protector of our king and country… Ready for your big moment?"

"Not sure I have a choice," says Benjamin with a smile.

Emmerick motions to Benjamin and he joins the other heroes on the stage. Tobi fastens the warrior's belt around his waist, and the humble shepherd admires the etching of the shepherd king in the silver buckle, the pride of Hallowed Hills swelling within him.

After the belt fastens, Benjamin kneels. King Emmerick places a black and yellow rope necklace around his neck. He taps the shepherd on the shoulder with his antique saber to signal his ascension, and Benjamin rises for the king's proclamation.

"I now present to you… The Sentinel of Issur!" announces Emmerick with a vigorous roar.

Hailing his valor, the crowd cheers Benjamin's new title. His fellow champions on the stage congratulate him, and he returns to Ashira's side. Her dark eyes twinkle from beneath her raven hair, and a glow emanates from her face. Her soft smile draws him near.

Benjamin prepares for the long-awaited kiss, but Ashira pecks him on his cheek instead. It's not the passionate kiss he hoped for, but he appreciates the innocence of the moment.

The midday sun illuminates Tizra with radiant beams that shine down upon the Remnant, on those who pierced the darkness of tyranny with the eternal light of liberty.

Appendix

Appendix A
The History of Issur

Concerning Metaphysics

This epic is about the duality of the human condition - matter and spirit. This epic is about the metaphysical journey of humans. (Metaphysics defined as moving beyond the material, transitioning to the spiritual.) Above all, this epic is about the quest of the Remnant to remember an ancient promise, a promise that was forged in ether and sealed in the eternal memory of the Goddess.

Concerning The Goddess,
Celestial Beings, and The Creation Age

In the beginning, Neshama created the ether world and the nephesh. In the latter, Neshama created the world and the humans.

The nephesh, the stewards and guardians of Neshama's creations, descended to the earth. They taught humans the skill to harness the power of the four elements: earth, wind, fire, and water. Human prowess allowed the nephesh to instill such knowledge as language, art, agriculture, metal-working, and so forth. Humans lived in harmony with their creator and her creation. They were stewards of the world and caretakers of one another.

The humans were secure in their utopia, free from evil,

until they failed to remember their creator. As time passed, humans forgot Neshama. They ravished the land without replenishing; they were cruel to animals and to one another. The nephesh ascended to Neshama, and the world was plunged into chaos. (The history of the first age, known also as The Creation Age, is told in shadow. There are no artifacts to support the creation age, making it nearly impossible to date these mysterious events surrounding the human genesis.)

Concerning The Prophetess and The Age of Grace

Issurian History began with Miriam, as most of her artifacts have been confirmed by The Hall of Knowledge.

Miriam was born in Hallowed Hills. A daughter of a shepherd, she was the oldest of five children. Shepherds dispute her clan ancestry, but most scribes agree that she was of the clan Tav (see Concerning Guilds). Miriam was the only follower of Neshama in Issur, possibly the world, when she was exiled into the mountains that now bear her name.

The prophets teach that Neshama offered Miriam a home in the ether world to reward her faithfulness, but Miriam chose to remain in Issur. Later, Miriam forged a covenant (an agreement) with Neshama. Miriam and Neshama agreed to remember one another. Miriam would no longer exist as a desolate woman, and Neshama's name would be remembered in Issur.

Miriam's covenant message was initially rejected, and she experienced a season of persecution before her religion eventually spread through acts of grace. Miriam's message flourished in Issur, and thousands remembered Neshama.

The Goddess revealed to Miriam the divine knowledge of ether. (Ether being a sort of medium believed to permeate the ether world, the heavens, and the world.) The impartation of this divine ability is a mystery that has baffled scribes, precepts, and even the most zealous of prophets. It's no mystery, however, that certain prophets have mastered the craft of manipulating ether through what Miriam called Pure Magic.

Miriam's death is often exaggerated by those of faith. The precepts teach that she did not die - Miriam was ushered into the ether world by a host of nephesh. The prophets believe that after her death she went directly to Neshama bypassing the ether world journey through a realm that they refer to as Emunah.

One should inquire of "The Book of Creation" and "The Book of Miriam" to read more on these matters.

Concerning The Order of the Prophets

Miriam's lasting legacy was not only felt for millenniums through the Covenant but through the influence of the order she established. It was the Order of the Prophets that guided Issur through the turmoil of the Second Age.

They appointed Moreb Ram to deal with Vilekin colonists from the east. (Little is known of the Vilekin. Most scribes agree that they worshipped a mystical sea hag and profited as slave traders.) Lord Moreb found initial success when he established a colony in Southern Issur and drove out the Vilekin. They returned, however, and burned Moreb alive along with his colony.

As fate would have it, Lady Mara Ram was out picking blackberries during the assault. Lady Mara built a new colony in the woods that bears her name. She also signed The Calcedonian Accord of 555, and within a few years the Vilekin were driven away.

The Order of the Prophets acted once more when the Vilekin returned in 703 to reclaim their colony and conquer Port of Arnor. They appointed Bera Korse "The Vintner" as High Chieftain to reclaim Port of Arnor and burn Vilekin Colony. Lord Bera, a man of the vine, turned bitter at the angst of sobriety. The Vilekin tasted of his bitterness and were no more in Issur.

From atop Miriam's Summit, the Order of the Prophets masterfully guided the affairs of Issur for the Second Age. (Miriam's Summit houses Summit Seminary, an ether training center, and the Conclave of Miriam.)

In 2010, a prophet known as Zithri 'The Invincible' conceived "The Book of Blight" and Issur was given over to great upheaval. Zithri's Dark Magic could not be contained by the order; neither could his adherents known as the Order of the Magi.

A master prophet known as Amiel 'The Voice' confronted Zithri in an ether duel, but Zithri triumphed over Amiel. Zithri put the House of Torn to the sword, and any prophets who challenged him were massacred.

Zithri built a fortress known as Blight, and his order spread the tenets of a new religion known as Melek worship. (A something-for-everyone religion, an inward religion, a religion of selfishness, pleasure, and disorder.) With no capable prophets and no House of Torn to stop Zithri, Melek worship thrived, Neshama was forgotten, and Issur was plunged into chaos.

The prophets derive their beliefs from "The Book of Neshama" and "The Book of Miriam." Their convictions are grounded in The Two Ways of Neshama: Grace (preferred path) and Justice (secondary path).

Concerning The Shepherd King and The Age of Justice

A remnant of the faithful in Issur cried out to Neshama

to remember the Covenant of Miriam. Neshama called Josiah from the shepherd family Tizra of the clan Tav to defend the Covenant. He was affectionately called thereafter 'The Shepherd King.'

A nephesh forged the sword Kurion (named after the maker of the sword, also nicknamed The Lord of Swords). Kurion presented this ether sword to 'The Shepherd King.'

Josiah marched his shepherd army on Blight. He beheaded Zithri 'The Invincible,' slaughtered the Order of the Magi, and razed the fortress Blight to the dirt. In time, the Synod of the Paladin Precepts purged Melek worship from Issur and the land had rest.

King Josiah built Tizra, a splendid capital, in adoration of Neshama. Among his many building projects was the Grand Chancel - A magnificent temple that housed a new holy order known as the Synod of the Paladin Precepts, a council of one hundred devout defenders charged with the mission of Issurian righteousness.

The Order of the Prophets pleaded with King Josiah to cease construction of the Chancel and to decommission this holy consortium, but he disregarded their wishes. King Josiah installed Zadok Zorn as High Precept. To encourage the disheartened prophets, he entrusted Kurion to their protection, a gesture that softened the apprehension between the prophets and the precepts.

Concerning The Synod of Paladin Precepts

It is said that the precepts enjoy merry givers, for they fancy themselves cheerful collectors of coin. Most find their sermons easier to swallow when their collection box rings not hollow. Though charity be the most touted edict, there are five total. These are recorded in "The Holy Writ of Issur." A testament that contains: "The Book of Neshama," "The Book of Miriam," "The Book of Josiah," and "The Book of Precepts."

The Five Edicts
(Of High Precept Zadok Zorn)

1. Truth. The path of truth unlocks the mind of Neshama.
2. Charity. The road of generosity flows from the hand of Neshama.
3. Forgiveness. The way of forgiveness leads to the heart of Neshama.
4. Veneration. The crossroad of veneration embraces the essence of Neshama.
5. Judgment. The journey to judgment ends at the feet of Neshama.

Paladin precepts worship Neshama with a fierce faith. Many faces of evildoers have been caved in by the consecrated maces of these zealots. After Kurion was entrusted to the prophets, the precepts rejected the wielding of bladed weapons (swords, spears, arrows, and so forth). They also refuse to wear helmets, hoods, masks, or face paints. Precepts believe that Neshama rejoices in their faces as they execute acts of divine justice.

Concerning Guilds
It should be noted that in Prehistory and the First Age, most guilds existed as tribes or clans led by a chieftain. It

wasn't until the golden age of grace, circa 1000, that the word guild became common language.

The Miners Guild:
The first Issurians were mountain dwellers and master miners (of garnet and sapphire). Sapphire was the first-known Issurian town. Since most mines in Miriam's Mountains have been depleted, the Miners Guild is in steep decline. Prominent lines include the House of Ram and the House of Kes. Located in Miriam's Mountains. Headquartered in Garnet atop Mount Crown. Guild Supervisor: Ludim Kes

The Shepherds Guild:
The first Issurians that came down from the mountains became shepherds. Leadership emerged from three prominent clans: Tav, Tsadi, and Resh. Despite an unstable environment, ravenous wolves, and shifty clansmen, the shepherds continue to thrive. Located in Hallowed Hills. Headquartered in Tsadi. Guild Masters: Nabal Tav, Ardon Tsadi, Jether Resh

The Foresters Guild:
Later Issurians that came down from the mountains became woodsmen. These frontiersmen formed four prominent houses: Boar, Elk, Owl, and Wolf. With lumber much in demand from Issur and the lands to the east, these reclusive foresters have prospered from their noble timbers. Located in The Forest of Elah. Headquartered in Elah. Guild Master: Erez Elk

The Merchants Guild:
In the golden age of grace, with the threat of Vilekin corsairs removed, the miners and foresters began exporting their

goods east. Soon after, merchant guilds were founded in various towns to protect Issurian commerce. Headquartered in Port of Arnor. Executor: Hamor Chug

The Farmers Guild:
Hesitant to form a guild, the farmers united at the prodding of Lord Bera Korse III 'The Portly' when the population thrived during the golden age of grace. The farmers work more and drink less in season; they work less and drink more out of season. The most prominent line to come from the Farmers Guild is The House of Korse. Located in The Heartland and Abilla's Orchard. Headquartered in Pella. Guild Master: Nebo Korse II 'The Pig'

The Scribes Guild:
Scribes have been around as early as 70 when the Order of the Prophets employed these archeologists as historians and copyists. When King Josiah II 'The Wise' constructed The Hall of Knowledge in 2065, the scribes became an official guild.

Concerning Zimri and The Age of Destruction
The past ages of Issur are creation, grace, justice. The present age of Issur is an age of oppression. Her children are shackled by the chains of slavery dangling from the reign of King Zimri 'The Backstabber.'

Religion and reason, faith and fact, both stand condemned by the court of ignorance. King Zimri makes a vile spectacle of Neshama's followers and intellectuals by burning them alive in front of rabid crowds in the black of night. Melek worship thrives, the Covenant dies, and Neshama is silent.

Appendix B
Timeline of Issur

The First Age: Creation "The Age of Neshama"
• Neshama created the world
• The Nephesh descended from the ether world and discovered humans
• The Nephesh were commissioned to enlighten humans on the four elements of earth, wind, fire, and water
• The Dark Age of Creation - Humans forgot Neshama and the Nephesh ascended to the ether world

The Second Age: Grace "The Age of the Covenant"
• Miriam's Birth – 1
• Neshama forged the Covenant with Miriam – 32
• Miriam established the Order of the Prophets – 57
• Vilekin colonists settled in Issur – 531
• The Order of the Prophets appointed Moreb Ram 'The Explorer' as High Chieftain to defend Issur from the Vilekin – 539
• Lord Moreb built the first settlement in Southern Issur – 545
• The Vilekin were driven out by Lord Moreb – 550

- Vilekin colonists settled in Calcedon – 552
- The Vilekin resettled in Issur and built a colony – 553
- The Vilekin burned Lord Moreb and his colony – 554
- Lady Mara rebuilt settlement in Mara's Woods – 554
- Lady Mara signed The Calcedon Accord – 555
- The Vilekin were driven out of Issur by the Issurian Calcedonian Alliance – 559
- The Vilekin reclaimed Vilekin Colony – 703
- The Vilekin captured Port of Arnor – 717
- The Order of the Prophets appointed Bera Korse 'The Vintner' as High Chieftain to reclaim Port of Arnor – 718
- Lord Bera reclaimed Port of Arnor and burned the Vilekin Colony – 720
- The last of the Vilekin colonists defeated in The Battle of Fog Swamp – 735
- Calcedonian King Carnek I 'The Corsair' broke The Calcedon Accord – 818
- The 1st Issurian Calcedonian War 819 - 901
- The Order of the Prophets rejected Gog Korse III 'The Drunkard' and the House of Korse – 898
- The Order of the Prophets appointed Tekoa Torn 'The Stag' as High Chieftain to lead the Issurian Army – 899
- Lord Tekoa killed King Carnek III 'The Sordid' – 901
- The Golden Age of Grace 904 – 2009
- Zithri 'The Invincible' expelled by The Order of the Prophets for initiating Dark Magic and conceiving "The Book of Blight" – 2010
- Zithri commissioned The Order of the Magi – 2015
- Zithri introduced Melek worship to Issur - 2016
- Zithri 'The Invincible' killed Ammiel 'The Voice' in an Ether Duel – 2018
- Zithri murdered the House of Torn – 2019
- The Conclave of Miriam dissolved – 2020
- Hundreds of prophets massacred in The Crimson

Onslaught – 2022

The Third Age: Justice "The Age of the Kings"

• The Golden Age of Grace (904 - 2009)
• Neshama called Josiah Tizra I 'The Shepherd King' – 2023
• A nephesh forged the ether sword 'Kurion' for Josiah – 2024
• Josiah reassembled the Conclave of Miriam – 2026
• Josiah marched the Shepherd Army on Blight – 2029
• Josiah triumphed at The Battle of the Pony Pasture – 2029
• Josiah 'The Shepherd King' killed Zithri 'The Invincible' and eliminated the Order of the Magi – 2030
• The fortress Blight razed to the ground – 2030
• At the behest of the people of Issur, The Conclave of Miriam anointed Josiah as King of Issur - 2032
• The King's Highway completed – 2046
• Tizra completed – 2050
• King Josiah erected the Grand Chancel of Neshama and commissioned the Synod of Paladin Precepts. Zadok Zorn was appointed as High Precept – 2053
• King Josiah entrusted 'Kurion' to the Order of the Prophets – 2053
• Zadok composed "The Holy Writ of Issur" and ordered the construction of chancels in every town and city – 2054
• The Synod of Paladin Precepts rid Issur of Melek worship in what Zadok proclaimed as The Glorious Scourge - 2057
• Neshama answered King Josiah's death bed request and filled all chancel ether fonts – 2057
• The Column of Kings completed by Josiah Tizra II 'The Wise' in honor of his father – 2063
• The Hall of Knowledge completed by King Josiah II – 2065
• The 2nd Issurian Calcedonian War 2219 - 2344
• The Issurian queen, Vashti 'The Buxom' killed the

Calcedonian king, Ekron 'The Lesser,' ending the war – 2344
• The Great Locust Famine – 2612-2614
• The Synod of Paladin Precepts blamed the Order of the Prophets for the famine – 2614
• The Golden Age of Justice 2615-3013
• King Aden Tizra IV 'The Deerstalker' drowned in Lake Resh while on a hunting expedition – 3013

The Fourth Age: Destruction "The Age of Melek"
• King Zimri Tizra I 'The Backstabber' inherited the throne – 3013
• King Zimri reinstated Melek worship – 3014
• King Zimri announced Zidon 'The Absolute' as High Magi and commissioned The Order of the Magi – 3014
• King Zimri declared war on The Order of the Prophets – 3014
• Neshama called guild master Oren Tav to defeat King Zimri and eradicate Melek worship – 3015
• The Shepherds Guild revolted – 3015
• The Southern Kingdom separatists backed Lord Emmerick Tizra I 'The Learned' – 3016
• Lord Emmerick and King Larz II 'The Wary' reinstated The Calcedon Accord of 555 at the Council of Carnek – 3016
• The Shepherds Guild battled Zimri's army to a draw at the Battle of Ephah's Field – 3016
• The Shepherds Guild accepted Zimri's truce – 3016
• The High Precept Shamgar Ram assassinated – 3016
• The Synod of the Paladin Precepts were hunted down in what King Zimri proclaimed The Scarlet Winter - 3016
• Neshama worship outlawed in Tizra – 3016
• High Magi Zidon sealed all ether fonts in the Northern Kingdom chancels – 3017
• The Grand Chancel converted to the Temple of Melek – 3018

• The Scribes Conspiracy felled – 3021
• The Hall of Knowledge razed to the ground – 3021
• The Pit constructed – 3022
• Summit Seminary raided, the Conclave of Miriam executed, and hundreds of prophets were slaughtered in what Zidon proclaimed as The Scarlet Revenge. – 3024
• Neshama worship outlawed in The Northern Kingdom – 3024
• The Grand Chancel rebuilt in The Southern Kingdom on Torn Hill - 3024
• Tizra's Merchant Guild Conspiracy felled – 3025
• The Merchant's Guild (Port of Arnor) and the Forester's Guild paid the tribute to purchase the Pact of Zimri – 3027
• Overseer Nebo Korse I 'The Bovine' led The Farmers Guild Revolt – 3030
• The Farmers Guild Revolt crushed – 3030

Current Date: Summer 3031 of the 4th Age